Praise for Cy

"Should be on your [summer reading list]."
—*Newsday*

"[Baxter's] neatly laid-out red herrings, charming heroine and surprise ending will not disappoint."
—*Romantic Times* (★★★★⭒)

"A thoroughly entertaining addition to Baxter's well-crafted mysteries . . . The murder mystery is cleverly constructed and chock-full of creative suspects and a surprising resolution. Mystery fans are in for a treat!"
—FreshFiction.com

"A cleverly constructed mystery chock-full of dysfunctional characters all hiding motives for murder . . . Readers . . . [will] savor this delightful cozy."
—*Publishers Weekly*

"The plot is multilayered and cleverly presented, with good characterization and pacing. It is the kind of story that draws you in immediately and keeps you reading eagerly. . . . HIGHLY RECOMMENDED."
—*I Love a Mystery*

"A very entertaining series with a menagerie of colorful human and animal characters."
—*Mystery Lovers Bookshop News*

"A pure gold mystery." —*Midwest Book Review*

"A wonderful mystery that packs a lot of action and red herrings into a slim volume . . . This is a great book to read while curled on the couch with your own four-legged friends." —TheBestReviews.com

"Cynthia Baxter knows how to write a good who-done-it complete with red herrings and enough twists and turns to keep the reader's interest." —Allreaders.com

"Cynthia Baxter has done it once again, and created an extremely enjoyable, laugh-out-loud-funny mystery that would please anyone." —*California Community Bugle*

"A real page-turner. If you love good mysteries or love animals or mysteries with animals, you'll love Baxter's *Putting On the Dog*." —*Long Island Times-Herald*

"Clever, fast-paced and well-plotted . . . Five paws up!" —Carolyn Hart, Agatha, Anthony, and Macavity awards winner

"Dead canaries don't sing, but you will after reading this terrific mystery!" —Rita Mae Brown, *New York Times* bestselling author

"A little bird told me to read this mystery, which is awfully good. For the record, I would shred any canary who insulted me." —Sneaky Pie Brown, *New York Times* bestselling cat

"*Dead Canaries Don't Sing* is top dog, the cat's pajamas, and the paws that refresh all rolled into one un-fur-gettable mystery entertainment." —Sarah Graves, author of the *Home Repair Is Homicide* mysteries

Also by Cynthia Baxter

Murder Packs a Suitcase

Cynthia Baxter

BANTAM BOOKS

MURDER PACKS A SUITCASE

A Bantam Book / November 2008

Published by Bantam Dell
A Division of Random House, Inc.
New York, New York

This is a work of fiction. Names, characters, places, and incidents either are the product of the author's imagination or are used fictitiously. Any resemblance to actual persons, living or dead, events, or locales is entirely coincidental.

All rights reserved
Copyright © 2008 by Cynthia Baxter
Cover art © Robert Giusti
Cover design by Marietta Anastassatos

If you purchased this book without a cover, you should be aware that this book is stolen property. It was reported as "unsold and destroyed" to the publisher, and neither the author nor the publisher has received any payment for this "stripped book."

Bantam Books and the rooster colophon are registered trademarks of Random House, Inc.

ISBN 978-0-553-59035-7

Printed in the United States of America
Published simultaneously in Canada

www.bantamdell.com

OPM 10 9 8 7 6 5 4 3 2 1

To Susan Breslow,
my editor at Honeymoons.about.com

Murder Packs a Suitcase

1

"A journey of a thousand miles must begin
with a single step."
—Lao Tzu

Graceful palm trees, an isolated white sand beach,
the gentle waves of the blue-green sea . . .

Breathe in, breathe out, Mallory Marlowe instructed herself, hoping that the breathing and visualiza-
tion technique her daughter had taught her would help
steer her toward something along the lines of relaxation.
Or at least ease her out of the state of near-panic in
which she found herself as she sat in the waiting area of
Paragon Publications, bracing herself for her first job interview in nearly two decades.

It wasn't working. The two cups of coffee she'd
gulped down before dashing for the 9:57 Metro North
train out of Rivington sloshed around in her stomach,
and the cream-colored silk blouse that had seemed so
fresh and polished early that morning already smelled
like something a construction worker would peel off his
back at the end of the day.

Forget Amanda's supposedly no-fail relaxation techniques, she thought grimly. Instead, Mallory fixed her gaze on the huge gold letters on the wall above the curved granite reception desk. *The Good Life,* they spelled out, proudly announcing the name of the magazine headquartered here on the twenty-fifth floor. Underneath, in letters only a few inches smaller, was the monthly publication's slogan, "Read *The Good Life* to Lead the Good Life!" along with half a dozen large, glossy photographs that represented some of the topics the magazine covered: fine wines, four-star restaurants, flashy cars, innovative home design, state-of-the-art speakers and televisions, and intriguing travel destinations.

Concentrating on the here and now wasn't working, either. With a sigh, Mallory concluded that it was time to resign herself to the fact that even if she breathed in every last molecule of oxygen in the entire building and imagined every tropical island she'd ever seen pictured in a tour company's catalog, she was still going to be a nervous wreck. Hardly surprising, she realized, since she'd never expected to find herself exploring new career opportunities at this stage of her life.

Then again, there were a hundred different things she hadn't expected to be doing in her forties. Like getting used to sleeping alone in a king-size bed. Making decisions about her two children completely by herself. And using that peculiar word every time she was forced to describe her status, the one that still didn't sound right whenever it emerged from her lips: *widow.*

Mallory's frame of mind didn't improve much as she observed the other two women who were perched on the tasteful caramel-colored leather chairs that formed a neat square in Paragon Publications's waiting area. One was flipping through a magazine, pausing every two minutes to glance at her watch and sigh. If she was trying to give the impression that squeezing in a job interview at one of the nation's top magazines was an inconvenience, she was doing a crackerjack job. The other woman kept punching the keys of her BlackBerry, scowling ferociously as if she was furious with it.

Their body language, which clearly communicated that they were both extremely important individuals whose time was worth a heck of a lot more than most other people's, was only part of what Mallory found so discouraging. Even more demoralizing was the fact that they were both so . . . well, young. Neither of them looked much older than twenty-three. And if perfectly taut skin and hair with nary a gray strand weren't bad enough, their clothes were of a trendy variety that Mallory wouldn't be caught dead in.

Reflexively, she glanced down at her own outfit. A plain dark skirt, the cream-colored silk blouse that desperately needed airing out, a classic beige blazer. The silk scarf she had tossed around her neck in what she'd hoped was a jaunty, self-confident manner could best be described as ecru. Even her dead-straight, light-brown hair, today worn in a low ponytail, was fastened with a neutral-toned tortoiseshell clip.

She was depressingly drab, she decided morosely. In fact, the only color she'd allowed herself was a few swipes of a recently purchased plum-colored lipstick, the result of having heard on *The View* that bolder hues for cheeks and lips were all the rage this season.

A wave of panic rose inside her as she suddenly contemplated the very strong possibility that she fit in here at *The Good Life* magazine's offices about as well as an elephant.

She was seriously contemplating jumping to her feet, striding over to the elevator, and just getting the heck out of there, but before she could will herself to take such definitive action, she heard a woman's voice say pleasantly, "Ms. Marlowe, Mr. Pierce will see you now."

Mallory stood up. But instead of making a beeline for the elevator, she dutifully followed the young assistant in the very short, very tight skirt, thinking that here was another woman who had yet to see the other side of twenty-five.

Who am I? she wondered as they walked through a corridor lined with giant framed versions of the magazine's past covers, which, like the artwork in the lobby, all featured delectable food or the latest electronic gadget or some other component of the good life. This wasn't really the best time to be experiencing an identity crisis, of course, but actually trying to answer that question might have a calming effect. She began with the most obvious response, that she was a mother of two healthy, self-sufficient children. Her daughter, Amanda, who was twenty going on fifty, was completing a double major in economics and political science at Sarah Lawrence while trying to decide which would be more practical, a law degree or an MBA.

In fact, it was Amanda who had insisted that Mallory start filling her days with new people and new experiences. As of late she'd been acting like a mother hen, reversing their roles by endlessly lecturing her about how it was high time Mallory venture back out into the world again. She had finally stopped telling her daughter about all the times she politely declined well-meaning friends' invitations to dinner or begged off a girls' night out at the movies, wanting to avoid the inevitable speech about how Mallory should really start acting like her old self again.

As for her eighteen-year-old son, Jordan, she supposed he could be considered self-sufficient, at least in a general sense. After all, he was able to microwave his own leftovers, successfully complete simple errands like buying milk and postage stamps, and even, if pressed, do his own laundry. Of course, since dropping out of Colgate

University just a few weeks after his freshman year was getting under way, he was also supposed to be looking for a job. So far, however, his only job, aside from keeping the couch warm and making sure the TV worked, was making excuses.

Mallory firmly reminded herself that during her forty-five years on the planet, she had done a lot more than give birth a couple of times. She was a college graduate with a degree in English. She had four years' work experience as an editor at a science journal. She also had nearly twelve years' experience as a freelance writer for the *Rivington Record,* covering every topic imaginable, from the Westchester County Garden Club's annual fund-raising tour to the antics of the local school board to the latest government scandal.

Surely a résumé like that qualified her to put together a monthly calendar of events that would help the magazine's readers cultivate something along the lines of "the good life." Especially since Carol at the *Record* had already put in a good word for her with the managing editor, who happened to be a longtime friend. Somehow, Carol had convinced him that Mallory was, indeed, someone who belonged on his staff. Whether it was because her boss was really that impressed with her work or, like Amanda, she simply felt it was time for her to jump back into life, she couldn't say.

Besides, how hard could the job be? Ever since she'd learned about the interview, she'd read every back issue of the magazine she could get her hands on. From the looks of things, she wouldn't be asked to write anything more complicated than "October 12–14, Annual Ragin' Cajun Crawfish Festival, New Orleans. For information, call 504–555–3423."

None of this was calming Mallory down in the least.

It wasn't until she was ushered into a large corner office with *Trevor Pierce, Managing Editor* on the door that she finally experienced something along the lines of relief. The man sitting behind the desk was a grown-up.

Probably in his fifties, she determined, judging from the flecks of silver in his dark hair and the crinkled laugh lines that appeared next to his hazel eyes as he smiled at her warmly.

But that wasn't all that surprised her. Mallory half expected to find the editor of an upscale lifestyle magazine like *The Good Life* wearing a silk smoking jacket and sipping champagne as he sat amidst framed photographs of his Ferrari, his vacation home on the Riviera, and his gorgeous model-thin wife.

Yet neither the man nor his office even hinted at the glamorous lifestyle the publication promoted. The photos on his desk were of two pretty young women in jeans and T-shirts who were grinning at the camera, and a large shaggy dog of unknown parentage. There appeared to be no room for any other personal effects on the desktop, given the haphazard stacks of paper that covered most of it. In fact, the only other clues as to who this man was when he wasn't playing the role of publishing mogul had been relegated to the windowsill: a New York Yankees cap, that morning's edition of the *Daily News,* and three cardboard coffee cups from Dunkin' Donuts.

As for the man himself, he seemed as unpretentious as his surroundings. For one thing, he chose to wear his hair a bit longer than most corporate types. Either that or he hadn't had time for a haircut in weeks. And while at the start of his day he'd probably been wearing a jacket and tie, they were both gone. The collar of his pale blue shirt was unbuttoned, and the sleeves were rolled halfway up his arms.

"So you're Mallory Marlowe," he pronounced, standing up behind his desk to shake her hand. "Carol has told me a great deal about you. You apparently impressed her as a very strong writer. Good at research, too. I've seen the clips she sent over, and I have to agree."

All this and I haven't even sat down yet, Mallory thought, feeling her cheeks flush.

"But please, have a seat," Mr. Pierce insisted, as if he'd been reading her mind.

"Thank you," she muttered.

"So," he said conversationally, settling back in his chair and folding his hands in his lap, "have you done much traveling?"

Mallory blinked a few times before realizing that it was probably a good idea to hide her surprise over his question. Carol certainly hadn't mentioned anything about having a passport being a requirement for the position. Must be some new outside-the-box technique for putting job applicants at ease, she figured. Chatting with them about their personal lives instead of getting right to the matter at hand . . .

"Uh, some," she replied.

"What kind?" he asked. "Adventure? Eco-tourism?"

"A little of everything." Launching into amusing anecdotes about the seven-island Caribbean cruise she and David had taken for their fifteenth anniversary didn't sound like a very good idea. Not when their biggest adventure had been almost missing the boat when the clerk at the duty-free store on St. Thomas couldn't figure out how to work the credit card machine. As for eco-tourism, the closest she'd come to eco had been packing her toiletries in small reusable bottles instead of using those plastic travel-size throwaways.

"Perfect," Mr. Pierce replied. "Exactly where have you traveled to?"

She hesitated again, aware that her answer wasn't exactly going to overwhelm him with her worldliness. As a child, she'd gone on the usual family vacations, traveling throughout the Northeast to visit relatives and making pilgrimages to Williamsburg and Gettysburg and Salem. But what she remembered most fondly were the trips to Florida over spring vacation, a three-day drive while packed into the backseat of her parents' Oldsmobile with her brother and sister.

Still, having spent her childhood exploring alligator farms and hot dog–shaped refreshment stands and gas stations that featured real live tigers in cages didn't exactly make her a world traveler. True, she'd always assumed that at some point in her life she'd see the Taj Mahal in India and the Great Pyramids in Egypt and all the other marvels the world had to offer.

Yet the trips she'd taken over the last couple of decades had leaned more toward the Disney World–Busch Gardens–Hersheypark variety, variations on the vacations that had been part of her own childhood. Throw in a few camping trips and a cross-country drive that involved almost as much bickering as sightseeing, and you'd pretty much have a complete list. In other words, most of her travel experiences had revolved around keeping the kids happy, which in turn kept her husband happy and therefore made for a peaceful few days all around.

As for Europe, Mallory and David had managed to sneak in a two-week overview of the great capital cities of London, Paris, Rome, and Amsterdam. But between getting on and off the tour buses and checking in and out of hotels, there had been little time left over to give the world's great monuments, art treasures, and historic wonders more than a glance. In short, she was hardly in a position to convince anyone that she was a seasoned traveler, especially the editor of a slick, glossy magazine like *The Good Life*.

Which brought her back to the question of why they were even having this discussion in the first place. Still, she realized she was warming to him. She was also slowly deciding that he was someone she could feel comfortable working for.

"Oh, the usual," she finally responded. "I've been all over the United States, Europe, the Caribbean . . ." She shrugged, hoping he would interpret the casual way in which she threw out the names of these places as a sign that she was practically Arthur Frommer himself.

"Excellent," Mr. Pierce replied with a satisfied smile. "And now for the sixty-four-thousand-dollar question: Do you *enjoy* traveling?"

Mallory had to think about that one for a few seconds. True, she had always found some aspects of travel stressful. The anxiety of standing on a street corner and poring over a map, struggling to figure out where you were and convinced you'd never find your way out of what was starting to look like a really seedy neighborhood. Not having access to your own coffeepot first thing in the morning. And always, it seemed, forgetting to bring the one thing that would have made such a major difference in one's comfort level: hand lotion, a nail clipper, that extra pair of shoes that was not nearly as likely to cause blisters.

Yet in the end, she invariably concluded that the thrill of experiencing a new place far outweighed the annoyances. Mallory could remember being awestruck as she gazed out over the Grand Canyon, so filled with emotion that her chest swelled and her eyes stung. She had gotten an adrenaline rush from wading in the warm, clear blue waters of the Caribbean Sea. She had even found Epcot exhilarating, simply because of all the creative thought that had gone into building it.

"Yes," she replied sincerely. "I love it. I can't think of any other experience that comes close."

Mr. Pierce nodded approvingly. Mallory was pleased that she seemed to have given the correct answer.

"So, given your past experience," Mr. Pierce continued, "it sounds as if you'd feel perfectly comfortable writing about a wide variety of destinations."

Something about the way he used *writing* and *destinations* in the same sentence made a lightbulb go off in Mallory's head.

"Mr. Pierce," she said cautiously, "I think there may have been a slight misunderstanding here." She used the word *slight* because she didn't want him to feel as if he'd completely wasted his time. After all, she was still hoping for the job she'd come all the way into New York to interview for, the one that involved nothing more demanding than reading press releases and organizing dates and accurately recording the phone numbers and websites required to receive additional information.

"First of all, please call me Trevor," the managing editor corrected her. "Only my newspaper delivery boy calls me Mr. Pierce. Second, I don't understand what misunderstanding you're referring to. I need a good travel writer, especially since our previous one quit in a huff three days ago and we've got deadlines to think about." With a little shrug, he added, "You seem to fill the bill. In fact, I think you'd be great."

"Me?" Mallory squawked, still trying to comprehend what she was hearing. "Why?"

"Because you're not some twenty-two-year-old who's right out of college and figures free travel means good beer, interesting clubs, and attractive locals to meet and greet," Trevor replied matter-of-factly. "You'll bring a more mature perspective to your articles. The magazine's readership is aging, just as the whole country is aging. The one theme that keeps coming up at meetings is that we've got to keep up with that trend and make sure we continue to communicate with our audience. You, Mallory Marlowe, can do that for me."

"But—but . . ." A hundred questions popped into her head. "How much traveling does the job require?"

"Just one trip a month," he replied. "We try to vary the places we cover, in terms of both geography and the kind of people they're likely to appeal to most. And the length of the trips ranges from a couple of days to close to a week."

"How about the articles? How long would they be?" Mallory imagined staying up until two a.m. night after night, putting together an in-depth report about a place she'd visited only for a few days.

"About two thousand words," he said. "Eight pages, double-spaced. But we're not looking for a detailed analysis. If you're familiar with the magazine, you already know that the tone we go for is lighthearted. While our primary goal is imparting solid information, entertaining our readers is at least as important. In other words, we'd want you to take a positive approach and make traveling to each of the destinations sound like fun."

Mallory sat frozen in her seat, just staring at him. But while her face and body were showing few signs of movement, her mind was racing.

I can't do this! she was thinking. I'm still having such a difficult time just getting through the day that I have to check to make sure I'm not still in my pajamas every time I leave the house! Taking on a brand-new career is light years beyond me right now.

Still, she couldn't ignore the fact that this man, this stranger with the impressive title of managing editor, apparently believed in her. Not only was he confident that she could do this job, he had just said in so many words that he thought she could do it better than someone twenty years younger.

The debate inside Mallory's head continued to rage. In fact, she felt as if somehow the fillings in her teeth had started channeling CNN, one of those news analysis shows featuring two snarling individuals on opposite sides of the political spectrum fighting like pit bulls.

Just because he thinks you can do this doesn't mean you can, one of the voices insisted.

But you've been writing for decades, the opposing voice countered. Trevor Pierce read your work and he liked it. And once upon a time, back when you were Amanda's age, you dreamed about working for a big national magazine.

What about all that traveling? the first voice demanded. For all you know, you'd be forced to cover extreme destinations like Antarctica and the Gobi Desert. Or countries with unstable governments and bad water and strikes every ten minutes that leave garbage piled on the streets and commuters stuck in subways. And what if you're assigned to write about a nudist colony? . . .

"What I need for the issue we're currently putting together," Trevor continued, oblivious to her hesitation, "is an article on Florida." He leaned forward and rested his elbows on his desk. "The old Florida, that somewhat hokey, somewhat tacky but always fun place so many of us remember with such affection from our own family vacations back in the fifties, sixties, and seventies. I'm thinking plastic pink flamingo lawn ornaments. Alligator farms with gator wrestling. Roadside attractions like caged tigers at gas stations. Hot dog stands shaped like giant hot dogs. The precursors of the giant theme parks, like haunted houses and talking mermaids.

"That's what I mean by the old Florida," he concluded. "Your job is to find out if it still exists despite Disneyfication, not to mention the Internet, computer games, iPods, and all the other high-tech toys that have become part of everyone's life."

Florida! For the first time since entering Trevor's office, Mallory felt herself starting to relax. Florida was something she could handle—if there was anything her limited travel experience *had* prepared her for, this was it. She couldn't help smiling as she found herself imagining a slide show that catapulted her back to her childhood.

She could remember the thrill of pulling into the parking lot of Horne's, a chain of roadside stops that popped up practically every five miles. Lingering over enticing displays of alligator wallets and pecan log rolls at Stuckey's, its number-one competitor. Begging to stay at the Mexican-themed South of the Border Motel, which was advertised by dozens of billboards along the interstate and was readily recognizable by the hundred-foot statue of the motel's sombrero-sporting mascot, Pedro.

And that was just driving there. She had fond memories of so many things that these days were considered kitsch—a term meaning "bad taste in good fun." Those alligator farms Trevor had mentioned, glass-bottom boats, snack bars shaped like giant ice-cream cones, Cypress Gardens with its thrilling waterskiing shows . . .

All that must have changed by now, Mallory reflected. All those quirky places that endeared Florida to me and a whole generation of young travelers have undoubtedly been put out of business by the Disney parks, SeaWorld, and Universal. Or maybe not.

"Of course, everything will be completely paid for," Trevor went on matter-of-factly, as if free trips like the one he was describing came along every day. "Tourist destinations generally do whatever it takes to get media coverage in their strongest markets, which means Florida's tourism bureau is picking up the tab for most of it. *The Good Life* will cover all your other related expenses, like getting to and from the airport and any meals that aren't comped."

"Comped?" Mallory repeated without thinking, then immediately regretted letting her ignorance show.

"*Comp* as in 'complimentary,'" Trevor explained,

without showing the tiniest shred of impatience. "In other words, free. Sorry to use jargon, but you'll catch on fast enough. And I should mention that you'll be part of a press trip. That's a group of travel writers who are hosted by the tourist bureau folks. On this trip, your base of operations will be Orlando. The fact that the Disney parks and Universal Studios have such a stronghold there has made the area a natural center for the family-oriented tourist industry—which means it's the ideal hunting grounds for the kind of attractions you'll be writing about."

He hesitated before saying, "I suppose I should mention that our writers generally travel alone."

Mallory frowned. "Sorry?"

"What I mean is, there's no budget for including spouses or other family members on these travel junkets," he explained. "Some writers run into difficulties because of babysitting problems or scheduling issues. Is that something we'd have to plan around?"

She realized he was trying to find a delicate way to ask about her availability without coming right out and asking if she was married or had children.

"No," she replied, not the least bit offended over what seemed like a completely legitimate concern. "My children are grown. And my husband died six months ago in an accident."

A startled look crossed his face. "I'm sorry," he said kindly. "That must have been extremely difficult."

Mallory nodded, surprised by how sincere he sounded. From the seriousness in his eyes, she got the feeling he had some firsthand experience with loss himself.

"You're right, it has been tough," she admitted. "But this job—writing travel articles for the magazine—sounds appealing. It also strikes me as something I'd be good at. I loved working for the *Record,* but after a while it got to be too much of the same thing. But travel writing . . . wow. That sounds like—"

"Like what?" Trevor asked, raising his eyebrows expectantly.

With a self-conscious laugh, she said, "It sounds like something that will impress even my kids."

Chuckling, Trevor gestured toward the photo of the two smiling young women. "I'm a parent myself, so I know how hard that is. But you're right. Travel writing may not be quite as glamorous as most people assume, but it definitely has its perks. Seeing places you wouldn't necessarily travel to on your own is just the beginning. You'll also end up viewing the places you go in an entirely different way. Even if you've been there before, evaluating them more objectively forces you to see them through new eyes. It's part of feeling responsible to your readers, as if you're venturing there first to see if they should follow."

"It sounds like you've done some travel writing yourself," Mallory observed.

"Some." He glanced around his office and sighed. "These days, I'm lucky if I can escape from these four walls long enough for lunch."

Suddenly Trevor's expression darkened. "In terms of this Florida trip, there is one tiny glitch."

Aha, Mallory thought. Not surprisingly, that old adage "If something sounds too good to be true, it probably is" was about to prove to be more than something grandmothers liked to say.

"What's the glitch?" she asked. She wasn't sure if she was disappointed or relieved that this entire fantasy was on the verge of dissolving as quickly as it had swelled her head. Either way, she chastised herself for having already started a mental To Do list that included "Check expiration date of last summer's sunblock, See if elastic on old bathing suit is still functional," and, for the first time in as long as she could remember, "Get legs waxed."

"You'd have to leave Sunday."

"This Sunday?" Mallory didn't even care that she was beginning to sound like a parrot. "But that's in three days."

Her head was spinning. Impossible, she thought. There's no way I can pull this off. I'd have to squeeze a million errands into the next seventy-two hours in order to get ready. And I'd have to leave the house unattended, plus cancel whatever I've got on my schedule. . . .

But she quickly remembered that Jordan was at home, so he could take care of anything that came up. As for her schedule, unless someone was throwing her a surprise party, there was nothing to cancel. It was even possible that she really could get herself ready in three days. She'd certainly accomplished more impressive tasks in the past, including staying up all night to sew a butterfly costume for Amanda's third-grade play and getting the scoop on whether Rivington's mayor planned to run for a second term by taking his wife out to lunch at Neiman Marcus's tearoom and plying her with white Zinfandel.

Maybe I really could do this, she thought tentatively. Besides, if I do fall on my face, the only people around to witness my failure will be a bunch of six-year-olds wearing mouse ears.

And then, even before she'd realized she was about to speak, she heard herself uttering the words, "I can be ready by Sunday."

Trevor responded with a grateful smile. "Perfect. I knew you were exactly what I was looking for. Welcome aboard, Mallory. I'll e-mail the Florida tourism folks ASAP that you're our new travel writer. Now if you'll just be patient while I get through some of the paperwork . . ."

A half hour later, Mallory rode down the elevator of

the Paragon Publications building, feeling dazed. She could hardly believe she had just said yes to a proposition that she now realized was completely ridiculous.

But it was too late. In her purse she had an e-ticket, the name and address of an Orlando hotel, the confirmation number of a car rental, and a cash advance for those extras Trevor had mentioned. She also had an official Assignment Letter printed on *The Good Life* letterhead that stated she was writing an article for the magazine. She'd glanced at it only long enough to see that it ended with the phrase, *Please extend to Ms. Marlowe all courtesies as a journalist.*

I have a job! she marveled. Like it or not, I'm a real live travel writer!

She wasn't sure whether she should be rejoicing or kicking herself. But one thing she was certain of was that simply repeating those words in her mind sent so much adrenaline surging through her veins that she doubted she'd ever need a cup of coffee again.

2

"The World is a book, and those
who do not travel read only a page."
—St. Augustine

"Next stop, Rivington. Rivington!"

As the Metro North train pulled into the station, Mallory took one last glance at the To Do list she'd scribbled during the ride home. It had grown considerably from the mental version she'd begun constructing in Trevor's office. "Get summer clothes out of storage. Schedule haircut. Get cash from ATM. Buy guidebooks. Shop for sandals. Write down important phone numbers for Jordan."

How am I ever going to get all this done in time? she wondered with alarm.

But preparing for her trip was only part of it. What she was really worried about was how her children would react to the news. She wanted to believe they'd be excited for her. Yet two decades in the mother business had taught her that the one thing children didn't like was change. Especially if it involved their parents.

"Jordan?" she called as she stepped into the foyer. She

dropped her keys and her purse on the marble table that was there expressly for that purpose. "Sweetie, are you home?"

She glanced into the living room, where her son was sprawled out on the couch. As usual, he was engrossed in some video game that enabled him to pulverize, mangle, and otherwise destroy a variety of digital bad guys merely by clicking a few keys.

"Jordan, did you—oh, my God!" Mallory froze, not quite believing what she was seeing. "Amanda? What are *you* doing here?"

"Frankly, I was hoping for a warmer welcome," her daughter replied sullenly.

Amanda stood in the kitchen doorway with one hand curled around a steaming mug. With the other hand she twirled a lock of her long, straight auburn hair, a nervous habit left over from childhood.

And a sign that something was wrong.

"Of course I'm happy to see you," Mallory assured her. "It's just that I didn't *expect* to see you."

She rushed over to give her a hug, still amazed that her firstborn child towered a good five inches above her. Amanda was also reed-thin, although the gawkiness that had plagued her during her teenage years was mercifully evolving into a willowy gracefulness.

"When did you get here?" Mallory asked, trying to hide her shock. "And more importantly, what are you doing home from college?"

"She just showed up a few minutes ago," Jordan informed her as he sauntered into the foyer, cradling a bag of some bright orange junk-food product. His baggy yellow T-shirt and equally baggy jeans looked rumpled, as they always did after a long session on the couch. His dark blond hair was similarly disheveled, making him appear as if he'd been engaged in hand-to-hand combat rather than merely fighting virtual enemies. "She's having an identity crisis."

"Wha—?" Mallory stared at her daughter, shaking her head in bafflement. "What on earth is he talking about, Amanda?"

Amanda took a deep breath. "Mother," she announced, pushing up the sleeves of the cream-colored cashmere sweater she wore with tailored black slacks, "I needed to get away from school. I'm taking a few days to decide what to do with my life."

I'm forty-five years old, Mallory thought ruefully, and I still haven't figured out what to do with mine.

But this wasn't about her, she reminded herself. This is about a twenty-year-old who up until this moment has never once strayed from any of the goals she set for herself.

Ever since she was tiny, Amanda had known exactly what she wanted, whether it was a yellow balloon as opposed to any other color or earning the highest SAT scores in her school's history. And once she'd set her sights on something, she exhibited amazing discipline in order to get it, acting as if reaching that particular goal was a matter of life and death.

Which made the fact that for once in her life, Amanda had stepped off that straight and narrow path of hers—even going so far as to have an "identity crisis," according to her brother—cause for alarm.

"Is there something in particular that precipitated this crisis?" she asked her daughter, trying to remain calm.

"As you know, I've been leaning strongly toward getting an MBA after I graduate from college next year," Amanda replied, as usual sounding more like a college professor than a college student. "But I just got my score for the law school admission test I took in the fall . . ."

"And?" Mallory prompted, still bracing herself for the bad part.

"I did better than I expected. *Much* better." Amanda paused for dramatic effect before adding, "I scored in the ninety-fifth percentile."

Is *that* all? Mallory thought, nearly falling over with relief. Here I was worried that she was in some kind of trouble—maybe even the kind that requires a lawyer. But it turns out that *her* crisis is deciding whether or not she wants to *be* one.

"If you're that smart," Jordan piped up, "why don't you just go to law school and business school at the same time? That way, you can make twice as much money—which is what all this is about, right?"

Mallory cast her son a dirty look. Sometimes he acted so much like a baby brother that she wondered if he was eighteen or eight.

"That's wonderful, Amanda!" she told her daughter sincerely. "That means you can pursue either one of them. So I don't understand why—"

"But that's the problem!" Amanda wailed. "Even though I've been thinking in terms of business school, it turns out I'm unbelievably well suited for law school. Everything is suddenly up in the air. I have a major decision to make, probably the most important one of my entire life!"

"Can't you go back to school and make your decision there?" Mallory asked, trying to hide her frustration over her daughter's tendency to overdramatize. Especially since this time around, it meant a major change of plans that affected them both. "The semester just started. You must be missing so many classes—"

"Actually, I thought it was much more important to return to my childhood home," Amanda replied, straightening her shoulders. "I felt it would give me an opportunity to get back in touch with my true self."

"Don't tell me," Jordan said, grinning. "Your inner child, right?"

Amanda cast her brother a scathing look. "Yes, as a matter of fact."

He groaned as he reached into the bag of mysterious junk food. "Do you think your inner child gives a hoot about whether you become an executive or a lawyer? I don't see a lot of little girls dressing their Barbie dolls in business suits and teeny-weeny briefcases."

Amanda tossed her hair in a way that said that one thing she *was* in touch with was the importance of ignoring her little brother. Widening her eyes at Mallory, she said, "This is a critical time for me, Mother. I'm facing a major crisis, possibly the biggest one of my entire life. And I need you to help me through it."

"Hey, I've got an idea." Jordan crunched through a mouthful of orange. "Why don't you toss a coin? Heads means law school, tails means business school—"

"Do you really expect me to take career advice from someone who spent less time in college than he did at Boy Scout camp?" Amanda asked icily, fixing her brother with a scowl.

"Hey, can I help it if college didn't turn out to be the way I expected?" Jordan shot back. "Besides, the timing for a major change in my life was a little awkward, don't you think? Since Dad just died six months ago?"

"If there's one thing Daddy would have wanted," Amanda countered, "it would be for you to get a college degree."

"Is that what it's about?" Jordan sneered. "The degree? What about all the important stuff I'm supposed to be learning?"

"Could you two please just stop?" Mallory cried. She put her hands over her ears, as if that could drown out the bickering she'd been listening to almost since Jordan first started talking as a baby. It was at that point that Amanda had realized she'd gotten more than a little brother—she'd gotten a sparring partner. Mallory knew her children loved each other, but they never seemed to tire of replaying the same script over and over again.

At the moment, she simply didn't have the patience for it. Not when she was doing battle with her own demons, the ones that kept bringing up the possibility that she was still too fragile to handle the new challenge she had suddenly been handed. For once, she wanted to focus on her own uncertainty and let her children deal with theirs by themselves, even if merely having that thought made her feel guilty.

"Amanda, I think you should enjoy the weekend at home, then go back to school Sunday evening," Mallory said firmly. "I understand that you've got a decision to make. But that doesn't mean you should be skipping classes."

"I don't care about my classes," Amanda declared, pouting. "Right now it's more important for me to take a break—one that includes spending some quality time with my mother. I thought you'd be thrilled that I came home for a few days. I figured we could, I don't know, go shopping at Bloomingdale's or . . . or go out for lunch. Aren't those things mothers and daughters are supposed to do together?"

No time like the present for Mallory to make her own announcement. "I'm sorry, honey. I would love to take you shopping, but I'm going away. I just got back from an interview at a magazine called *The Good Life*. The editor offered me a job as a travel writer."

Amanda gasped. "You didn't take it, did you?"

Mallory's eyebrows shot up. "I certainly did," she replied indignantly, wondering at what age children finally figured out that their parents had lives, too. "My first assignment is writing an article about Florida. I'll be away for five days—all of next week. And to be perfectly honest, even though I'm a little nervous, I'm actually looking forward to it."

"Cool, Mom," Jordan said. Then he frowned. "Wait a minute. Does that mean I'll have to, like, take out the garbage and stuff like that while you're away?"

"You've been taking out the garbage since you came back home," she pointed out.

"Yeah, but you've always been around to remind me what day."

"Travel writing? That's so . . . so extreme!" Amanda exclaimed. "Your job at the *Rivington Record* is nice and safe. You don't even have to go beyond the town limits!"

Mallory was growing increasingly impatient. She could practically see the list she'd been composing in her head. And of all the things she had on her list, arguing with her children about whether or not she was capable of flying to Florida for five days to write about alligator farms and seashell earrings wasn't on it.

"Sweetie," she said, her exasperation beginning to seep through, "you're the one who's been on my case about meeting new people and having new experiences."

"Well, yes, but . . . but . . . when are you going?" Amanda demanded.

"Early Sunday morning."

"But Mother, you can't just *leave* me!" Amanda cried, tears welling in her eyes. "I *need* you!"

"Which day is recycling?" Jordan asked, suddenly agitated. "I can never remember if it's Tuesday or Thursday."

Mallory sighed. She'd so desperately wanted Amanda and Jordan to be happy for her. Or at least accepting. If anyone knew how David's death had affected her, it was the two of them. They'd witnessed her transformation from a confident, self-reliant woman to someone who was so unsure of herself that deciding what to make for dinner had become overwhelming.

Then again, they were children. *Her* children. Up until this point, she had always been available to them, thanks to her flexible schedule as a freelancer for the *Record*. She'd had the time to drive Jordan all over Westchester County for his soccer games and the energy to bake chocolate chip cookies with Amanda after she learned she'd missed becoming class valedictorian by one thousandth of a point—even if it was ten o'clock at night.

"Just call your new boss and tell him something came up," Amanda urged.

Mallory glanced at her purse, still lying on the front table. In it were her e-ticket and her itinerary. Not long before, those pieces of paper had made her feel excited, if apprehensive, about the fact that she was about to embark on a brand-new chapter of her life.

"I'm sorry, Amanda," she said gently. "Maybe the timing isn't right for you, but it couldn't be better for me." With a little shrug, she added, "I'm going."

• • •

Out with the old, in with the new, Mallory thought as she sat in the waiting area at JFK Airport early Sunday morning. She wondered if she was being overly dramatic by thinking that the plane she was about to board would carry her away from her old life and into a brand-new one, one in which she played the role of travel writer.

A very busy travel writer. The last seventy-two hours had been the whirlwind she'd anticipated. She'd freshened up warm-weather clothes that hadn't seen the outside of a cardboard box since September. She'd gotten a haircut along with the leg waxing and, as a last-minute splurge, a pedicure, making a statement about this new chapter of her life by opting for cherry-red toenails— although she'd drawn the line at her pedicurist's suggestion that she add a tiny palm tree on each toe. She'd bought three different guidebooks, then spent both Friday and Saturday nights reading them cover to cover, flagging the important pages with Post-its.

But while she did her best to enjoy herself, she'd carried out all her preparations under the watchful and disapproving eye of her daughter. A daughter who trailed after her the same way she had when she was four years old, talking about the pros and cons of business and law so incessantly, she wished she could pop a bottle of apple juice into her mouth. Mallory had had no idea an identity crisis could be so noisy. She only hoped she hadn't been so distracted that she hadn't packed sensibly. She could imagine opening her suitcase in Orlando and finding it contained six pairs of pajamas, two tubes of toothpaste, and a wool ski sweater.

As for Jordan, he demonstrated his annoyance over the fact that his mother was making an attempt at reestablishing a life for herself by acting like one of Orlando's best-known residents: Grumpy. He made a point of letting out a loud sigh every few minutes. He also refused to engage in any of their conversations, including the few that Mallory managed to steer away from the topic of careers.

As she climbed into the airport van before the sun came up, she felt as if she finally had a chance to catch her breath for the first time since before her job interview. But that didn't mean she was leaving her apprehensions behind with her sleeping children.

True, it was hard to imagine a destination more user-friendly than Orlando. She told herself the folks from the mega-corporations that dominated central Florida's tourism industry undoubtedly put a great deal of time, effort, and money into making sure that nothing bad ever happened to visitors.

But she hadn't been to that part of the country since Amanda was eight and Jordan was six. And on that trip, the Marlowes stuck to the theme parks. There had been little decision-making, and even less risk, since their trip had consisted primarily of shuttling from their Disney hotel to the various parks on a monorail, waiting in line for one attraction after another, and consuming every single one of their meals on Disney property. In fact, the most daring thing she could recall doing on that trip was going on the Space Mountain ride.

Now, as she waited at the airport gate, her stomach was in knots. The fact that she seemed to be odd man out didn't help. Not surprisingly, she was the only person sitting alone amidst a crowd of couples, families, and every other possible combination of travelers, all of them chattering away excitedly either to one another or to the faceless beings they spoke to on cell phones. She kept reminding herself that there was something to be said for the feeling of autonomy that came from traveling alone, something she hadn't experienced since before she'd married David. She certainly didn't envy the parents of children who were too young to contain their excitement. Case in point was the frazzled-looking mother of the little boy who was already wearing a pair of Mickey Mouse ears. "I want Goofy *now*!" he screamed during his Category Five temper tantrum.

Mallory grimaced, relieved when it was finally time to board. After all, as long as she was earthbound, she could still back out of this crazy adventure. She shuffled through the plane behind the other passengers, checking the seat numbers.

As she neared 12C, she saw that the aisle seat was already occupied. Quite comfortably, too. Sprawled across it was a tall man in his late fifties or early sixties, his face gaunt with leathery skin and his longish gray hair slicked back over his head. He looked like a caricature of a tourist, thanks to his gaudy Hawaiian shirt splashed with orange, yellow, and green parrots and his khaki Bermuda shorts that had so many pockets he probably hadn't needed luggage.

"Excuse me," she said politely. "I believe you're sitting in my seat."

He didn't even glance up.

"Excuse me," she repeated, this time in a louder voice. "I believe you're—"

"I heard you the first time," he shot back.

"Then why are you still sitting there?" she countered with a smile that she hoped was more pleasant than she actually felt.

"You can take my seat," the man told her. "Twenty-three B."

"I don't want a middle seat, thank you. I want an aisle seat—like this one."

"Hey, I've got long legs. I need an aisle seat." To prove his point, he stuck out both legs. They were long, all right. They also had exceptionally knobby knees and pasty white skin that looked as if it hadn't been exposed to sunlight in months.

"In that case," Mallory said, by this point openly letting her impatience show, "you should have requested an aisle seat when you made your reservation."

"Is there a problem?" the flight attendant who had just appeared from nowhere asked.

"There doesn't have to be," the man said. "Not if this lady will go sit in twenty-three B."

"This is my seat," Mallory said. "See? Here's my boarding pass."

The flight attendant glanced at it. "Sir, I'm afraid you'll have to move. This isn't your seat."

"What difference does it make?" he shot back. "I have long legs and I need to sit on the aisle."

"I'm sorry, sir, but this seat belongs to this woman." By this point, most of the other passengers in the vicinity had stopped chattering. The altercation that had brought the boarding process to a standstill was evidently much more interesting than anything they had to say to their traveling companions.

"Why can't she just sit in twenty-three B?" the man demanded.

"She's made it quite clear that she prefers the seat she was assigned." The flight attendant looked ready to strangle him with one of those oxygen masks that drop from the ceiling in the event of an emergency. "Now, if you'll please get up and go back to your own—"

"I'm writing down your name," the man barked. "I'm going to notify the airline of your unprofessional behavior as soon as we land. You obviously don't know who I am, do you?"

"Sir, our policy is the same for everyone," the flight attendant insisted.

"Whatever." He stalked off to his assigned seat, muttering under his breath the entire time.

Mallory had a feeling she wasn't the only one who was relieved. She was also glad his real seat wasn't anywhere near hers.

As she sat down in the seat she'd fought so hard for, she tried to push the uncomfortable interlude out of her mind. In fact, she forced herself to picture a relaxing setting the way Amanda had taught her, even though she hadn't had much luck with it the last time around. She was determined to do everything she could to make this trip a success, not only to prove to Trevor Pierce that she could do it, but also to prove it to herself.

She settled back and fastened her seat belt. It was time to take off.

• • •

"Welcome to Orlando, Ms. Marlowe," the car rental agent said warmly. Frowning at his computer screen, he added, "I see a compact car has been reserved for you. For only eight dollars a day more, we can upgrade you to a mid-size." Beaming at her across the counter, he added, "How does a PT Cruiser sound?"

"No, thanks," Mallory replied, irritated by his sales pitch. Do I look *that* naive? she wondered. "A compact is just fine."

The rental agent clicked a few keys. "Are you sure? It only comes to an additional forty dollars."

"I'll stick with the compact, thanks." The fact that *The Good Life* had reserved the least expensive class of rental car indicated that they clearly preferred to keep her expenses down. Thriftiness aside, she really was just as happy with a compact car. Somehow, it seemed simpler to maneuver in an unfamiliar place, not to mention easier to park.

"Actually," the rental agent said, clearing his throat, "we don't have any compact cars available at the moment. How about if I give you the PT Cruiser for the same price?"

"That's fine," she agreed, hiding her amusement.

It wasn't until he walked her over to the shiny, cherry-red car parked right outside that she realized that motoring around Orlando in a car like this was going to be a lot more exciting than it would have been in the usual stodgy rental car—especially a car that matched her shiny new toenails. In fact, once she was flying along I-4 with the windows open, luxuriating in the feeling of the Florida sunshine warming her face and the wind messing up her hair, it occurred to her for the first time that this whole trip was going to be fun.

She realized that up until this moment, she had been thinking of her first press trip as kind of a test, a way to see whether she was hardy enough to take her place in the land of the living again. Yet now that she was actually here, it seemed like it could be just as enjoyable as going on a real vacation.

As she merged into the fast lane, speeding past palm

trees, she marveled over how much a simple change of scenery was altering her mood. Not only did the New York winter feel far away. So did her nervousness over accepting this job, and even the argument she'd had with the obnoxious stranger on the airplane. Most surprisingly, her guilt over leaving Amanda and Jordan behind also seemed like something in the distant past.

When she turned onto International Drive, the main thoroughfare of Orlando's tourist district and the location of her hotel, Mallory was startled by the kaleidoscope of color that suddenly surrounded her. The street was lined with a hodgepodge of billboards and neon signs. Set farther back from the road was one over-the-top building after another, each as outrageous as anything that could be found in Fantasyland. The same thrill she remembered from her childhood trips to Florida was shooting through her like a jolt of electricity.

Her eyes widened as she cruised past a tremendous store called Bargain World, its entire facade covered with gaudy murals. The artwork featured kids on a roller coaster and an eagle as big as a small airplane sporting an Olympic gold medal. For some inexplicable reason, a giant flying saucer hovered over the entrance. As if all that wasn't startling enough, gigantic statues of Michael Jordan and David Beckham were poised in front, each one well over a story high, as if these larger-than-life figures had literally become larger than life. The discount-ticket shop next door, which was housed in a bright orange-red lighthouse, seemed practically ordinary by comparison.

Farther down the road, she passed a Hawaiian-themed miniature golf course, complete with a fake volcano, tiki torches that blazed even in daylight, and a rickety wooden footbridge that crossed a waterfall. Right next door was a tremendous white building with dignified columns and a large staircase leading up to the front door—the whole thing built upside down. She recognized it as WonderWorks, a hands-on science museum she'd read about in her guidebooks.

Orlando is definitely kitsch headquarters, Mallory decided, almost embarrassed to admit what a kick she was getting over seeing it all for the first time in over a decade. This was truly the home of bad taste, all in the name of good fun—just as Trevor suspected.

As she turned into the parking of the Polynesian Princess Hotel, still feeling a little like Dorothy on day one of her trip to Oz, she saw that her hotel fit right in with all the other architectural flights of fancy surrounding it. A profusion of plants lined the front, tropical flowers in bright pinks, oranges, and yellows that were interspersed among a variety of lush, healthy-looking palm trees.

The open-air lobby was smothered in Polynesian-style artifacts, none of which came even close to looking authentic. Elongated masks that would have been frightening if they hadn't worn big, welcoming grins better suited to smiley faces than primitive tribes hung above the entrance to the gift shop. Barrel-shaped drums decorated in petroglyph-style motifs served as trash cans. Clutching a sign indicating the direction of the Tiki Tiki Teahouse was a smirking tiki god carved from wood and painted in Day-Glo colors—perhaps the god of gluttony, or at least twenty-four-hour dining. The forbidding-looking spears affixed to the walls didn't do nearly as good a job of screaming "Welcome." In fact, they were a harsh reminder that Polynesian culture was about more than cheerful tiki gods and multipurpose drums.

Yet all these fake tributes to the South Seas were dwarfed by the lobby's focal point: a tremendous volcano. The black, rocky mountain that emerged from a tangle of thick green foliage towered over two stories high. Hot orange lava, or at least some synthetic substance that looked like it, oozed out of the top, beneath a cloud of black smoke. The volcano was framed by two waterfalls that splashed over rocks she assumed were made out of anything but real stone, then spilled into a dark pool that meandered toward the front desk.

Is the whole trip going to be this intense? Mallory wondered as she slid her key card into the lock of her room after checking in. She was getting such a kick out of the faux-Polynesian decor that she hoped the same designer had been given free rein in the guest rooms. Sure enough, the brown-and-black bedspread on the king-size bed had a primitive motif that, like the design on the lobby's trash cans, had clearly been borrowed from ancient petroglyphs. The wastebasket was made of plastic that was molded to look like bamboo.

She was tickled to find a gift basket on the dresser, no doubt a special welcome for the visiting writers from the hotel. Through the cellophane wrapping, she could see a chocolate-and-macadamia-nut candy bar, a bottle of coconut-scented body lotion, and a grass skirt—the basic necessities for a pretend trip to the South Seas.

Once she'd completed her tour, she hung up her clothes, dazed and a bit giddy over being in a new place—especially one that tried so hard. At the same time, she was grounded enough to appreciate modern touches like hangers that had been integrated into the Polynesian experience, even if they were the two-piece contraptions designed to be absolutely useless in the real world. As she laid out her toothbrush and cosmetics on the bathroom counter, she was similarly relieved that modern plumbing had been substituted for thatched outhouses.

Before stashing her suitcase in the closet, she hesitated, debating whether to unpack the last thing she'd stuck into her suitcase before slamming it closed. Deciding the item in question would bring her more strength than sadness, she finally took out the framed photograph of the four Marlowes posing on a beach in Jamaica. It had been taken by one of the hotel lifeguards on what turned out to be their last family trip.

She studied it as she lowered herself onto the edge of the bed. She was standing in the center, her wet hair clinging to her face and the strap of her bathing suit peeking out from the neckline of her white T-shirt. David stood next to her with his arm slung around her shoulders. The fact that he was grinning emphasized the lines that crisscrossed his tanned face. He hadn't shaved in days, and she remembered teasing him about the black-and-white stubble that she claimed made him look like a buttoned-up Manhattan attorney turned beach bum. His upper torso was lean and muscular. In fact, he looked like the picture of health.

It was hard to believe that only a few months after this picture was taken, he was dead.

It was just as hard to believe that the happy children in this photo were about to have their entire world change. They looked like any other teenagers who were ecstatic to be on vacation. Amanda, who was on spring break, had plastered zinc oxide all over her nose. Her straw sun hat was pulled down so far that it collided with her sunglasses, making it hard to tell who she was. Only her lustrous reddish-brown hair, which Mallory had insisted she free from its elastic band for the photo, gave a clue about her identity.

Jordan, meanwhile, had insisted that sunblock and sun hats were for sissies. He was bareheaded, his dark blond hair bleached nearly white and sticking up at odd angles. He, too, was beaming at the camera, making him look even more like his father than usual.

Mallory touched David's face lightly. "You would be proud of me right now," she whispered.

Gently she placed the photograph on the night table,

right next to the digital clock, so it would be the first thing she saw when she opened her eyes every morning. Then she took out her notebook.

"For those without the means to take a trip to the South Pacific, a stay at the Polynesian Princess Hotel is the next best thing." She scribbled the words quickly, keeping in mind Trevor's directive about being both positive and lighthearted. "Of course, having a sense of humor helps, especially when it comes to appreciating some of the more over-the-top touches, such as trash cans shaped like primitive drums and fake tiki gods painted in colors that don't actually appear in nature. . . ."

She paused mid-sentence, blinking as she stepped out of herself for a moment.

I'm good at this, she marveled. Trevor was right. I can do it.

But what struck her even more was the fact that she was actually having *fun* doing it.

And that having fun turned out to be one of those things it was possible to learn to do all over again.

3

"I have found out that there ain't no surer way
to find out whether you like people or
hate them than to travel with them."
—Mark Twain

It wasn't until Mallory was about to meet the rest of
the writers on the trip that the wave of anxiety she'd
been bracing herself against finally descended. Precisely at one o'clock that afternoon, she stood awkwardly at the entrance of the Tiki Tiki Teahouse, her
stomach fluttering uncomfortably as she peered inside,
trying to identify the group of people who would be her
traveling companions for the next few days.

The itinerary Trevor had given her included a list of
the other journalists and the publications they wrote for.
Admittedly, none of the magazines or websites had the
same status as *The Good Life*. But that didn't keep her
from fearing that all four writers would be much more
seasoned and sophisticated than she, and that she'd end
up feeling like a geeky kid on her first day at a new
school.

The only plus she could see was that she'd automatically have someone to eat lunch with—even if it was in an ersatz teahouse. After the hostess sat her at an empty table for six, Mallory took stock of her surroundings. The Tiki Tiki Teahouse was really just a coffee shop that had been dressed up with a scattering of potted palm trees, wicker furniture, and more of those tribal masks with expressions as friendly as smiley faces. As for sophistication, it didn't exactly appear to be the order of the day. Not with the toddler in the corner tossing his hamburger bun as if it were a Frisbee and another young child at a neighboring table dipping her Cinderella doll's head into her dish of chocolate ice cream.

To mask her discomfort over sitting alone, Mallory pulled out her notebook.

"The Polynesian Princess Resort is extremely child-friendly," she wrote, continuing her quest to find the fun in everything she experienced. "No pompous waiters shaking their heads disapprovingly here. Instead, the coffee shop off the main lobby, the Tiki Tiki Teahouse, offers the perfect spot for a relaxing meal. Even the menu is geared toward young visitors, with entrees like Banana-Fana Pancakes and Tiki-Tacky Tuna, which youngsters are guaranteed to enjoy. . . ."

She jerked her head up when something bumped against the table.

"You'd think after all these years, I'd have learned to bring earplugs whenever I come to Orlando," the short, barrel-shaped woman complained in a gravelly voice. She seemed completely oblivious to the fact that she'd nearly sent the small vase of brilliant red tropical flowers at the edge of the table flying. "The worst thing about Orlando is that it's crawling with kids. If they could fix that, it wouldn't be half-bad."

At first glance, Mallory assumed the woman was in her fifties. She wore a rumpled white blouse and an unflattering gray pleated skirt that hung unevenly from her thick waist, an outfit that made her look as if she'd just mugged a Catholic school student. Her black hair was pulled back into a crooked bun and held in place by a plastic contraption that operated like a giant binder clip. Loose wisps that hadn't quite made it inside hung down haphazardly. Yet upon closer study, Mallory realized that the woman's face was youthful enough to put her somewhere in her thirties.

Peering at Mallory through squinting eyes, the woman asked, "Are you here on the press trip?"

"Yes, I am," Mallory replied, smiling. "How did you know?"

"You're sitting alone at a table for six, you don't have any kids with you, and you're taking notes," the woman replied tartly.

She dropped into the seat opposite Mallory, smashing her big, clumsy black pocketbook against the edge of the table. "I'm Annabelle Gatch," she announced. "*Travel on a Shoestring* magazine." She shook Mallory's hand, offering only three limp fingers.

"Nice to meet you. I'm Mallory Marlowe. I write for—"

She stopped mid-sentence, distracted by an older woman she'd suddenly spotted wandering around the restaurant, looking confused. She was barely five feet tall, dressed in a purple sweat suit with silver sequins running up the sides of the baggy pants and along the collar of the zippered jacket. Her white sneakers, which made her feet look almost as big as Mickey Mouse's, were festooned with shiny silver patches and tiny red lights that lit up each time she took a step.

"Someone should help that poor woman," Mallory remarked. "She seems completely disoriented."

"What are you talking about? That's Frieda Stein," Annabelle said. "Frieda!" she cried, waving her arms in the air and half standing. As she did, she bumped against the table, once again sending the vase of fake red anthuriums trembling. "Over here, Frieda!"

Mallory cringed. Even if Frieda happened to be hard of hearing, there was no way she could have missed the grating sound of Annabelle's voice. So Mallory wasn't surprised that the older woman made a beeline for the table, although her pace was closer to a snail's than a bee's.

"Goodness, I was afraid I was late," Frieda said in a singsong voice that sounded almost like a child's. "But I see I'm not the last to arrive."

Up close, Mallory saw that her bright orange-red lipstick wasn't the only makeup Frieda Stein wore. She had also applied brown eyeliner. Unfortunately, the thick, uneven lines that squiggled like caterpillars were perched about a quarter of an inch above the actual edge of her eyelids.

Gesturing toward the newcomer with her thumb, Annabelle said, "Frieda here writes for *Go, Seniors!* magazine."

"That's right," Frieda agreed in her melodious voice. Patting her silver pageboy primly, she added, "And we seniors are no longer spending our vacations playing shuffleboard on cruises or golfing from dawn to dusk. We're trekking in the Himalayas. We're hang gliding in Jamaica. We're bungee jumping in the Grand Canyon!"

"Not this trip," Annabelle said. "The only thing around here that's likely to raise your blood pressure is the Revenge of the Mummy roller coaster at Universal."

"Nonsense," Frieda returned indignantly. "Last time I was here, I went skinny-dipping in the World Showcase Lagoon at Epcot. That was for my article 'Grin and Bare It.' " Winking at Mallory, she added, "Almost got myself arrested by a very handsome police officer. But I managed to flirt my way out of it."

"So you must be *The Good Life*'s new travel writer,"

Annabelle said. "The Florida tourism people e-mailed us on Friday, saying there was a replacement."

"That's me."

"That's not a bad magazine. Not bad at all." She sounded impressed. "Who did you write for before?"

Mallory paused to take a sip from her water glass. She wondered just how forthcoming to be.

But the moment passed when she and Annabelle and Frieda all turned their heads at the unexpected sound of an argumentative voice just a few feet away.

"Whaddya mean I can't smoke in this stupid restaurant?" a man in khaki shorts and a garish Hawaiian shirt sputtered. "This is a coffee shop, for God's sake. What goes better with coffee than a cigarette?"

"Must we go through this every time you're a guest at my hotel?" another middle-aged man asked crisply. He couldn't have looked more different from the other man. He was impeccably dressed in a beige suit that, despite the fact that it was linen, was as smooth as if it had just been run over by a steam roller. Even more distinctive, however, was his yellow bow tie, which was splattered with big black polka dots.

"If I'd wanted to be tortured by people who act like smoking cigarettes is in the same category as shooting heroin, I'd have stayed in California," the first man shouted.

Mallory immediately recognized him as the man she'd seen on the plane—the one who had tried to steal her seat and then been so rude the flight attendant had looked ready to throw him off. It appeared that he didn't limit his boorish behavior to the friendly skies; he'd brought it along to the hotel, keeping it with him like a carry-on bag.

"Here at the Polynesian Princess," the second man said haughtily, "we strive to create an atmosphere that's pleasing to everyone. That includes children, senior citizens, and asthmatics."

"What about smokers?" the testy traveler shot back. "Where are our rights?"

"Never a dull moment, eh?" a deep male voice interjected.

Mallory had been finding the scene unfolding in front of her so horrifying—and so enthralling—she hadn't noticed that someone had sat down next to her. She turned and saw a man with ridiculously blue eyes and salt-and-pepper hair directing a warm smile at her.

"But that's one of the things I like best about traveling," he added. "You're always encountering something you didn't expect."

"Anyone who's ever spent more than five minutes with Phil expects him to act like that," Annabelle insisted.

"You know him?" Mallory asked.

"Sure. That's Phil Diamond. He's one of the writers on this trip."

Great, Mallory thought, groaning inwardly. So I have five whole days of Malice in Wonderland to look forward to.

"He's probably cranky from the trip," Frieda said tartly. "Then there's the fact that he's not exactly working for a top-of-the-line publication these days. What's that website he's been writing for lately?"

Annabelle snorted. "It's got some silly name, like I'dRatherStayHome-dot-com."

"Actually," the newcomer to their group said, "I believe it's called BeenThereDoneThat-dot-com. It's geared toward the experienced traveler who's covered all the usual destinations and is looking for something new."

"What about you?" Mallory asked him. Talking to Blue Eyes about Blue Eyes seemed like a lot more fun than discussing their surly traveling companion. "Who are you and who do you write for?"

"I'm Wade McKay," he replied, shaking her hand. "And I'm not really a writer. I publish a lifestyle magazine called *Living Well*. It's very much like *The Good Life,* in fact."

She raised her eyebrows. "How did you know I'm the one who writes for *The Good Life*?"

"Process of elimination. You don't look like you write for seniors or travelers on a budget. And you're clearly not Phil Diamond." Once again he rewarded her with a smile that was so engaging she half expected his teeth to glint. "I also know you used to write for the *Rivington Record*."

Startled, she asked, "How do you know that?"

"I always do my research. I made a point of finding out whatever I could about everyone who was coming on this trip with me. And that included you. At least, after the Florida Tourism Board e-mailed all of us to say you'd be replacing the magazine's former travel writer. You'd be amazed at all the cool stuff you can learn by Googling someone's name."

"In that case, I don't know if I should feel flattered or paranoid," Mallory commented.

He grinned. "If I had a choice between the two, I'd definitely go with flattered."

"So you're on a press trip even though you're not a writer," Mallory said, trying to deflect what she thought might have been a compliment.

"Guilty as charged. Actually, I usually send someone from my staff on travel junkets like this one. That is, whenever the opportunity to travel to a destination that seems right for our readers comes up. But Toronto gets pretty gray in January, so I decided to take advantage of this one."

"Ah. You're Canadian," Mallory observed.

"That's right." Grinning again, he added, "But my

English is good enough that I can usually pass myself off as American."

She laughed. "It sounds as if you don't get to do much traveling."

"I'm starting to do more." He hesitated before adding, "I recently got divorced, and I suddenly find that my schedule is a whole lot freer."

"Do you believe this place?" Phil Diamond plopped down at the head of the table and glared at the other four journalists. "How do they expect people to have a good time if they can't even light up a cigarette? And I've already had a hell of a day. Would you believe it started in Milwaukee, where I spent two days researching a piece on some ridiculous ice-sculpting competition? This morning, I flew to JFK at dawn, then got stuck on this ridiculous overbooked flight run by sky Nazis. . . . It's enough to make anybody need a cigarette."

"Perhaps you should consider giving up smoking, Phil, dear," Frieda suggested. "It's such a nasty habit. And so bad for you, not to mention everyone around you."

"Speaking of things that are bad for you," Phil grumbled, snapping his fingers at the waitress, "I could definitely use a drink. Anyone care to join me?"

Once again, his eyes drifted around the table. When they reached Mallory, they suddenly narrowed.

"Oh," he said disgustedly. "It's *you*."

"I didn't think you two knew each other," Frieda commented.

"Are you kidding? We're old friends," Phil replied, his voice curdling with sarcasm. "Just this morning, this delightful lady and I had the pleasure of flying into Orlando together."

Fortunately, their waitress came trotting over, her pad and pen in hand. "Is there something I can get for you, sir?" she asked Phil.

"Can I get a gee-and-tee, pronto?"

The waitress, who looked young enough to be en route to Disney World herself instead of working at a restaurant, immediately became flustered. "I'm sorry, sir. I don't know what that is."

"You don't know what a gee-and-tee is? It's a gin and tonic. The recipe's simple. See, you take gin—a lot of gin—and you add tonic. Voilà!"

"I'm afraid we don't serve alcohol here."

"*What?* How in hell am I supposed to—"

"Well, it looks like you're all having fun!" chirped a young woman who'd just trotted over to their table. "I'm Courtney Conover, and on behalf of the Florida Tourism Board, I want to welcome each and every one of you!"

She clutched a clipboard in one hand, and with the other nervously pushed her overly long bangs out of her eyes. Mallory noted that she didn't look much older than their waitress. And thanks to her straight platinum blond hair, courtesy of Clairol, and her bright emerald-green eyes, courtesy of Bausch & Lomb, she looked more like Barbie's little sister than someone in a position of authority.

"Sorry I'm late," Courtney continued. "Things got a little crazy at the office this morning. But I want to start out by telling you how thrilled we are to have all of you here."

"Y'know, there's such a thing as being too damned jolly," Annabelle muttered. "Especially before lunch, when everyone's blood sugar is low."

"Now, now," Frieda returned. "She's just cheerful. There's no law against being cheerful."

"Before I start boring you with details," Courtney said, "there's someone I'd like to introduce. Mr. Farnaby," she called across the room, "could you please come over here? If you have a moment, I'd like you to meet our distinguished group of writers."

Mallory glanced around the table, blinking. *Distinguished?*

Mr. Farnaby was all smiles as he scurried over to the table. "Well, of *course* I want to meet my honored guests!" he gushed.

"Everyone, this is Desmond Farnaby, general manager of the Polynesian Princess Hotel." Courtney introduced him with the same drama one would expect for the presentation of the Queen of England.

The writers mumbled a greeting. All except Phil.

"I believe you already know Phil Diamond," Courtney said.

The two men glowered at each other.

"This is Annabelle Gatch," Courtney said quickly. "She writes for *Travel on a Shoestring.*"

"Is that Miss or Mrs. Gatch?" Desmond asked.

"Miz-z-z-z," Annabelle hissed.

"Ms. Gatch, then," Desmond said graciously, shaking her hand. "I think you'll find the Polynesian Princess offers its guests excellent value."

"Hmph," Annabelle replied. "The complimentary shampoo is microscopic. And there's no sewing kit, no shoe shine kit, no nail care kit—"

"I'll look into all of it," the hotel manager said diplomatically. Turning to Frieda, he asked, "And you are...?"

"Frieda Stein, *Go Seniors!* magazine."

She stuck out her hand, as if to shake. Instead, Desmond grasped her fingers and brought them to his lips.

"*Enchanté,*" he murmured.

Frieda giggled. "My goodness! What a charmer you are, Mr. Farnaby!"

"Thank you, my dear. And I hope you're equally charmed by our lovely hotel."

"This is Mallory Marlowe," Courtney said, stepping

behind her chair and placing her hands on her shoulders. "Mallory writes for *The Good Life*."

"Ah. A fine magazine. It's a real pleasure to have you as our guest, Ms. Marlowe."

When Desmond shook her hand instead of kissing it, Mallory didn't know whether or not to be insulted. In the end, she decided it was better to be treated like a professional than a femme fatale.

"And last but certainly not least, this is Wade McKay, the publisher of *Living Well*. It's a Canadian magazine that's based in Toronto."

"Wade."

"Desmond."

The two men shook hands. Phil looked on, scowling.

"I hope you all make yourselves at home," Desmond said, spreading his arms in a welcoming gesture. "If there's anything I can do to make your stay more enjoyable, please don't hesitate to ask."

"How about that nail care kit?" Annabelle muttered.

"Thank you, Mr. Farnaby." Beaming, Courtney added, "We'll be seeing more of Mr. Farnaby later on, at the reception this evening. If you have any questions about the hotel, he'll be happy to answer them then.

"As for the other aspects of your visit," she continued, focusing on the group once Desmond had left, "I want you to feel you can come to me for anything you want. You're our guests. So I encourage you to think of me as much more than just your tour guide and point of contact here in Orlando. Think of me as your family. Your sister or your daughter—"

"Too bad incest has such a bad name," Phil wisecracked. "I can't remember the last time I was on a press trip with such a hottie."

Courtney froze. Mallory winced as she watched the young woman's face turn as red as the anthuriums that decorated the table.

"Hey, part of your job is to make sure all of us have a good time, right?" Phil went on, smirking. "I've already got a few ideas. And the fact that we're in a hotel makes them a lot easier to put into practice, if you catch my drift."

Mallory glanced around the table. All the writers had the same stricken looks on their faces.

"The people who read my website are always looking for new and unusual things to do," he continued. "So I hope you're open to trying new things. It just so happens I packed a copy of the Kama Sutra in my suitcase."

"I—I wasn't going to admit this," the young tour guide stammered, "but this is the first time I've run a press trip all by myself." She was addressing all of them, but her eyes were fixed on Phil. "My *husband* told me not to let on. But I'm hoping that by being straight with you, maybe you'll be willing to cut me some slack."

"First time, huh?" Phil guffawed. "So I guess that makes you a virgin. Hey, I noticed that there's a volcano in the ballroom. That looks like a great place to sacrifice virgins, so you'd better watch out! Of course, you'd probably need to be a virgin in every sense of the word, but if they need somebody to check you out, I'm their man!"

Courtney remained silent, twisting her mouth and wrinkling her forehead in a way that made her look like a rubber-faced elf—an elf who was about to burst into tears. She reminded Mallory of Amanda when she was four years old. And Phil's bullying suddenly brought back the year Jordan was constantly tormented by a schoolyard toughie.

Before she'd even had a chance to think about what she was doing, she stood up and turned to Phil.

"Look, we're all here because we're professional writers," she said, her voice controlled but her feelings clear. "That means that even though this hotel looks like it was designed by somebody on LSD, as far as our little group goes, it's a workplace. Which means everyone here is expected to act in a professional manner. That translates to no sexism, no tasteless jokes, and if it's at all possible, no stupidity. From this point on, we're all going to show our host the respect she deserves. Got it?"

Her blood still boiling, she turned to Courtney and said, "Now, if you'll be kind enough to continue, Courtney, I'm sure we're all interested in what you have to say."

After she plopped back down in her seat, everyone at the table remained silent for what seemed like a very long time. And then Wade started to applaud.

"Here, here," he said. "I think Mallory speaks for all of us."

Mallory glanced over at Frieda and saw that she was nodding. Annabelle had pink patches on her cheeks, but the fact that she was staring at the table, avoiding making eye contact with Phil, implied that she, too, agreed with Mallory.

Courtney cleared her throat, then pushed her hair back again. "Okay, then. Let's, uh, continue. This press trip is going to be a particular challenge, since you all have such a different focus. Annabelle, you write for *Shoestring,* so you'll be looking for low-cost activities, special deals, that kind of thing." With a little smile, she added, "And your editor e-mailed me that your birthday is on Tuesday, so we'll have to be sure to schedule in a little party. I understand it's a big one, too."

"Uh, yes." Annabelle lowered her head and muttered, "The big four-oh."

"Wow!" Courtney exclaimed. "That definitely calls for a birthday cake!" She made a note on her clipboard. "Frieda, you'll be focusing on activities that are of interest to seniors, including those who are traveling by themselves—that is, without their grandchildren. And, uh, Phil, since you're writing for the seasoned traveler, you'll be looking for anything that's new or off the beaten track. I can help you with that."

Mallory cast him a meaningful look, just in case he hadn't quite gotten the point and decided to toss out a few more unwelcome witticisms. Instead, he stared right back. And then, smiling crookedly, he held up his hands and shrugged.

"Wade writes for a Canadian audience," Courtney continued. She flashed him a shy smile, then added, "So part of my job will be convincing you that our neighbors to the north are more than welcome to visit us here in the good old U.S. of A."

She turned to Mallory. "And last, but certainly not least, Mallory, I understand this is your very first press trip, too."

"That's right." Mallory smiled self-consciously. "But I think I'm already getting the hang of it."

She was grateful when Frieda and Wade laughed.

"*The Good Life* is a terrific publication," Courtney went on, "and we're thrilled to be getting coverage in it."

"It has great circulation," Frieda commented, beaming. Impishly she added, "Unlike so many of my peers."

Mallory was beaming, too. She was convinced she'd done all of them a favor by taking Phil to task, not only Courtney. Here she'd felt as if she was just getting to know all the other kids on her first day at a new school, and with more guts than she would have thought she possessed, she'd handled the fact that some of them hadn't learned all they needed to know in kindergarten.

"You should all be settled into your rooms by now," Courtney went on. "Please let me know if there's anything at all I can help you with."

"Aside from the substandard amenities, my room is much too cold," Annabelle complained. "I think the air-conditioning is broken."

"The bathtub in mine doesn't have handrails!" Frieda piped up. "That's important for us senior travelers."

"My room overlooks the parking lot," Phil complained. "But I guess I'm not about to get it changed."

For a moment, Mallory felt as if she'd gone back in time and was traveling with Amanda and Jordan again, back before iPods and video games were enough to silence them for hours at a time. She could hardly believe that not long before, she'd been worried about being less sophisticated and worldly-wise than her fellow travel writers.

"I'll ask Mr. Farnaby to look into all those things," Courtney replied, jotting notes on her clipboard. Mallory was relieved that Courtney's sparkle was back, and that neither Phil's boorishness nor her attempt to keep it in check had thrown her. "And you're welcome to mention them to him at the reception we're throwing tonight. It's at seven o'clock in the Bali Ballroom, right here at the hotel. Dinner follows right afterward. The hotel's executive chef is preparing a special tasting menu for the occasion, and it's guaranteed to be absolutely fabulous.

"Now, let me hand out these press kits. Inside, you should find all the vouchers you'll need during your stay, plus a whole bunch of booklets that I think you'll find useful, a photo CD, and an official Orlando key chain and nail file."

When lunch was over, Annabelle stood up and announced, "Bye, everyone. I'm off to Epcot. I've got ten bucks in my pocket, and my goal is to spend the entire afternoon there and still come home with change." She reached into her clunky black purse and pulled out a Ziploc bag containing cubes of cheese and half a dozen broken Stoned Wheat Thins. "This is my afternoon snack. I'm going to have to sneak it past Security."

Frowning, she mused, "The Diet Coke is going to be much trickier because of the metal can."

There's something to remember, Mallory thought wryly. Skinflint Hint #382: Feel free to break the rules by sneaking your own food into places in which it's not permitted. She was glad she worked for a magazine whose readers could actually afford the vacations they took.

"I'm going to the Magic Kingdom this afternoon," Frieda said as she rose from the table and pushed in her chair.

"What happened to the bungee jumping?" Annabelle asked with a smirk.

"Even our most adventurous readers are young at heart," Frieda replied defensively. "They enjoy a ride in the teacups as much as the next person. Even if the next person *does* happen to be five years old."

Phil didn't bother to share his plans for the afternoon. Mallory wondered if they consisted of doing research at the hotel bar.

"I'm off to tour some of Orlando's luxury hotels," Wade said. "The ones that are targeted at grown-ups, with great spas, saunas, and four-star chefs." Smiling at Mallory, he asked, "What about you?"

"I'm spending the afternoon at an attraction called Titanic: The Experience," she replied.

Unfortunately, Phil overheard. "My heart will go on-n-n and on-n-n..." he crooned in an irritatingly shrill falsetto. "Hey, make sure you wear a life vest. Better yet, bring along a couple of lifeboats." He burst into raw laughter over what he clearly believed to be his remarkable cleverness.

Mallory forced a polite smile. She may have tamed the beast, at least temporarily, but she certainly hadn't silenced him.

"If you don't mind," Courtney piped up, "I think I'll join you. Believe it or not, I've never been to the Titanic."

She giggled. "Oops, I mean the attraction, not the ship. Of course, I haven't been to the ship, either."

"I'd enjoy the company," Mallory said, even though inwardly she was groaning. She didn't know if she could handle an entire afternoon of Courtney's perkiness. I guess there's no such thing as a free lunch, she thought grimly. Or a free trip.

After she and Courtney agreed to meet at the base of the volcano in fifteen minutes, Mallory stood up to leave. "Have fun, everyone," she said. "I'll see you tonight at the reception."

As she wove among the tables, she felt someone touch her arm. She turned, surprised, and saw that Wade had caught up with her.

"Good job," he said. "Putting some limits on that idiot, I mean. You did us all a service."

"Thanks," she said, suddenly shy.

"I'm glad we have someone as spunky as you on our trip. It should make things much more fun."

"Spunky, huh?" She laughed. "No one's ever called me spunky before."

He just winked. "Catch you later," he called as he headed out of the coffee shop.

By that point, Phil had slithered up to her. "Have fun on the *Titanic*," he commented. "I just hope you're a good swimmer."

And then, in a much lower voice, he added, "And I promise you'll be seeing a lot more of me. You and I will definitely have the chance to get to know each other a lot better."

"Jerk," Mallory muttered after he'd strutted away.

But as she left the restaurant, it wasn't annoying Phil that she was thinking about. It was the Canadian. Wade.

Interesting fellow, she thought.

She immediately asked herself if the reason she'd gotten that impression was that he had an exciting career publishing his own magazine—or if it was because he was recently divorced and had divine blue eyes and a luscious smile.

You're here to do a job, Mallory reminded herself firmly. You've come to Orlando to uncover the old Florida, not flirt.

Still, she realized it was the first time she'd come even close to having such thoughts since David had died. She was surprised to find that she was still capable. She was even more surprised by how good it felt, as if the warm Florida sunshine was thawing something deep inside her that had been frozen for much too long.

4

"Happiness is a direction, not a place."
—Sydney J. Harris

What better place to seek out the old Florida than at an attraction built around the world's "Ship of Dreams"? Mallory mused a few minutes later as she and Courtney pulled into the parking lot of the first attraction on her list, Titanic: The Experience.

The ticket office was housed in an oddly shaped geometric building in front of an open-air shopping mall with Spanish-style architecture, called the Mercado. A painting of what was arguably the most famous ship in history hung above the entrance, with a sign identifying it for anyone who had just arrived from another planet. Jutting upward from the building's flat roof was a gigantic inverted triangle that was covered with circles and had a metallic look.

"That's such a funny-looking building," Courtney commented, scrunching up her nose. "I can't imagine what they were thinking."

"I can." Now that Mallory had a chance to study it,

she realized that the strange building was the architect's version of the *Titanic*. A tad abstract, perhaps, but at least the designer's approach had been more creative than simply copying the actual ship's design. "It's supposed to be the *Titanic*. See? The upside-down 3-D triangle shape is a re-creation of the hull. The circles symbolize the bolts."

"O-o-h," Courtney said vaguely, as if she didn't really see at all. She was about to open the car door when she paused and said, "By the way, Mallory, I wanted to thank you for sticking up for me before. That was really nice of you."

"No problem. Phil was bothering all of us, not just you."

"Still," Courtney persisted, "if I had more experience, I might have handled it better. I'm actually pretty nervous. About being in charge of a press trip for the first time, I mean."

"It's a big responsibility," Mallory said sympathetically. "All those details to juggle—and all those different personalities. But you're doing just fine." She heard herself speaking in a motherly tone, no doubt because Courtney wasn't much older than her daughter. "Besides, if anyone was acting unprofessional, it was Phil. In fact, he was behaving like a junior high school boy on his first trip away from home. You'd think that by now he'd know better."

As they walked inside the building, she was annoyed that the nasty scene from lunch was seeping into the rest of the day. As if talking about Phil Diamond wasn't bad enough, she couldn't get his off-key rendition of the theme song from the James Cameron movie out of her head. Of course, the piped-in music, a Celine Dion wannabe crooning a song that sounded just different enough from the famous one not to precipitate a lawsuit, didn't help.

Still, she was determined to forget about the oafish journalist and concentrate on the famous disaster. She smiled at the ticket seller, a young man dressed in period costume consisting of black pants, a black vest, and a white shirt and tie.

"One, please," she said, proffering the voucher she'd found in her press kit.

"And I'm with Florida Tourism." Courtney flashed an ID card the same way cops on TV were always flashing their badges.

Her credentials clearly had just as much clout here in Florida, where sightseeing was the official state pastime.

"The next tour begins in fifteen minutes," the young man advised, pushing two tickets toward them. "These are each printed with a name of one of the *Titanic*'s actual passengers. At the end of the tour, you can check the Memorial Wall to find out whether or not you survived."

Mallory expected to be a scullery maid or one of the other third-class passengers who, in the movie, was kept behind a locked gate as the great ship went down. Instead, she saw that for the next hour or so she would be the Countess of Rothes, also known as Lucy Dyer-Edwards.

"I'm a countess!" she exclaimed. "Who are you?"

"Mrs. Latifa Baclini." Frowning, Courtney noted, "I'm traveling third-class."

"Oh, she's a good one," the ticket seller gushed. "Latifa was Lebanese and didn't speak English. She and her daughters weren't even supposed to travel on the *Titanic*. They had tickets on another liner. But while they were in Cherbourg, France, one of the girls got pink eye and they had to delay their departure until she got better."

"What about the countess?" Mallory asked.

"Definitely first-class. She was British, married to the

nineteenth Earl of Rothes, mother of two sons. A real lady, from what I understand."

Mallory walked just a little more gracefully than usual as she wandered over to a glass display case, which held a copy of the *New York Times* dated Tuesday, April 16, 1912. The headlines read:

Titanic Sinks Four Hours After Hitting Iceberg
866 Rescued by Carpathia, Probably 1250 Perish;
Ismay Safe, Mrs. Astor Maybe, Noted Names Missing

Ismay, she recalled from the movie, was the muckety-muck who ran the White Star Line, the company that owned and operated the *Titanic*. The Astors were house-hold names simply because they were so rich. As for the number of casualties, she knew from the reading she'd done before coming to Florida that it was even larger: 1,503.

But she copied down the headline, word for word, in case she decided to include it in her article. As she wrote, she overheard a man who had just come into the ticket office.

"So what exactly is the experience?" he asked the man behind the counter. "Do you, like, get wet?"

Maybe I should be writing an article on macabre Florida, she thought.

"We have a few minutes before the tour starts," she told Courtney. "Let's check out the gift shop."

Mallory quickly decided that the gift shop also belonged in an article on macabre Florida. After all, there was definitely something unseemly about a retail establishment whose theme was one of the worst tragedies of the twentieth century.

Still, she couldn't resist a store of any kind, much less one with a clerk dressed like a maid from the early 1900s, in a long black dress and crisp white apron and cap.

Mallory wandered among the displays, wondering if Jordan would appreciate a fluffy white bath towel embroidered with *White Star Line—Titanic*.

Maybe a reminder of how fragile life is would prompt him to hang it up every once in a while, she thought, instead of leaving it on the bathroom floor in a mildewing heap. When she spotted the price tag, however, she decided there had to be cheaper ways of training an eighteen-year-old boy.

She reached for a long thin box sporting a picture of the doomed ship. *Inflatable Titanic,* the box read. *Twenty inches. Educational and fun.*

Very educational, Mallory thought grimly. It teaches the lesson: Go by airplane.

The box also warned, *Do not use as a flotation device,* which she decided was excellent advice.

Nearby she spotted a plastic replica of the famous ocean liner, one that was apparently battery powered. *Cruises on surface* the copy on the box noted.

That, Mallory concluded, was undoubtedly designed to calm potential customers who feared the toy would go under the very first time it was used.

But showtime was imminent. As she and Courtney waited in line with two dozen other tourists who were part of the tour, their eyes were glued to a video with actual footage of the great ship.

"The ship was nearly four city blocks long," the narrator reported with pride. "Its passengers included famous names like Guggenheim, Astor, and Strauss."

"I'm surprised you've never been here before," Mallory commented, figuring that part of being a good travel writer was making conversation with the people who had sponsored her trip.

Courtney scrunched up her nose again. "Actually, it's been a really busy year for me. I just graduated from college last May. And then Greg and I got married in

August. Planning our wedding was a huge job. But it was worth it.

"You should have seen it!" she gurgled, just assuming Mallory would be interested in the details. "We got married at this really gorgeous hotel, outside in the garden. We had almost three hundred guests, and a million flowers.... My wedding cake had five tiers. Five! It was like something out of a fairy tale—or the food channel!"

"It sounds wonderful," Mallory said politely.

"Oh, it definitely was. Then, right after our honeymoon, I started working for the Tourism Board. So I've spent the past few months getting used to both a new job and my new status as a married lady. All of a sudden, I had this completely different life, compared to my four years at college."

"Did you go to school in Florida?" Mallory asked.

Courtney nodded. "Florida State University. I majored in Communications. I also had some really cool part-time jobs. I worked for a local radio station my first two years. Then I moved to a public relations firm. I ended up learning a lot."

"Sounds like a tough schedule," Mallory observed, thinking of all the hours Amanda logged in at the library. "Being a full-time student plus working, I mean."

Shrugging, Courtney replied, "But I got such great experience. When I graduated, it helped me get exactly the job I wanted."

Without going to law school *or* business school, Mallory couldn't help thinking. "It sounds as if you really enjoy working in the tourism field."

"Ooh, I love it!" Courtney gushed. "It's *so* much fun. I get to meet all kinds of interesting people and go to fun places—like today! I'm having a great time. Aren't you?"

By that point, the group had started shuffling forward. When they reached the front of the line, their tour guide, the same young man who had played the role of ticket seller, ripped her ticket in half.

"Welcome aboard, Countess," he greeted her.

In response, she bowed her head. She wondered with amusement if she could induce her son to start addressing her the same way. As for her daughter, she was undoubtedly a lost cause.

Yet Mallory found her cynicism dropping away as the tour group entered the first room of the exhibit, the offices of J. Bruce Ismay. The caption underneath his portrait, which hung on the green-and-white-striped wall, explained that he was the son of Thomas H. Ismay, cofounder of the White Star Line. Junior became the manager of the company when his father died in 1899.

J. Bruce Ismay—or at least the handsome, mustached actor who was portraying him—suddenly appeared on the video screen above the huge wooden desk. The actor managed to make him seem suitably arrogant as he announced that the ship formerly known as R.M.S. No. 401 had just been launched. He smugly explained that the 882-foot ship made from 45,000 tons of steel was the most luxurious and safest ship ever built and that it was practically unsinkable.

"Eight hundred eighty-two feet...forty-five thousand tons of steel..." Mallory muttered as she copied down the facts she thought she might need for future reference. "Most luxurious and safest..."

She continued taking notes as the group was led through the Belfast Shipyard, where a reproduction of the ship's giant propeller was on display. Next came the boarding area in Southampton, England, where, the tour guide explained, all passengers, including those traveling first class, were checked for head lice. She snapped some photos inside the elegant black-and-white Verandah Café, with its glass displays of china and silverware.

Then the group entered a room that contained a reproduction of the ship's Grand Staircase, which everyone recognized from the movie. A plump woman in a floor-length black dress, a black hat trimmed with feathers, and an overabundance of jewelry burst into the room.

"I'm Molly Brown," she introduced herself energetically. "You may have heard of me."

Sure, Mallory thought. You're a famous historical figure who's best known for not dying on the *Titanic*.

Actually, Mallory had read about her in one of her guidebooks, so she knew there was a lot more to her. The real Molly Brown was the daughter of Irish immigrants who'd fled the famous potato famine of the 1840s. At age thirteen, she got her first job in a tobacco factory in her hometown of Hannibal, Missouri. She moved to Colorado and married a mining engineer named J. J. Brown, who became a millionaire after inventing a method for digging deeper in the gold mines. Even though the Browns began hobnobbing with the Vanderbilts, the Whitneys, and the Astors, she never stopped fighting for improved labor conditions and women's rights and even ran for Congress.

This version exhibited the brash personality that became Molly Brown's trademark. She explained that the solid oak staircase spanned seven flights and that first-class passengers used it to reach the dining room, where they enjoyed ten-course dinners and champagne. Mallory had to admit that so far, the exhibits had managed to capture all the glamour of the ship.

But of course it couldn't last. Molly Brown led the group through the lower deck, where they could hear the ominous rumble of the engine. As they passed the iron gate that blocked off the quarters of the third-class passengers, the lights began blinking on and off.

The mood darkened even further when the group stopped in front of an actual iceberg.

Mallory glanced around and saw that everyone in the group appeared to be enraptured.

"Put your hand on it for fifteen seconds," Molly Brown instructed. "It feels cold at first, but then it starts to burn. It's thirty-two degrees in here. The night the *Titanic* sank, the air was thirty-one degrees and the water was twenty-eight degrees. Adults can last ten to twenty minutes in that temperature before hypothermia sets in and they suffocate."

I guess this is part of the Experience, Mallory thought, jotting down the gruesome figures the tour guide had just rattled off.

She was disappointed that the exhibits included a real life iceberg, which struck her as the height of bad taste. But her attitude changed once she dutifully filed over to it with the rest of the group and pressed the palm of her hand against it.

The iceberg was torturously cold and frighteningly solid. In fact, it was only when she had actually touched the enormous chunk of ice herself—*experienced* it—that she fully understood what a formidable foe it had been.

The re-creation of the deck was almost as cold. Once the group had gathered around the ersatz Molly Brown, she pointed out that here, as on the real *Titanic,* there were stars in the sky but no moon. As Mallory stood shivering in the dark, frigid air, she could really relate to the horror of that night.

Maybe this is a little *too much* of the *Titanic* experience, she thought, shivering as Molly Brown launched into a detailed description of the horrors that occurred as the ill-fated ship went down. It wasn't until she was explaining that the passengers had never had a lifeboat drill, since it wasn't scheduled until later in the trip, that she noticed that some of the children on the tour were turning blue and moved them along to the next room.

"Model of the propeller," Mallory wrote as she shuffled along with the others. "Molly Brown, actual iceberg, cold then hot..."

As promised, there was a Memorial Wall near the end that listed all the passengers. The survivors' names were in bold letters. Mallory was relieved to see that both she and Courtney had made it out alive.

"Look, we survived!" she cried. "See, here's my name, Lucy Dyer-Edwards, Countess of Rothes. And here's yours, Mrs. Latifa Baclini."

She glanced over at Courtney, expecting to find her rejoicing in their good fortune. Instead, tears were streaming down her cheeks.

"Courtney, are you okay?"

"It's so sad!" she cried. "Wives lost their husbands, children lost their fathers—"

"It was a terrible tragedy," Mallory agreed. She glanced around, slightly embarrassed that Courtney had chosen this particular time and place to mourn an event that had taken place nearly a hundred years ago.

"To us, it's just an interesting historical event," Courtney sniffled. "But I'm sure it's something those poor people who lost their loved ones never got over."

Why hadn't Courtney done this when she saw the movie, Mallory wondered, like everybody else?

She handed her a tissue, then led her to the final room of the exhibit. Fortunately, it focused on the tragedy's commercial aspects. Hanging on the walls were posters from the various movies about the *Titanic* that had been made since the 1940s, along with photos of the actors who starred in them. The final display was a reproduction of one of the ensembles Kate Winslet wore in the most recent film, along with Leonardo DiCaprio's actual costume.

By the time they left the exhibit, Courtney was her usual cheery self again.

"That was quite moving," she chirped. "I'm glad I

came with you. I'll definitely recommend this to everyone who visits Orlando."

And I'm sure the tourists will appreciate it, Mallory thought. After all, there's nothing like death to bring in the crowds.

• • •

After an entire afternoon of Courtney's chattiness, Mallory welcomed the silence of her hotel room. The Florida Tourism Board reception wasn't scheduled to start for a couple of hours, so she sat down at the small round table, intending to read through the notes she'd taken that afternoon. But she couldn't resist reorganizing them, then jotting down her impressions while they were still fresh in her mind. When she finally finished and surveyed what she'd written, she found that she'd filled six full pages.

I had no idea I had so much to say, she thought, astounded by how easily this was coming to her. To think I was worried that I wouldn't be able to do this—and now that I'm here, it turns out there's no stopping me!

She stood up to stretch, exhilarated by what she'd accomplished on her very first day as a travel writer. When she glanced at the clock, she realized that she'd worked for almost a solid hour.

Travel Writing: the Experience, she thought giddily as she headed into the bathroom to get ready for the reception. After a long, steaming hot shower, she slathered on the coconut-scented body lotion the hotel provided, deeply inhaling its delightfully sweet scent. Then she spent longer than usual blow-drying her hair, agonizing over the strands in front until she finally got them to curve gently around her face.

At twenty minutes to seven, she slipped into a black halter-top dress splashed with red flowers. She smiled as she remembered what David said the last time he'd seen her in it: that it made her look like one of those women in the L'Oréal ads who claimed, "I'm worth it." Then she slipped on a pair of strappy red sandals with heels that were much higher than she was used to. When she'd spotted them at Macy's, she hadn't been able to resist trying them on. When she saw how long they made her legs look, she'd had no choice but to whip out her charge card.

The final touch was makeup. She put on more than she'd bothered with in months, with the exception of her interview at *The Good Life*. It was hard to believe that it was only days earlier that she'd ridden up the elevator with butterflies in her stomach. Now here she was, standing in front of a bathroom mirror more than a thousand miles from home, agonizing over which pair of earrings looked better, the white pearls or the red chandeliers.

And enjoying every minute of the trip. In fact, she suddenly stopped what she was doing to marvel once again over how much fun she was having—and to recognize how little fun she'd had since David's accident.

She understood that she'd needed time to mourn. That in fact she was still mourning. Yet she was dealing with even more than grief. She also had to cope with the feeling that everyone she loved was deserting her.

It was something that dated back to before David's death. She'd spent so many years catering to the needs of her family that once they vanished, one by one, she had found herself floundering for a new way to define herself. When Amanda went off to college, Mallory had felt as if a part of her body had been physically cut off. But she still had David and Jordan with her at the dinner table every night. Then, when Jordan was only a couple of months away from going off to college, David was suddenly gone, too.

Even her son's return only a few weeks after leaving for school hadn't helped the aching in her heart. True, he was living in her house again. But he didn't belong there.

He was just stopping in while he decided where to go next, like someone who was idling in a No Parking zone.

The result was a feeling of emptiness that never quite went away. At least until now. Before coming on this trip, Mallory had been afraid that being thrust into a new and unfamiliar situation would cause her to lose whatever sense of balance she still clung to. Instead, she abruptly found herself being forced to play a completely different role. And her personal life didn't matter one bit. Whether or not her children were at home, whether or not she had a husband—in this context, none of it was the least bit relevant. All that mattered was what Wade and Annabelle and Courtney and the others could see: that she was a travel writer working for a well-respected publication, here to do a job.

The question that kept nagging at her was whether or not she could rise to the occasion. Yet here she was, doing exactly that. She was holding her own in a situation that a lot of people would find downright intimidating. She wasn't surprised that she was managing to handle herself just fine. What did surprise her was the ease with which the old Mallory was resurfacing, pushing aside the timid, uncertain Mallory who had appeared from nowhere when David died.

Still marveling over the attractive, self-confident woman staring back at her in the mirror, she decided that tonight she would quietly celebrate her unexpected return to her old self. Surely a reception in a big, flashy hotel would include champagne or some other appropriately festive drink. She vowed to make a toast to the return of Mallory Marlowe, a woman who only hours before a virtual stranger had characterized as "spunky."

• • •

The Bali Ballroom, Mallory discovered as she teetered inside on her red high heels, had the same faux-Polynesian decor as the lobby. The walls were covered with coarse straw mats that she assumed were supposed to look as if they'd been woven in huts made of the same material. More artifacts from the South Seas dotted the walls—the usual assortment of tiki gods, masks, and weaponry. But the centerpiece was the ceiling-high waterfall, which splashed over fake rocks and then spilled into a dark pool that was surrounded by a low stone wall.

There were also signs of the festivities to come. A long table against one wall was lined with empty chafing dishes, and a small bar was tucked into one corner. Clustered around it were small round tables covered in fabric that looked very much like the bedspread in her hotel room.

As she headed in that direction, she stumbled. "Klutz," she muttered, assuming her ineptness with impractical shoes was to blame. But when she glanced down, she saw that she'd tripped on a spear.

She automatically leaned over and picked it up, figuring there was no reason for anyone else to trip on it. Besides, she'd spent half a lifetime cleaning up after other people, moving Jordan's gargantuan sneakers out of the hallway and Amanda's heavy textbooks off the dining room table.

Once she was holding it in her hands, she saw that it was made of metal, unlike the wooden spears the natives of the South Sea Islands undoubtedly used to kill one another. She also noticed that it was discolored at the end. It looked as if it had been dipped in something red. Dark red.

But before she had a chance to examine it any further, the sound of a human voice—a very perturbed human voice—prompted her to turn around.

"Oh, my God. Will you *look* at those horrendous tablecloths? Whatever possessed them to use those ancient things?"

Desmond Farnaby stood in the doorway, his hands on his hips. "If I told them once, I told them a thousand times: You can't—oh, hello. It's Mallory, isn't it?"

She nodded. "Hello, Desmond." Holding out the spear, she added, "It looks like this fell off the wall. You might want to—"

"Oh, my God!" he screeched, this time with considerably more vehemence. "Oh, my *God*!"

Mallory just stared at him, puzzled over what indecent thing any tablecloth could possibly have done that would cause the hotel's general manager's hands to fly to his cheeks like the child star in *Home Alone*. But something about the look of shock on his face told her it was the result of something a lot worse than outdated fabric.

She followed his gaze to the waterfall. It was only then that she noticed something unusual protruding out of the little pond surrounding it. Something large. Something oddly shaped. Something brightly colored.

Mallory's forehead creased as she tried to make sense of what she was looking at. And then, in a flash, she realized that Phil Diamond was floating facedown in the pool of water.

And from where she stood, he looked very, very dead.

5

"Embrace the detours."
—Kevin Charbonneau

"Oh, my God!" Mallory cried, dashing toward the waterfall. "Is he breathing? Is he still alive?"

Even though the sight of a man floating face-down in the water was horrific, she forced herself to look more closely. It was difficult to tell if he was dead, although the fact that he wasn't moving certainly made him look as if he was. Unless, of course, he was simply playing some perverse joke.

But there was another bad sign: a large bloodstain on the back of his garish Hawaiian shirt. The brightly colored, flowered fabric was soaking wet, which oddly enough caused it to puff up like a life preserver. Visions of that afternoon's excursion to the *Titanic* exhibit pushed their way into her head.

"What should we do?" Mallory asked frantically, trying to push any association with over-the-top tourist attractions right back out again. "Should we pull him out and try to resuscitate him? I haven't taken a CPR course since my kids were practically babies. And I certainly don't want to tamper with a crime scene if he was mur—"

"We can't have this!" Desmond shrieked, his eyes wild. "This is a family resort!"

"We have to do *something*!" Mallory insisted. "I'm going to call the police. Or do you want to do it, since you're the—?"

"No!" he screeched. "No police! Not yet! Not until I have a chance to get this place in order . . . Goodness gracious. Will you look at this? There's water splashed all over the place! And—oh, my God, is that *blood*? All over the carpet?"

Mallory decided not to wait another second. She stepped into the corridor outside the ballroom, afraid that if Desmond saw what she was doing, he'd rip the cell phone away from her. Her hands trembled as she dialed 911.

"I'd like to report an accident," she said in a voice that was as shaky as her hands. "At least, I think it was an accident. It could have been murder. I'm at the Polynesian Princess Hotel. . . ."

After explaining the situation in as few words as possible, she headed back into the ballroom. She expected to find Desmond frantically calling hotel security or cordoning off the waterfall to make sure no valuable evidence was destroyed.

Instead, he was on his hands and knees, energetically scrubbing the carpet with a white rag. Beside him was a large plastic jug that Mallory concluded contained an industrial-strength cleaner.

"What are you *doing*?" she demanded.

"I'm positive this is blood!" he cried in a panicked voice, holding up the rag. It was indeed tinged with red. "The Polynesian Princess can't host an elegant reception with *blood* on the carpets!"

"Desmond, I don't think the reception is going to take

place," Mallory pointed out. "Even more important, you shouldn't be touching anything! The police will be here any minute, and it's crucial that they find everything exactly the way it was when Phil was—when this horrible thing happened!"

"You don't understand," Desmond insisted. "This hotel has standards! You have no idea how hard we've worked for our four-star rating!"

"But—but you're tampering with a crime scene!"

He cast her a scathing look. "What I'm doing is trying to restore some semblance of normalcy to my hotel." He looked around frantically, his eyes lighting on the spear lying on the floor a few feet away from him. "Will you look at that? There's more nasty blood on the spear!" He grabbed it and frantically began rubbing it with the rag.

"Desmond, *stop*!" Mallory cried. "That spear could have been used to kill Phil! For heaven's sake, get control of yourself! Someone was *murdered*!"

"Exactly!" he screeched. And then, as if he'd suddenly remembered that he was trying to make the situation better, not worse, he lowered his voice to something more along the lines of a hiss. "How do you think something like this will affect the future of the Polynesian Princess Hotel? You obviously don't know this town. Here in Orlando, a serious crime is somebody making off with Minnie Mouse's bow or . . . or smashing bulbs on the Snow White float right before the Light Parade."

"Yes, but—"

"When word gets out that someone's been murdered, all hell will break loose!" he continued. "This place will be crawling with reporters and photographers and news teams from all the television stations. And they'll be reporting live. *Live!* How will it look if they walk into the fabulous Polynesian Princess and instead of the South Seas fantasy our guests expect, they find a badly dressed travel writer lying in the crowning glory of the Bali

Ballroom, the Gitgit Waterfall? What do you think that will do to bookings? What do you think it will do to my annual evaluation? Something like this could destroy a property like this—not to mention an entire career!"

Mallory stood frozen to the spot, wondering what to do about the fact that even as he spoke, Desmond was destroying something himself: evidence. She wondered if she should call hotel security or make a citizen's arrest or perhaps try to wrest the spear away from him.

But before she could decide what to do, Annabelle Gatch's grating voice interrupted her thoughts.

"It would have been nice if Courtney had told us in advance that we'd be going to a fancy reception," she complained loudly. From the sound of her voice, it sounded as if she was right outside the Bali Ballroom. "My readers travel on a budget, so they stick to bargain entertainment. I never bring dress clothes, since fancy receptions like this one aren't the kind of thing they go to when they're on vacation."

"You look absolutely lovely," Frieda assured her. "Not everyone can wear brown, you know. Especially such a *dark* shade. But your coloring is perfect for earth tones. In fact—oh, my! What's going on?"

Frieda froze as soon as she entered the ballroom, causing Annabelle to bump into her.

"Umph!" she cried. "Frieda, what do you think you're—*agh!* What *is* that?"

"Get them out of here!" Desmond snarled, even though there was no one around to perform that particular task.

"Desmond," Mallory exclaimed, her tone reflecting her frustration, "you can't hide the fact that Phil is lying in a waterfall, dead!"

"Phil is *dead*?" Annabelle cried.

"Are you sure?" Frieda rushed over to the waterfall. "Let me have a look. Believe me, I've seen my share of dead bodies. When you get to be my age, you suddenly find yourself a member of the Frequent Funeral Club." She peered at Phil's floating body for only a second or two before her eyes grew wide and her hands flew to her mouth. "Oh, my. You're absolutely right. Deader than the proverbial doornail. Poor Phil!"

At that moment, two uniformed cops burst through the double doors, their walkie-talkies squawking. Two EMTs hauling life-saving equipment tromped in right behind them.

"Somebody reported a murder," one of the police officers barked. "Is this the correct location?"

Without a word, Frieda and Desmond moved aside, revealing Phil Diamond's floating corpse.

"Aw, jeez," the other police officer said. "Better get Martinez over here."

The person he was referring to had apparently already gotten wind of the incident at the Polynesian Princess Hotel, since only minutes later a tall man with the muscular build of someone who worked out regularly strode in.

"Detective Martinez," the first cop greeted him with a nod. "Looks like we got a DOA."

"Rope off the crime scene," Martinez ordered, running his hand over his jet-black crew cut. Surprisingly, it didn't appear to contain a single gray hair, even though he looked as if he was in his mid-forties. "I'll get Forensics over here."

Mallory realized that under normal circumstances, she would have thought he was attractive. But circumstances had stopped being normal the moment she saw Phil Diamond's dead body floating under the fake waterfall.

Desmond rushed over to Detective Martinez, the blood-covered rag still clutched in his hand. "Detective, I hope you can get this body out of here ASAP. This situation is completely unacceptable. I simply cannot have something like this floating around in the Gitgit Waterfall. Not only is it bad for business—"

"Who are you?" Detective Martinez demanded.

"Why, I'm Desmond Farnaby," he replied indignantly. "The general manager of this hotel. As I was saying, I'm sure having something dead in the Gitgit Waterfall violates some health code, so it's critical that you—"

"Whoa," Detective Martinez interrupted again. "What's that word you keep saying? The one right before *waterfall*?"

Desmond looked puzzled. "Oh," he finally said. "You mean *Gitgit*." With a haughty toss of his head, he said, "I thought everyone knew the Gitgit Waterfall. It's the largest waterfall in Bali."

"I'll be sure to jot that down in my travel journal," Detective Martinez replied dryly. "But for now, I want everybody out of here. This is a crime scene. We need to let Forensics do their thing before the EMTs remove the body.

"In the meantime," he added, briefly making eye contact with Desmond and all three journalists, "no one is to leave. Mr. Farnaby, is there a room nearby where all of you can wait? I'll also need a second room where I can question each of you, one at a time."

His last words sent a shock wave through the small group. Mallory glanced at Frieda, then Annabelle. They both wore the same horrified look she suspected was on her own face.

"Detective Martinez," she said in a soft voice, "surely you don't think any of *us*—"

"Standard procedure," he replied curtly. "I need to find out everything I can about the victim, as well as what took place this evening. I'll start by taking statements from the four of you. Officer Langley, I'd like you to accompany me."

"What about the other writer who came on the press trip?" Desmond piped up. "I would think you'd want to talk to him, too."

Detective Martinez cast him an odd look, as if he wasn't used to his murder suspects being so helpful. "Of course. And I'd like the names of any other guests or hotel staff who knew the deceased."

"Don't forget Courtney," Frieda said. "She might know something useful."

"She works for the Florida Tourism Board," Annabelle explained. "She's in charge of our group."

"Mr. Farnaby," the detective asked, "can you get in touch with her as well?"

"Of course," Desmond replied. "She's probably somewhere in the hotel. I'll try her cell phone. Detective Martinez, I want you to know that I'm prepared to cooperate fully. Now, if you'll all just follow me."

He led the group into a modest-size room furnished with a gleaming oval-shaped conference table, gray padded chairs, and enough electrical equipment to stage Cirque du Soleil.

"I'll see if I can get Courtney and the other journalist, Wade, down here pronto," Desmond offered. "If you want to get your interrogation under way, Detective, you can use the room right next door, the Pago-Pago Party Room. The Feinbergs had booked it for a party celebrating their son's bar mitzvah, which was yesterday, but they called a couple of hours ago to cancel. Apparently poor Stuart fractured his tibia on his skateboard this morning."

Drawing his lips together in a straight line, he added, "I suppose it's just as well, with a dead body right down the hall and all. That doesn't exactly scream 'Happy Birthday,' does it? Still, if they expect to get their deposit back, they'd better be prepared to provide me with a letter from his doctor. On *letterhead*."

Detective Martinez didn't seem interested in the details. "Who's the woman who called 911?" he asked as soon as Desmond left. He glanced around the conference room, where Mallory, Frieda, and Annabelle were perched on the edge of gray upholstered chairs as if they were waiting for a business meeting to begin.

Mallory gulped. "That's me," she said meekly, raising one hand.

"Then I'll start with you." Nodding at the uniformed cop, he added, "Officer Langley?"

Mallory followed Detective Martinez and the other officer into the room next door.

HAPPY BIRTHDAY, STUART! MAZEL TOV! A huge banner festooning the back wall shouted its greeting as they walked into the Pago-Pago Party Room. The Feinbergs had embraced a black-and-silver color scheme for their son's bar mitzvah, one that seemed oddly suited to the somber occasion the space was now being used for.

Mallory followed the others through an archway made of black and silver balloons. More balloons in the same colors had also been used in the centerpieces. The half-dozen floating above each of the twenty or so round tables gave the room a dreamy look. The tables themselves were draped with black tablecloths topped by large squares of a shiny silver fabric. A black cardboard gift box decorated with a silver embossed Star of David sat at each place.

The three of them were silent as they settled into chairs that were supposed to have been occupied by Stuart Feinberg's friends. Mallory half expected a waiter to come by and offer them all virgin piña coladas.

"Ms. Marlowe, isn't it?" the detective began.

"That's right. Mallory Marlowe." She did her best to

sound confident, as if she wasn't the least bit rattled by being questioned as part of a homicide investigation.

"Would you mind telling me how you knew the decedent?"

"I—I met him for the first time today," Mallory replied. "At lunch, right here in the hotel. It was the same time I met all the other travel writers who are down here."

Detective Martinez looked confused. "Can you tell me about the nature of this trip?"

"This is a press trip," she explained. "My first, actually. We're all here because we're writing travel articles about Orlando. I just started working for a magazine called *The Good Life,* which is based in New York. I came to Orlando to . . . to do a piece about tourist attractions in central Florida."

"How long will you be staying?" Detective Martinez asked.

"Until Friday."

"At this hotel? The whole time?"

"Yes, that's right."

He paused to make a few notes. Then, abruptly, he said, "Tell me about what happened when you walked into the Bali Ballroom earlier this evening."

"Well," she began, choosing her words carefully, "we were all supposed to meet for a reception at seven. I got there a few minutes early. In fact, I was the first to arrive—"

"What prompted you to arrive at the ballroom early?" Detective Martinez interrupted.

"Uh . . ." His question threw her. "Nothing in particular." She shrugged. "I was ready, and I figured there was no point hanging around my hotel room."

"Go on."

Mallory cleared her throat. "Anyway, I was the first one there. When I walked in, I noticed that one of the spears that had been hanging on the walls—you know, as part of the Polynesian decor—was lying on the floor. In fact, I nearly tripped over it. It was such a surprise that without even thinking, I leaned over and picked it up. Once I did, I noticed there was something that looked like blood at one end.

"Actually, I didn't realize it was blood at first," she corrected herself. "I didn't know what it was. Everything happened so quickly after that—"

"Exactly what do you mean by *everything*?" Detective Martinez asked.

"I'd only been holding the spear for a few seconds when Mr. Farnaby walked in. As soon as he did, he let out a yell, which prompted me to look over at the waterfall, which seemed to be what he was staring at. That's when I spotted Phil."

"You sound as if you immediately knew the victim's identity."

She nodded. "It was his shirt. I remembered it from earlier today. You've got to admit, it's pretty distinctive."

Detective Martinez didn't look as if he was about to admit anything.

Still, she seemed to have gotten through the worst of his interrogation, since he switched to easy questions, like her home address and her cell phone number.

Routine procedure, she told herself, feeling her anxiety level drop. Just like he'd said.

"Thank you, Ms. Marlowe." The detective snapped his notebook closed. "Please go back and wait with the others. I'd like you to stick around until I've had a chance to speak with everyone."

"Not a problem." As if I have a choice, she thought.

"And would you please ask one of the others to come in?"

Desmond was back in the conference room, whining to Frieda about how difficult it was going to be to explain this to his boss. Courtney sat in the corner in silence.

Mallory figured she was probably agonizing over how something like this had ever managed to slip into her carefully prepared schedule. Wade was also there, dressed in a dark-blue linen blazer that for some reason impressed her as something James Bond would wear.

"Detective Martinez is ready for his next victim," she announced. "Who wants to go?"

"I will," Annabelle volunteered, dragging herself to her feet. "Might as well get this over with."

Mallory waited while the others went into the party room one by one, first Annabelle, then Frieda, then Desmond, then Courtney, and finally Wade. As the minutes passed, she slumped lower and lower in her chair, gradually becoming overwhelmed with exhaustion from her long day. She could scarcely believe she'd woken up in her own bed that morning, far, far away in New York. And now, more than twelve hours later, she found herself thinking longingly about the king-size bed that was waiting for her in her hotel room.

In fact, she was imagining the feeling of sliding between the starched white sheets when her reverie was interrupted by Detective Martinez's voice.

"Ms. Marlowe?" he said crisply. "Would you mind stepping next door again?"

She could feel all the blood running out of her face. "What for?" she asked, her voice about three octaves higher than usual.

Detective Martinez remained stone-faced. "I have a few more questions."

Instantly her fatigue vanished. It was replaced by something that very closely resembled panic. In fact, she made a point of avoiding everyone else's eyes as she stood up from the table.

He probably just forgot to ask for your zip code, Mallory told herself as she walked back to the party room. Besides, you're innocent. Innocent people have nothing to worry about. It's just that all this is such a strange experience. That's why you're finding this so nerve-wracking. . . .

She had barely sat down at the same table before the detective said, "Ms. Marlowe, one of the other people I spoke with mentioned that you had quite an argument with Mr. Diamond shortly before he was murdered. You want to tell me what that was about?"

She blinked a few times. "It . . . it wasn't exactly an argument," she stuttered. "I just . . . gave him some advice. All the travel writers met for lunch, and Phil immediately started making embarrassing comments to our tour guide. I simply told him we'd all feel more comfortable if he'd stop."

"Would you describe the nature of your interaction as angry?"

Was this a trick question? She was tempted to point out that what one person perceived as anger could actually be frustration or simply strong feeling. But she decided to keep her answers simple.

"Yes, I suppose I was angry."

"Exactly what did you say to Mr. Diamond?"

"I—I'm not sure." Mallory struggled to replay the scene in her mind. But the truth was that she had been so upset and so caught up in the moment that she hadn't bothered to think through her tirade. The words just came out, completely on their own.

"Something about how we were all professionals and the hotel was temporarily our workplace, so sexist comments and jokes that were in bad taste weren't appreciated."

"But you said it angrily," Detective Martinez repeated.

"It's possible I was a little hard on him," she admitted. "But I was probably still upset about the argument we'd had on the plane."

She'd barely gotten the words out before she realized she had just made a major tactical error.

"I see," he said without a flicker of emotion. "Tell me about what happened on the plane."

"It was nothing," she said, trying to keep her tone light. "Not even worth mentioning. It was just some confusion about who belonged in which seat."

"Yet you just said a second ago that you were still angry about it."

That word again. "Not angry, exactly. More like frustrated."

"Frustrated," Detective Martinez repeated.

"I didn't kill Phil Diamond," she cried. "I barely knew him! I never laid eyes on the man until today!"

"I'm going to ask that you remain in Florida until you hear otherwise," Detective Martinez said icily. "And that you continue to stay at this hotel. I'll be getting in touch with you again. For now, you're free to go."

As Mallory left the room, she felt like someone had slipped her a very powerful drug, one that had engulfed her entire brain in fog. She bypassed the conference room, not wanting to see anyone, not wanting anything except the solitude of her room. She certainly didn't want to deal with the swarms of reporters Desmond Farnaby was expecting.

Once she was alone, however, she didn't feel the least bit better.

She sat on the edge of the bed, staring at the photograph of her family without really seeing it.

Someone obviously told Detective Martinez about the way I lit into Phil at lunch, she thought. It could have been anyone on the press trip who told him. It could even have been *everyone* on the press trip.

But at least one person had made it sound as if Mallory had been more than a little irritated with Phil.

It could even have been the real murderer.

She swallowed hard, suddenly aware of how dry her mouth had become. Up until this point, she'd simply assumed that Detective Martinez had questioned each one of the writers simply because they'd all been in the hotel around the time Phil Diamond was murdered. But she realized with a jolt it was possible that someone in the group was the killer.

The thought sent a chill through her that was even colder than the iceberg at the *Titanic* exhibit.

I don't even know these people, she thought, fighting off a wave of panic. Yet here I am, stuck in a hotel with them, eleven hundred miles from home. . . .

She focused on the photograph, hoping that somehow the faces of her children and the man who had been her husband for more than two decades would give her strength. Instead, she thought, This was supposed to be a dream job. Instead, I suddenly find myself living in a nightmare.

Detective Martinez's final words kept echoing through her head. *For now, you're free to go.*

The implication was that at some later date, she might not be.

Mallory couldn't imagine how she would ever manage to concentrate on writing a lighthearted article about Florida's whimsical tourist attractions. Not when the mere thought that she was a suspect in a murder sent her into a tailspin.

And then, through the fog that encompassed her brain, an idea occurred to her: Maybe I can figure out who murdered Phil.

She had no idea how she could ever accomplish something like that. She didn't know a soul in this town, aside from the people who were involved in the press trip. She didn't know how to make her way around Orlando, either, aside from driving from the airport to the hotel. For that matter, she hardly knew anything about the victim.

Yet she couldn't simply assume that Detective Martinez would clear her name by tracking down the real perpetrator. True, it was possible. But at the moment, she was feeling anything but optimistic—and the stakes were too high to sit back and hope that just because this was Orlando, the story in which she suddenly found herself a character would have a happy ending.

6

"All journeys have secret destinations
of which the traveler is unaware."
—Martin Buber

W hat a way to start a press trip!" Annabelle declared over breakfast the next morning as she
emptied three packets of sugar into her coffee.
"This is worse than the time my flight to Cancún was
canceled because of snow and I had to spend the entire
night sleeping with my head on a Ziploc bag full of
pennies."

She makes it sound as if Phil got himself murdered
just to be rude, Mallory thought crossly, hiding her scowl
behind her mug. She's acting if he was simply indulging
in another one of his annoying habits, like chain-
smoking or making obnoxious comments.

Still, she couldn't help paying close attention to
Annabelle's behavior, along with everyone else's. The
odds were good that one of the people sitting at this table
this morning—Annabelle, Frieda, Wade, or Desmond—
was responsible for Phil Diamond's murder. Of course,
she knew perfectly well that they all thought *she* could be

the killer. All in all, the bountiful serving of suspicion on the breakfast menu hardly made for a festive mood.

"I mean, how creepy is that?" Annabelle continued. "The way he just up and died—at the foot of a tacky fake waterfall, no less!"

Desmond and the other journalists watched in silence as she helped herself to at least a dozen more sugar packets and dropped them into her purse.

"You're right, Annabelle," Frieda finally agreed. Despite the somber mood that hovered overhead like a rain cloud, she looked anything but funereal. She'd arrived at the Tiki Tiki Teahouse dressed in a white T-shirt emblazoned with *Party Girl!* in rhinestones, and electric pink hot pants that revealed some remarkably wrinkled knees. "Somehow, murder just doesn't fit in with the ambience of the Polynesian Princess Hotel."

Glancing around, she added, "Just look at this place. Everything is perfect. There's not a speck of dust on any of the tiki gods, not a single weed among the tropical flowers . . . even the waterfalls are designed not to splash any of the guests!"

"But all of Florida is that way," Wade interjected. "It's as if the entire state is dedicated to enabling people to escape from their real lives and anything bad that may be part of them—which is why when something terrible happens, it seems so out of place."

"That's not true!" Desmond protested. "Florida is *filled* with creepy things." He sounded offended by the notion that the state in which he lived was close to perfect, even if only from a tourist's point of view. It was an interesting contrast to the Desmond Farnaby of the night before, the one who'd scrubbed the bloodstained carpet at the scene of the crime to keep from having points taken off his next job evaluation form.

"You mean like the long lines at every attraction and that ridiculous sun that doesn't quit?" Annabelle asked archly, meanwhile eyeing the stack of jellies in tiny plastic tubs as if calculating how many of those to add to her stash.

"I happen to know about some *truly* creepy things here in Florida," Desmond said. He paused dramatically before lowering his voice and asking, "Have any of you ever heard of the Skunk Ape?"

When no one responded with a hearty "Yes," he continued, "It lives in the Ocala National Forest, although there have been sightings in other places." He sounded like a twelve-year-old boy who was having a blast scaring the bejeezus out of the other kids sitting around the campfire. "Back in the 1950s, three terrified Boy Scouts on a camping trip came running out of the woods, claiming they'd just seen a giant creature with the body of an ape and the face of a man. They said it smelled terrible."

Are you sure it wasn't the Cub Master? Mallory was tempted to ask.

"Then," Desmond continued, his eyes growing big and round, "in the early 1970s, five archeologists came up with an identical story about Skunk Ape. They reported that a white hairy creature destroyed their campsite and then ran into a swamp. They said it was eight feet tall and weighed around seven hundred pounds. Over the years, there have been a number of sightings, including one by a police officer. Some people have taken photographs of the beast, and some have made castings of its footprints."

"Sounds like Big Foot," Frieda observed, nodding as if she actually believed the tall tale.

"It's Florida's own version of Big Foot," Desmond replied proudly. "In fact, in the late seventies, the Florida legislature introduced a bill to protect Skunk Ape."

These are the people who decide how to spend taxpayers' money? Mallory thought, trying to keep a straight face. Wade caught her eye and grinned, as if he'd had similar thoughts.

"We've also got our own ghosts," Desmond continued in the same dramatic voice. He was clearly enjoying being the center of attention. "There's a haunted road in a town called Lady Lake. A glowing lady dressed in white has been seen crossing the street. According to legend, she was murdered by her jealous lover after she told him she was marrying someone else. Some people have also reported seeing a second ghost: a man dressed in black."

"Maybe that's the undertaker," Wade suggested. Dryly he added, "According to legend, he never got paid."

Desmond ignored him. "There's another haunted road in Wauchula, with a bridge that's known as Bloody Bucket Bridge. According to legend—"

"Another legend," Mallory noted. This time, she caught Wade's eye and smiled.

"A former slave from Georgia once lived around there," Desmond insisted enthusiastically. "She delivered hundreds of babies. But after a while, people suspected she'd started smothering some of the newborns, especially when the parents already had more children than they could manage to feed. She buried them by the bridge, in the woods near the river. The townspeople eventually caught on, and that put an end to her midwifery career. She went crazy, and from then on spent her days sitting next to a bucket that was filled with blood— blood she claimed was from the babies she'd murdered. Of course, nobody else besides her ever saw any blood. To them, the bucket looked empty. But she kept emptying it into the river, then claiming it would fill up again. Finally, she fell into the river and drowned."

Mallory wished she'd stayed in her room and ordered room service. She was finding Desmond's gory folktales disturbing, no doubt because of the horrific events of the night before. Dead people, even legendary dead people, just didn't strike her as very amusing.

"Then we have Magnolia Creek Lane in Montverde," he said dramatically, "where two hundred people died in a train crash in the late 1800s. Late at night, you can hear their screams—"

"It's all very creepy, Desmond," Annabelle interrupted, "just as you promised. But I don't see what any of it has to do with Phil's murder. Which, I seem to remember, is how we got onto this tasteless topic in the first place."

Desmond shrugged. "Nothing, aside from the fact that people think of Florida as either a fantasy world for kids or a place for senior citizens to retire. I was simply pointing out that it also has a dark side."

"I think we all found that out in the 2000 election," Frieda commented.

Desmond ignored her. "Of course, Florida has other notable sights that are much more cheerful," he continued. "Like America's Smallest Post Office, in Ochopee. Would you believe it's only eight feet by seven feet and only ten and a half feet high? Then in Carrabelle there's the World's Smallest Police Station, which is no bigger than a phone booth. As a matter of fact, that's what it originally was."

"I'll take the bloody bucket over the tiny post office any day," Wade said. "It's not that strange a concept, given how high Florida real estate prices are these days." He leaned across the table and, in a voice soft enough that no one else could hear, asked Mallory, "Speaking of horror stories, how are you holding up after last night?"

"Fine." She forced a smile. "At least, as well as can be expected."

"I don't blame you," he said. "The whole situation is horrendous. What you need is to get away from all this."

"Away from the hotel—or away from the company I've been keeping?"

"Both. In fact, I'm starting to feel as if I need to get away myself."

"Me, too," she agreed. That was the very conclusion she'd come up with herself after spending a sleepless night in her huge, king-size bed. She'd scarcely been able to believe the contrast between her arrival at the hotel, which had seemed like the beginning of an exciting adventure, and how she felt about being in Florida now that she was considered a suspect in the murder of a man she barely knew.

"Then how about having dinner with me tonight?" he asked. "It'll be good for both of us. Not to mention a lot of fun."

Mallory froze. Dinner? she thought, her mind racing. As in a *date*?

She told herself she must have misunderstood. That she was reading way too much into Wade's casual suggestion that two journalists who were far from home—and suddenly found themselves in the midst of a murder investigation—grab a bite to eat someplace other than the hotel that had begun to feel confining to them both.

Then again, it certainly *sounded* as if he'd just asked her out on a date.

Yet *Mallory* and *date* struck her as two words that definitely did not belong in the same sentence. After all, decades had passed since she'd thought about herself that way—*that way* meaning someone who could ever be considered even remotely attractive to a member of the opposite sex.

Much less someone who went out on dates.

Which is why she was absolutely dumbstruck when she heard a voice that sounded very much like hers saying, "Sure. Dinner sounds great."

A wave of relief suddenly rushed over her as she

remembered she had a perfectly valid excuse not to follow through on the plan she'd just made so cavalierly.

"Wait—I can't," she said. "I'm sorry, Wade. I totally forgot that I already have plans for tonight."

Wade looked crestfallen. "Don't tell me I have competition."

"As a matter of fact, you do," she replied, considerably more relaxed now that she knew she wouldn't actually have to go through with something as nerve-wracking as a date. "Some handsome, swarthy men who can really impress a girl by swinging from the mast of a schooner and . . . and showering her with gifts of gold dubloons."

Wade blinked. "You're having dinner with pirates?"

Mallory laughed. "Courtney even got them to comp me. See that? They're not nearly as bad as most people think. Besides, they love to have a good time, especially if rum is involved."

Wade looked amused. "I had no idea you were such a party animal."

"I can be," she assured him, cocking her head to one side. "In fact, maybe I should be wearing Frieda's T-shirt instead of her."

She suddenly clamped her mouth shut. I'm *flirting*! she thought, alarmed. I'm one step away from batting my eyelashes at this guy. I've been away from home a little more than twenty-four hours and I'm already turning into Betty Boop!

Folding her hands primly in her lap, she said, "What I mean is, I'm supposed to go to the Pirates Adventure theme dinner tonight. I'm hoping to include it in my article."

He leaned even closer, as if he was about to share a secret. "Don't tell anyone," he said in a conspiratorial tone, "but back home in Toronto, I'm considered quite the swashbuckler. How about some company when that pirate ship of yours sails tonight?"

She cast him a surprised look. "You mean you'd actually come along to something like that?"

"Sure. It sounds like fun. Besides, you'd be there, right?"

Mallory could feel her cheeks growing warm as she said, "Okay. I'll ask Courtney if she can get a second voucher."

"Shiver me timbers," Wade said with a grin. "I've got me a dinner date."

• • •

"I need a drink," Frieda announced after Wade, Annabelle, and finally Desmond had excused themselves one by one, each claiming to have something to rush off to.

Mallory, who had remained at the table to finish her second cup of coffee, gave a startled laugh. "Don't we all."

"Just a little something to take the edge off," Frieda said earnestly. "Care to join me at the Bora Bora Bar? I'd enjoy the company. Besides, it's never a good idea to drink alone."

And here I thought she was joking, Mallory marveled. "I'd be happy to join you," she said, suddenly a lot less interested in increasing the amount of caffeine in her veins than she was in picking Frieda's brain.

She was curious about whether the hotel bar would actually be open at this hour. Much to her amazement, it turned out Frieda wasn't the only tourist who needed a little extra something in her morning glass of juice in order to get going. A surprising number of people had bellied up to the bar, which looked like an island hut, complete with a straw-covered roof. Most of them were working on what looked like traditional brunch drinks, screwdrivers and Bloody Marys and mimosas. But a few were hitting the harder stuff, slurping clear brown liquid out of highball glasses, looks of desperation in their eyes.

Mallory hovered a few feet away, not quite able to bring herself to join the early-morning bar scene. But Frieda rushed past her and plopped down on one of the wooden stools. By the time Mallory slid onto the seat next to her, Frieda was waving coyly at a bleach blond bartender with a surfer boy look.

"What can I get for you lovely ladies?" he asked, sliding a flowered cocktail napkin in front of each of them. The Hawaiian shirt he was wearing made him look as if he and Phil used the same fashion consultant.

"You first," Mallory urged.

She expected Frieda to be a mimosa girl. Instead, she barked, "Whiskey, neat."

The bartender just nodded. "Any particular brand?"

"Johnny Walker Black. And supersize me."

He was already filling a glass as Mallory said, "I'll have a glass of cranberry juice."

"You got it," Surfer Sam replied.

Mallory had barely taken her first sip when she glanced over at Frieda and saw that she'd already gulped down half her drink. She had a feeling she'd just stumbled upon the secret behind the woman's eternal cheerfulness.

At the moment, however, Frieda's ebullience was nowhere in sight.

"I can't believe Phil is dead," Frieda said morosely, staring into what remained of her Scotch. "And what a way to go! Imagine, being stabbed with a spear. And it wasn't even a *real* spear!"

"I overheard one of the cops saying he might have drowned," Mallory commented.

"You think that's better?" Frieda countered. "Drowning in a fake waterfall is better than being stabbed to death with a fake spear?"

"The whole thing is an unspeakable tragedy." Mallory hoped her comment would steer the conversation away from a debate of the merits of one undignified way of dying compared to another.

Frieda took a few more gulps of her version of the Breakfast of Champions. Then, reaching over and putting a comforting hand on Mallory's wrist, she said, "I know the police consider you a suspect. But I know better. You never even met Phil until yesterday, right? That means you didn't have enough time to develop a festering hatred for the man, the way so many other people did."

Mallory's eyes widened at the woman's bluntness. Then she noticed that Frieda was starting to slur her words. Which, she decided, made this the ideal time to pump her for information.

"I thought you and Phil were friends," she said. "At least, that's the impression I got from watching you two interact."

Frieda let out a snort that was hardly the thing anyone would expect from a woman who easily fit the Sweet Little Old Lady profile. "Phil Diamond didn't have any friends. He used people."

"I guess that doesn't surprise me," Mallory said. "How long did you know him?"

"Forever," Frieda replied. "At least that's how it feels. I first got to know Phil in the eighties, back when he was still writing for a newspaper here in Florida called the *Orlando Observer*. I met him at some conference. Atlanta, I think it was. Anyway, we spent a few nights hanging out at the hotel bar together. That pretty much solidified our friendship, especially since after a few drinks most people start looking a lot better. Of course, the *Observer* is long gone. But back in those days—and I'm talking at least twenty years ago—Phil was really somebody. At least in the world of travel journalists."

"Are you serious?" Mallory was surprised that the surly, chain-smoking string bean of a man had ever been somebody in any world.

"Sure. He had a lot of clout. He became one of the *Observer*'s most popular columnists. He called his column 'Diamond in the Rough' because he was famous for telling it like it was, with no holds barred. Phil Diamond was somebody who could launch a hotel and make it the one place everybody wanted to go. The other side of the coin was that one bad review from him could mean that a hotel or a restaurant or even an entire Caribbean island would have a bad season."

Shrugging, she added, "But then, he disappeared into thin air. A few years ago, his name suddenly started popping up again. He'd moved to California and was writing for newspapers, magazines... nothing that was considered top of the line. It looked to me like he'd hit the bottom of the barrel."

Frieda paused to finish her drink, then signaled the bartender for another. "One thing about Phil: He was a survivor. The next time he resurfaced, he was writing for the Internet. He was certainly smart enough to jump on that bandwagon. Once computers came onto the scene, everything changed. All of a sudden, the opportunities for travel writers exploded.

"Of course, most of the time there isn't much money in it. But for somebody like Phil, who was addicted to travel, just having the chance to live a life of globetrotting was more than enough. As far as I know, he was happy writing for second-rate websites, like the one he was currently tied up with, just because it kept him in the game."

"BeenThereDoneThat-dot-com isn't a good website?" Mallory asked.

"Nope. See, there's a hierarchy in the journalism business," Frieda explained. She paused to pounce on her fresh drink. "The *New York Times* is always at the top, along with the other big name newspapers like the *Washington Post* and the *Philadelphia Inquirer*. So are the

glossy magazines like *Condé Nast Traveler* and *Travel +
Leisure*.

"Lifestyle magazines like *Food & Wine* and *Gourmet*
offer some opportunities, too, since they write for a
pretty sophisticated audience. The same goes for major
magazines with a general readership, like *GQ* or *Elle* or
Vogue. From there, the list of top media depends on your
field. For athletic types, for example, *Outdoors* is big.
Pays well, great exposure, good assignments.

"Of course, some of the papers and magazines frown
upon travel junkets—free press trips, like the one we're
on. They pride themselves on only accepting articles
from journalists who haven't accepted any freebies. They
think it keeps the writers from being influenced. You
know, that they'll be reluctant to write anything bad. I
suppose they have a point. The problem is that travel is
expensive and writers aren't exactly known for having
tons of money. And while some magazines and newspapers pay travel expenses, most don't. The bottom line is
that a lot of places would never get any exposure in the
press if they didn't invite writers as their guests, all expenses paid. Personally, I have no problem with that.
After all, movie reviewers don't pay for their own tickets
and restaurant reviewers don't pay for their own meals.
So what's the difference?"

"It's true that practically all travel articles are positive,
though," Mallory mused. "You never read one that says
'This is a place you shouldn't go.' "

"My feelings exactly." Frieda took a few more gulps,
then commented, "The magazine you're writing for, *The
Good Life*, is terrific. Especially for somebody like you
who's just getting started. You really lucked out."

"I kind of fell into it," Mallory admitted. "How did
you start out?"

"Back in the sixties, I started writing for a couple of
local papers in Brooklyn. I wrote about anything I got

assigned. My goal was to put together a bunch of clips. As I built up my portfolio, I kept pitching ideas to bigger and better outlets. Before long, I could pick and choose my assignments, writing about whatever I chose."

Frieda had just about finished her second drink. All of a sudden, it was as if she'd hit her limit. Her eyes became glazed, her shoulders slumped, and her words went from slightly slurred to barely comprehensible.

"It's getting late," Mallory said, dismayed by Frieda's rapid disintegration. She took some cash out of her wallet and tucked it under her empty juice glass. "I'd better get going. But it was fun talking to—"

"Where y'goin'?" Frieda asked, shoving her hand into her purse and fumbling around.

"Actually, I'm checking out an attraction that sounds really fun," Mallory replied brightly. "It's a wildlife preserve and alligator theme park called Gatorland. But it also has other types of reptiles, especially crocodiles. I understand it has other animals, too, like exotic birds and llamas."

"Sounds great," Frieda mumbled. "At least if you like crocogators...Hah! Didja hear what I just said? Crocogators! Hey, I'm a comedian!"

Mallory smiled wanly. Amazing what a few whiskey smoothies for breakfast can do for one's creativity, she thought.

Sliding off her bar stool to show she was serious, Mallory pointedly said, "I really have to get on the road."

"Hey, y'mind if I come, too?" Frieda asked. "I'm supposed to go over to the new Disney theme park this morning. Whazzit called? Animal Kingdom? A lot of people who read *Go, Seniors!* are roller coaster fanatics, and they're supposed to have a really wild one called...I forget. But for some reason, I'm not feeling so great. My stomach's a little queasy. Must have been something I ate. So maybe I'll just tag along with you instead, okay?"

Mallory hesitated, trying to think of a polite way to Just Say No. Unfortunately, she couldn't come up with a single one.

"Sure," she finally agreed.

If nothing else, she thought, accompanying me sightseeing will get her away from the bar. And maybe she can stretch out in the backseat and sleep off her breakfast binge.

But just in case Frieda decided to duplicate her famous Epcot skinny-dipping routine in one of Gatorland's swamps, she resolved to keep her away from the alligators and crocodiles.

The crocogators, too.

• • •

"Fasten your seat belt, Frieda," Mallory said once Frieda had followed her out to the parking lot and collapsed into the passenger seat of the PT Cruiser. "We want you to be safe."

"Shafe," Frieda repeated. After fumbling with the strap for an excruciatingly long time, she finally managed to buckle up.

"We're off!" Mallory cried with the same forced cheerfulness.

She was about to put the car into reverse when her cell phone trilled. She grabbed it out of her purse and flipped it open. She didn't bother to check the screen, since she assumed either Jordan or Amanda was calling.

"Hello?" she said, wondering what on earth she was going to say. She wasn't exactly anxious to tell her children that one of the other writers on her trip had turned up floating in two feet of water, the homicide detective investigating the case had placed her on his list of suspects, and at the moment she was shuttling around town with a drunken senior citizen wearing sparkly rhinestones that were the same shade of silver as her hair.

So she was startled when she heard Trevor Pierce say cheerfully, "Good morning, Mallory. I was just calling to see how things are going with my favorite travel writer."

7

"The traveler sees what he sees,
the tourist sees what he has come to see."
—Gilbert K. Chesterton

Trevor!" Mallory cried. "What a surprise!"

Surprise was an understatement. Hearing her boss's voice was more like a shock. The last thing she wanted was for him to know she'd landed herself in the middle of a murder—not to mention a murder investigation. At her job interview, he'd made it clear he believed in her more than she believed in herself. Yet she wasn't exactly doing a crackerjack job of handling things, and she couldn't help feeling she'd let him down her very first time out.

"So how's the fearless travel writer faring in the wilds of Orlando?" Trevor asked, chuckling.

"I'm doing fine!" she exclaimed, trying to match her boss's upbeat tone. "Absolutely great, in fact."

"See that? I knew you could handle this assignment."

"Piece of cake," she replied, the words sticking in her throat.

"I knew I made a good choice," Trevor continued.

"The moment you walked into my office, I could tell I'd found someone who could take care of herself. Get the job done, too."

I can't let him down, Mallory thought, blinking hard to stop the stinging in her eyes. I don't even want him to know that I've come under the scrutiny of a homicide detective.

Being reminded of Trevor's confidence in her made her more determined than ever to find the real culprit.

"Well, don't hesitate to give me a call if anything comes up," Trevor continued. "The Florida tourism people are pretty sharp, but it's always possible you'll run into something unexpected."

"I'll certainly let you know if that happens," Mallory assured him.

As she snapped her cell phone shut, her sidekick for the day let out a loud snort. Alarmed, Mallory glanced over at the passenger seat, and saw that Frieda had dozed off and was slumped to one side, so that the car window served as her pillow. If it wasn't for Frieda's seat belt, Mallory suspected she would have sunk to the floor. Her mouth was wide open, and through it she emitted a sound more fitting to Fred Flintstone than a sparkly senior citizen.

At least she's breathing, Mallory thought, wondering how she'd ever let herself get into this situation.

She'd just begun to appreciate the silence when Frieda burst forth with, "Schlovely out, zint?"

It took Mallory a second or two to realize that that translated to *It's lovely out, isn't it?*

"Yes, Frieda," she agreed. "It's a very nice day."

She groaned internally. Earlier, Frieda's choice of Johnny Walker as her breakfast companion had worked wonders—just as Mallory had hoped, she'd spilled her guts about Phil Diamond. But now that the two of them were about to spend the day at a park filled with the type of creepy-crawlies that usually play starring roles in nightmares, Frieda's inebriated state was bound to be a major liability.

"Tell me again where we're going." Frieda glanced around, looking confused about why she was sitting in a car.

"Gatorland," Mallory replied, trying to keep her irritation in check. "It's a preserve that bills itself as the 'Alligator Capital of the World.'"

Mallory decided to do most of the talking, since at least she still had the ability to pronounce words correctly. Drawing upon the history she'd found on the attraction's website, she explained, "A couple named Owen and Pearl Godwin founded it back in the 1940s. Owen had several different jobs, including butcher and postmaster, but he was fascinated with alligators. He even dug a pit in his own backyard and invited visitors to come view a mother alligator and her babies."

"Cute," Frieda mumbled. "Baby gators, I mean."

"But Owen wanted to open a real alligator preserve," Mallory went on, encouraged by the fact that at least some of what she was saying seemed to be penetrating Frieda's drunken haze. "He raised money by bringing a thirteen-foot alligator named Cannibal Jake up north during the summer and charging ten cents to see him. But his fund-raising really took off when he acquired a crocodile named Bone Crusher that was even bigger. Fifteen feet long, in fact. He weighed something like twelve hundred pounds and was supposed to be the largest captive crocodile in the world. Owen offered a thousand dollars to anyone who could prove otherwise, which never happened."

"Wouldn't wanna measure a crocodile." Frieda still sounded as if her mouth was stuffed with cotton. "Maybe if he was shleeping . . ."

"When the Godwins opened this place in 1949,"

Mallory continued, "it featured an Indian village along with the reptiles. The Seminoles who lived there wrestled alligators. In fact, alligator wrestling is still part of the entertainment, along with a bunch of other shows."

Frieda brightened. "Maybe they'll ask for volunteers from the audience. It would be great if I could include my firsthand experience in my article!"

The image of Frieda in her hot pink hot pants and rhinestone Party Girl T-shirt engaging in hand-to-claw combat with a humongous slithering reptile was chilling. Of course, the strong smell of alcohol that wafted from Frieda's mouth every time she opened it was likely to send even the toughest alligator fleeing in the opposite direction.

"I guess it depends on how liberal their insurance coverage is," Mallory replied politely. Anxious to move away from the topic of Frieda's daredevilry, she said, "Steven Spielberg filmed some of the scenes from his Indiana Jones movies there, you know."

She was relieved that they'd finally reached their destination. Near an odd assortment of buildings nestled amidst what looked like swamplands, she spotted a gigantic pair of alligator jaws that was clearly visible from the road. They were wide open, and it appeared that entering the park required walking through them, taking care not to hit one's head on the huge, pointed teeth.

If that isn't the old kitsch Florida, Mallory thought with amusement, I don't know what is. She pulled out her camera to snap a few photos, meanwhile making a mental note to write about the gigantic gator jaws in her article.

It wasn't until she was about to turn into the parking lot that she noticed a group of at least twenty picketers on the side of the road. They marched back and forth angrily, thrusting placards into the air so passing motorists could see them, chanting a slogan Mallory couldn't quite make out.

Up ahead she spotted a cop wearing a uniform and a disgusted look. She switched off the air-conditioning and rolled down the window.

"What's going on?" Mallory asked.

"Drive to the back," he instructed, waving her toward the section of the parking lot that was farthest away from the protestors.

"Is there a problem?"

"Nothing to worry about," the policeman informed her. "Gatorland is open for business as usual. Please move on."

Mallory drove away slowly, craning her neck to get a better look at what all the fuss was about.

" 'Boycott Gatorland!' " she read aloud. " 'Textiles for Reptiles!' 'Put Vipers in Diapers!' 'Stamp Out Animal Nudity!' "

"Hrumph!" Frieda barked. "Looks like those idiots from PANTS are at it again."

"PANTS? What's that?" Mallory pulled the PT Cruiser into a parking space in the very last row, since she didn't know if her car insurance covered scratches made by picket signs.

"It's an acronym. Stands for 'Put Animal Nudity To Shame.' "

Mallory just stared at her. "You're not serious."

"Yup. Very serious. PANTS is a bunch of crazies who believe it's obscene for animals to walk around naked," Frieda explained. The commotion seemed to be sobering her up. At least, if her improved pronunciation was any indication. "A few years back, their founding members started a movement to make dogs wear pants. They claimed it was obscene for canine genitalia to be on view. Their slogan was 'Trousers for Bowsers.' Since then, they've expanded their focus. They want *all* animals to wear clothes, just like people."

Peering out the car window, Frieda mused, "Looks like they've added reptiles to their list. Frankly, I don't remember seeing any alligator's private parts. Come to think of it, I wouldn't even know where to look. And how on earth would you keep a pair of tighty-whiteys on a snake?"

No matter how ridiculous PANTS's concerns seemed to both Mallory and Frieda, their protest had attracted media attention. A small white van with WFTV ORLANDO printed on the side was parked near the picketers, and positioned right outside was a cameraman with a huge video camera balanced on one shoulder. A half-dozen men and women carrying notepads stood nearby, chatting and laughing as if covering a story this absurd was the equivalent of a coffee break.

Reporters. Mallory's heartbeat quickened. She wondered if any of them might know something about someone who'd been a reporter a long time ago. Someone named Phil Diamond.

Studying them more closely, she saw that only one looked old enough to have been doing anything besides learning to read twenty years earlier, back around the time Phil was a well-known columnist based in Orlando. This particular man looked as if he'd said good-bye to fifty long ago, thanks to a heavily lined forehead that was highlighted by a seriously receding hairline. His outfit— baggy gray pants worn with a brown belt and a rumpled white shirt with rolled-up sleeves that revealed exceptionally hairy arms—made him look as if he'd been dressed by Lou Grant's costume designer.

She was suddenly itching to talk to him. "Frieda," she said, trying to sound matter-of-fact, "why don't you go ahead and get our tickets? Here are the vouchers Courtney put in my press kit. I'll join you in a minute."

"What's the problem?"

Actually, what Frieda had said was *Wazza problem?* Mallory realized with chagrin that the older woman wasn't nearly as far along in the sobering up process as she'd hoped.

"I want to go talk to those reporters," she said. Thinking fast, she added, "I want to see if I can get some additional information about Gatorland's history. For my article."

"Okay," Frieda agreed sullenly, opening the car door and unfastening her seat belt. As soon as she did, she rolled out of the car and sank to the ground, where she lay in a heap.

"Frieda!" Mallory yelled. "Are you all right?"

Much to her relief, the older woman started to giggle. "Oops!" she exclaimed. "Guess I lost my balance!"

Right, Mallory thought crossly. Must have been that mysterious something you ate.

At least she's not hurt, she told herself, searching for a silver lining. But she knew there was no way she could follow through with her plan of cornering the reporter who looked about Phil's age. Not when Frieda wasn't even capable of standing up, much less finding the ticket booth and carrying out a business transaction.

She watched mournfully as the cameraman from WFTV gathered his gear and headed into the van. The reporters, meanwhile, began wandering off in different directions.

A terrific opportunity, she thought, down the drain.

As she half carried, half dragged Frieda across the parking lot and through the tremendous alligator jaws with her teeth gritted, she wondered how many visitors got tossed to the hungry, snap-happy creatures every year by friends and family. She immediately felt guilty—or at least hopeful that Detective Martinez hadn't somehow planted a computer chip in her head that enabled him to hear her thoughts.

Still, once she and Frieda were inside, Mallory decided to make the best of it. After all, she was here for a reason: to evaluate Gatorland and determine whether or not it captured the funky flavor of the past.

Besides, she'd immediately found herself transported to another world, one that resembled the Forest Primeval— or at least the old Florida. The grounds were covered with dense greenery: palm trees, bushes with leaves the size of snowboards, flowering shrubs that were as big as cars. Scattered throughout were swampy ponds that served as home sweet home to the preserve's animal residents. One was occupied by coral-colored flamingos perched on tall, skinny legs that looked more like stalks than part of anyone's anatomy.

But the stars of the show were the alligators—even though they weren't exactly acting like stars. They lay as motionless as if they were merely plastic models of the real thing, some half submerged in the water and others strewn across islands like logs.

Mallory found them so grotesque that she wasn't even sure she wanted to stare at them. But at the same time, there was something fascinating about them. Studying them was like watching the most frightening scene in a horror movie: she couldn't look away, even though she wasn't sure she wanted to be there in the first place.

Running along one side of what appeared to be a very large pool of water were zoo-style displays of the other animals exhibited at Gatorland: tropical birds with brilliantly colored feathers, a black bear named Judy, and a bright yellow snake coiled inside what looked like a doghouse. Then there was Dog Gone Gator, a huge black beast that had caused a ruckus when he was running free, since his idea of a tasty snack was munching on somebody's beloved house pet. Apparently it had been decided that the best solution, short of sending him to the great swamp in the sky, was incarceration.

All of it was fascinating, and as close to the old Florida as she'd been since she arrived. The fact that the attraction dated back to the 1940s certainly helped. But because it was a preserve, it had remained undeveloped. Its rustic character made it timeless—and exactly the kind of place she'd hoped to find still flourishing.

There were other old-style touches, as well, many of which definitely fell into the kitsch category. On display was a sign from the early days, a crude alligator cut out of plywood, painted bright green, and labeled 13 MILES. WORLD FAMOUS GATORLAND. "LEGENDARY." A life-size, startlingly lifelike model of an alligator was perfect for photo sessions that were guaranteed to impress the folks back home. The walls inside and outside the rest rooms were painted with a jungle scene.

Mallory loved all of it. Five flamingos, she decided. Gatorland definitely captures the old Florida. No neon, no white-knuckle thrill rides, no special effects. Just alligators in their natural environment.

Still, the fact that Frieda kept swaying from side to side whenever the two of them stopped to look at something prompted Mallory to keep her viewing time to a minimum. When the older woman caught her balance by leaning against a gate with a sign that read, DO NOT ENTER OR YOU WILL BE EATEN, Mallory quickly checked the map she'd been given when she entered.

"How about riding the train that goes through the Jungle Crocs of the World exhibit?" she suggested, thinking that sitting down for a while might not be a bad idea.

"Nah, too boring," Frieda scoffed. "That's for babies and old codgers. My readers hate that kind of thing."

"Then how about the Swamp Walk?"

"Sounds buggy."

Mallory sighed. Keeping Frieda entertained was turning out to be as difficult as spending the day with a fussy toddler.

"Maybe we can check out one of the shows," she tried, "like the Gator Jumparoo Show."

Frieda brightened. "Hey, look at that sign over there! We're just in time for gator wrestling!"

Mallory cringed. She wouldn't put it past Frieda to thrust herself into the limelight in order to get the story she was after—even though it carried the risk of being turned into Purina Gator Chow. Yet Mallory had come to see what Gatorland was all about, and that meant checking out everything.

"Then gator wrestling it is."

She and Frieda followed the other tourists who were shuffling into the small arena that, appropriately enough, was called Gator Wrestlin' Stadium. Tiers of bleachers surrounded a sand "stage" edged with metal fencing that no doubt was meant to keep the performers safely separated from the audience.

"Let's sit inna front!" Frieda demanded.

"Uh, I think there's less sun in the back—"

But Frieda had already plopped down in the front row. "I wanna make sure they see me when I put my hand in the air."

Before Mallory had a chance to talk Frieda out of it, a blond young man stepped onto the patch of sand that served as the stage. He wore jeans, a khaki shirt with GL embroidered over the pocket, and an Indiana Jones–style hat.

"Welcome to Gatorland, everybody!" he cried, cracking a whip. Mallory jumped. So did everyone else in the stadium. Everyone except Frieda, who was still enjoying the benefits of a major muscle relaxant.

"Many people don't realize that cattle was once big in Florida," he continued in the same booming voice. "The cattle herders used to crack whips to round up the cattle and keep them in line—which is how southerners came to be called crackers." To emphasize his etymology lesson, he cracked his whip loudly a few more times.

"Okay, folks, we've got a great show for you today. My name is Doug and this is Lisa, who'll be demonstrating just how friendly gators can be." A tiny blond woman who wore an identical outfit, minus the hat, but probably weighed a hundred pounds less smiled and waved. "Anybody here want to see some alligator wrestlin'?"

The audience yelled out, "Ye-e-ah!"

"Anybody want to volunteer?"

This time, the response was nervous laughter. Only Frieda thrust her hand into the air, yelling, "Pick me! Pick me!"

Fortunately, sacrificing senior citizens wasn't on the program. "How about you, young man?" Doug asked, reaching out to a little boy sitting with his family in the third row. "Want to come up so we can see how brave you are?"

"Rats," Frieda muttered. "They always pick the kids for these things."

"What's your name, son?" Doug asked.

"Kevin," the recruit answered in an uncertain voice.

"And how old are you, Kevin?"

"Six."

"Six! That's great! So you've already lived a long and rewarding life." He paused while the audience laughed. Little Kevin, meanwhile, didn't look particularly amused. "Now, here's what I want you to do, my good man. See that opening over there? That leads to the alligator pit where we keep our meanest, toughest alligators. I'd like you to crawl in there and pick out the biggest, scariest one you can find and drag him out by his tail. Okay?"

Kevin's eyes grew wide. And then, after glancing at his mother, he nodded.

"Nah!" Doug insisted. "You don't really want to do that, do you? I think we'll leave the wrestling to somebody really tough. Somebody big, somebody strong... Lisa, you want to take over while Kevin goes back to his seat?"

Relief was written all over poor Kevin's face. He didn't even seem to notice that the audience rewarded him with enthusiastic applause as he scurried back to his seat.

"Hi, everybody," Lisa cried, leaping into center stage. "Before I get down and dirty with one our gators, let me give you some basic facts. Most gators are seven to eight feet long and weigh 120 to 180 pounds. But they're ninety percent muscle. They also have a brain the size of a lima bean, which means they're about as smart as one."

She reached into the opening to the pit and pulled her opponent out by the tail. She then immediately sat on his back and held his mouth closed. "This guy has fifteen hundred pounds of pressure in his jaws. Inside his mouth he's got eighty-two teeth for grabbing his prey. Alligators don't chew their food, they swallow it whole. So if you ever get caught by a gator, at least you won't hurt going down!"

Lisa's act consisted of wedging the alligator's mouth underneath her chin and throwing both arms out, as if to say, *Look, Ma! No hands!*

As Doug took over once again to do some more showing off, Frieda stood up to leave.

"Whatta disappointment," she mumbled. "Let's get outta here. I was so sure they'd let me do a few tricks with those gators. I'm a lot stronger than I look, you know. I've got really strong bones because I take an osteoporosis drug regularly."

They'd walked only a few steps along the path leading

out of the stadium when they heard someone ask, "Did you ladies enjoy the show?"

Mallory turned and saw that the person who'd posed the question was a scruffy-looking man who, like Doug and Lisa, wore a shirt with a *GL* embroidered over the pocket. But he could have been their grandfather. He had a shock of white hair that puffed upward and a mottled red nose that reminded Mallory of a potato.

"It was great," Mallory replied.

"Except I didn't get to wrestle a single alligator," Frieda said petulantly.

"That's too bad. But maybe I can make things up to you two lovely ladies." He sashayed up to Frieda and said, "Let me introduce myself. I'm Zeke—better known as Alligator Zeke."

"Hello, uh, Alligator Zeke," Mallory said politely. She needn't have bothered. Zeke clearly had eyes only for Frieda.

And Frieda seemed to be loving it. "I'm Frieda Stein." Cocking her head to one side flirtatiously, she added, "Seems to me a man with a nickname like that must have earned it."

Zeke chuckled. "I admit, I've had my share of close encounters with the cute little critters. Got the scars to prove it, too." Leaning toward Frieda, he added, "I'd be happy to show 'em to you, if you're interested."

She giggled like a twelve-year-old.

"But for now," Zeke offered, "how about if I personally show you lovely ladies some of Gatorland's highlights?"

"Ooh, I'd *love* that!" Frieda cooed.

"Thanks, but I think I'll pass," Mallory said. She knew perfectly well *she* wasn't the lovely lady he was interested in impressing, and she had no interest in being a third wheel. "If you don't mind, I'll just duck into the gift shop."

"Be my guest," Zeke said. "Now, Frieda, if you'll just step over here into the Snakes of Florida exhibit..."

Anxious to make a quick getaway, Mallory dashed into the gift shop. Not surprisingly, it was filled with alligators made of every possible material. She couldn't help stroking one of the cute, fuzzy alligators that had somehow morphed from reptiles into mammals. She also spotted a stuffed mommy gator with two babies Velcroed on, which struck her as a terrific way of keeping one's offspring close by. She wished someone had thought of that when Jordan was little.

She pulled out her pad and took notes on the merchandise: a bean-bag gator with a goofy expression; a foam-rubber mask that made it possible for any human to be mistaken for an alligator; a floating version for bathtub enjoyment, billed as "28 BIG inches of rubbery reptile fun!"

Mallory was tempted to buy Jordan one of the official Gatorland T-shirts on display. But she couldn't decide between the one printed with *Chasin' Tail—Gatorland Orlando, Florida* and the considerably more tasteful one that said, *Official Gatorland Gator Patrol—If You See Me Running, Try to Keep Up!*

In the end, she decided to chuck the shopping spree and instead take advantage of her last minutes of freedom from Frieda by grabbing some lunch. Even though they hadn't been at the park very long, it was already close to noon and her stomach was growling more loudly than Judy the bear.

After checking her map once again and weighing her options, she decided that Pearl's Patio Smokehouse sounded like the best bet for chowing down—even if the menu did include smoked gator ribs and deep-fried gator nuggets.

As soon as she walked into the outdoor eatery, her heart leaped into her throat. The reporter she'd noticed earlier was sitting at a picnic table, an outdoor snack bar, dousing a sandwich with sauce.

She'd just started to head toward him when Frieda came over and placed her hand on Mallory's arm.

"Mallory, dear, would you mind if Zeke took me on a private tour? He has something special he wants to show me. Something that the general public doesn't get to see."

Mallory didn't even want to know what that was. Thank you, Zeke, she thought.

"Of course I don't mind," she said aloud. "Have a ball. Meet me at the ticket booth whenever you're ready to leave."

Frieda just winked, then hurried away.

As soon as she was out of view, Mallory sidled over to the reporter, who at the moment had an extraordinary amount of brown sauce dripping down his chin.

"Is the food here any good?" she asked casually.

"Sure, if you like gator meat."

"You're kidding!"

"Yeah. This is regular old pulled pork. It's really good, though. I highly recommend it."

"Thanks for the review."

She ordered her own lunch, then carried her tray back to his table. "Mind if I join you? I hate eating alone."

Since his mouth was full of half-chewed pork, he grunted and made a welcoming gesture.

"You're a reporter, aren't you?" Mallory asked as she unwrapped her straw. "I noticed you out front when I came in."

He swallowed loudly. "Yup, that was me." Rolling his eyes, he added, "That's what happens on a slow news day. You end up giving crazies a bunch of publicity they don't deserve. Fortunately, I can pad the piece with some legitimate news. Coming here today gave me an excuse to interview some of the employees about the park's recovery from the serious fire they had here a while back."

"I guess your job is never boring," Mallory commented. She bit into her sandwich. He was right. The pulled pork at Pearl's was excellent. "Have you been doing it for a long time?"

He snorted. "Sometimes it seems like forever. But I guess it's more like, what, thirty-five years?"

Which meant she'd been right about his age. "I don't suppose you ever ran into a reporter named Phil Diamond who wrote for the *Orlando Observer*?"

"Phil Diamond?" he repeated, startled.

Mallory did her best not to react. "Did you know him?"

"As a matter of fact, I did." He frowned. "I guess you know he was murdered last night."

She nodded. "I'm one of the travel writers who came down on the same press trip. We're all staying at the hotel where he was killed." She decided not to mention that she was also a suspect, since that probably wasn't the best way to get him to open up. "I'm Mallory Marlowe. I write for *The Good Life*."

"Al Zimmerman. *Orlando Sentinel*." He stuck out his hand, then drew it back as if he'd realized it was too sticky for human contact. "Nice to meet you."

"Same here." She hesitated. "I understand that Phil Diamond had a pretty successful writing career back in the eighties. He had his own column, didn't he?"

"That's right. He called it 'Diamond in the Rough.'" Smirking, he added, "I don't know how well you knew Phil, but that name fit him pretty well."

"I didn't know him well at all," Mallory replied. "Actually, I just met him yesterday."

"Yeah, well, I knew Phil forever. He and I actually started out in the newspaper business together. I was just out of college with a degree in journalism. As for Phil, I seem to recall he didn't graduate from college. He was one of those 'pull yourself up by your own bootstraps' types. I think he'd taken a few writing courses somewhere, but he mainly learned the writing trade by working for local papers. They didn't pay much, but he was willing to do whatever they asked to learn the business.

"Phil was a decent writer, but not a great one. To give him credit, he did get better as time went on. But what he was best at was getting the story."

"You mean he was good with people?" Mallory asked, surprised.

Al smiled crookedly. "More like he had a certain ruthlessness when it came to beating people down. He was one of those guys who had no problem showing up at a murder victim's home at two o'clock in the morning and asking his mother, 'How do you feel about your kid being shot to death two hours ago?'"

"But isn't that a necessary skill in the newspaper business?"

"For certain kinds of reporting. The problem with Phil was that he didn't know when to let it go. He was a diamond in the rough, all right. And not only at work. Unfortunately, he carried it into every part of his life, including his personal life. His marriage was the perfect example."

Mallory pricked up her ears. "It didn't even occur to me that Phil might be married."

"He's not—or I guess I should say he *wasn't*. At least, not anymore. He and Patrice got divorced a long time ago. Early nineties, I think. It was pretty ugly, from what I understand."

"Was she a reporter, too?"

"Patrice? Nah. I seem to recall that she tried a couple of different things. Eventually, even she got caught up in the tourism business. After the divorce, she opened one of those ice-cream stands that's actually shaped like a huge ice-cream cone. After that, I don't know what happened."

Mallory was about to press Al for more details about Phil's failed marriage, but he said, "Anyway, Phil got to be pretty popular at the *Observer*. Readers loved him because he always got the story. He had no problem telling it like it was, no matter whose toes he might have been stepping on. But his columns were so abrasive that our editor, Jim Tillson, got loads of angry phone calls from the local citizenry. Politicians, too. The cops, even. When it came to offending people, Phil didn't discriminate.

"After a while, Jim got pretty tired of it. But by that point Phil had a big enough following that Jim didn't want to let him go. So he came up with the idea of giving him his own column."

"A travel column, right?" Mallory asked.

"He covered travel, but it was actually more of a lifestyle column," Al replied. "Phil wrote about anything he felt like writing about. It was mostly stuff about the local scene. Restaurants, trends, the growing tourism trade, the long-term repercussions of Disneyfication, and the tremendous growth that was changing the face of central Florida."

Mallory's eyebrows shot up. "Don't tell me Phil was concerned about preserving Florida's past. Or that he was worried about what overdevelopment might do to the environment."

"Ha! Not Phil. He was much too self-serving. But so are a lot of people, and I guess he put in print what many of them were thinking. That's what I meant about developing a following. People liked his curmudgeonly style. It was something different, something a big portion of the paper's readership could relate to."

"If he was that popular, why did he give up his column and leave Florida?"

"I'm afraid that's where there's a hole in my story," Al said. "Phil seemed pretty happy being a big fish in a little pond. As for me, when I suddenly saw the big three-oh staring me in the face, I decided I wanted more. So I applied to the Journalism program at Columbia University. I figured having a Master's degree from a name school would help me move into the big league. I went up to New York for a couple of years, and Phil and I lost touch.

"After that, I worked at a bunch of papers all over the country. It's only recently that I came back. I think of myself as semiretired. The work here isn't that demanding, and I live in a nice condo with my wife. We've got a pool, a clubhouse, the whole shebang."

"But what happened to Phil?" Mallory persisted. "Why did he leave Florida?"

The creases in Al's forehead deepened. "I don't know the details. All I know is that I heard through the grapevine that Phil was suddenly out on his keister."

"He was fired?" Mallory exclaimed. "Why? What happened?"

"He apparently got involved in some scandal. Something pretty serious, too, I understand. But it was all kept very hush-hush. I guess the people who were in power at the time were afraid it would hurt the paper's reputation. All I know is that one day Phil Diamond was the golden boy, and the next day he'd vanished."

So good old Phil had gotten into some kind of trouble, Mallory thought. Before she managed to press Al for more details, he crumpled up all the barbecue sauce–streaked napkins he'd used and pushed back his bench.

"Speaking of vanishing, I've got to get out of here. Big press conference at the mayor's office. Seems he found a new way to cut taxes without cutting services—or so he claims." As he stood up, he added, "Nice chatting with you."

"Same here."

"I'll keep an eye out for your article. Hey, I like living the good life as much as the next guy."

Mallory was about to respond when her cell phone

erupted into its signature melody. She was about to answer when she noticed the number. It was Trevor Pierce, calling her again.

I got off easy with the last call, she thought. I may not be as lucky this time around.

So instead of answering, she waited until the words 1 NEW MESSAGE appeared on the screen. Then she punched in her password and listened.

"Mallory, Trevor Pierce again. Would you mind telling me what the hell is going on down there?"

8

"Stop worrying about the potholes in the road
and celebrate the journey!"
—Fitzhugh Mullan

Cringing, Mallory listened to the rest of Trevor's
message.

"I just logged onto the *Orlando Sentinel*'s website to check out the weather," he continued. He sounded
as if he was doing his best to remain calm but wasn't doing that great a job of it. "I wanted to see if you had any
rain down there. But instead of getting the weather report, I read in the headlines that a journalist who sounds
like he's on the same press trip you're on was *murdered*
last night! For God's sake, Mallory, call me!"

Mallory hesitated for only a moment before turning
off her cell phone and tossing it into her purse.

*Okay, so he knows I wasn't exactly telling the truth
when I said everything was going well,* she thought
guiltily. *But right now, I have enough to deal with without
trying to explain my situation to my boss.*

*And that included dragging a libidinous senior citizen
away from her gator-filled love nest.*

"You should see how strong Zeke is!" Frieda cooed as she toddled through the parking lot a little behind Mallory, after turning up at the ticket booth much later than Mallory would have liked. At least she no longer appeared to be intoxicated. At least, not on alcohol. "And how brave he is! He actually picked up an alligator and held it in his arms like a baby! Of course, it *was* a baby. And the little guy's teeth didn't look much bigger than mine...."

As soon as Mallory managed to strap Frieda into the front seat, she snapped on the car radio.

"Police have no leads in the death of Phil Diamond, the seasoned journalist who was visiting Orlando to write an in-depth investigative piece on the city's tourism industry...."

Okay, that's just one station, she thought, fighting the wave of anxiety that was rapidly descending and pressing the Seek button. And a local station, at that.

"According to Desmond Farnaby, general manager of the Polynesian Princess Hotel, security has been stepped up and the hotel staff is doing everything possible to cooperate with police...."

Another local station, Mallory thought desperately, punching Seek again. Al Zimmerman told me himself that today was a slow news day.

"This is National Public Radio," a dreamy female voice said, *"and today's top story is the murder of journalist Phillip Diamond, the voice of the highly respected travel website BeenThereDoneThat-dot-com...."*

"Sounds like poor old Phil getting bumped off is big news." Frieda cackled. "Frankly, I'm surprised it didn't happen a long time ago."

Mallory kept jabbing buttons until she finally found a country station. It wasn't her favorite type of music, but she gritted her teeth and turned the volume up enough that it discouraged any further conversation.

"Our lo-o-ove is like a di-a-mond, shiny and strong..." an ersatz cowboy caterwauled.

Biting her lip, she snapped off the radio. He's everywhere, she thought, trying to quell the anxiety rising in her chest by taking deep breaths. I can't get away from him.

Amazingly, Phil Diamond is turning out to be even more trouble dead than he was alive. But while I have no control over how the rest of the world deals with him, the one thing I can do is spend every waking moment trying to get him out of *my* life.

• • •

"Thanks for taking me to Gatorland," Frieda said as she and Mallory strolled through the Polynesian Princess lobby, toward the elevators. "I'm sure it'll be one of the highlights of the entire trip."

"I'm glad you enjoyed it," Mallory replied. "It's nice that Zeke made the time to give you an insider's view. Who knows? Maybe you two will even keep in touch."

Frieda cast her a surprised look. "Zeke and I are going out tonight. He promised to show me some of Orlando's hot spots."

"That should be something your readers will be interested in," Mallory said politely, wondering how many of those hot spots were located on Zeke's body.

"Ha! Forget my readers. I'm taking the night off, baby. Party on!"

When the elevator doors opened, Frieda stepped in. "Time for my nap," she announced. "Not a long one, just twenty minutes to recharge the batteries."

Mallory hesitated. Up to this point, she had been looking forward to returning to her hotel room, the only place in town that afforded her a room with a door—a door that could shut out the rest of the world. Yet now that she was back, she realized there was a much better way to use her free time: paying a visit to the scene of the crime.

While she couldn't anticipate what she might find—and in fact didn't even have a very good idea of what to look for—she'd seen enough crime shows on TV to know that viewing the crime scene was a crucial element of any investigation. Besides, even if she didn't manage to spot anything the cops had missed, something in that room might spark an idea or give her a clue as to who had been there when Phil was murdered.

"Going up?" Frieda asked crossly, stabbing the Open Door button with resignation. That nap was clearly something she needed.

"On second thought, I think I'll get some coffee," Mallory lied. "I'll catch up with you later."

"Suit yourself."

When Mallory reached the Bali Ballroom, she saw that the double doors were closed tight. She turned one of the knobs halfheartedly, expecting to find the door locked. Instead, it opened.

Inside, the lights were off. Even though she didn't dare switch them on, there was enough light from the hall that after waiting a few seconds for her eyes to adjust, she could see fairly well.

The Bali Ballroom seemed as lifeless as Phil's body had been as it floated in the pool. Bubbling water no longer cascaded down the waterfall, and the potted flowers that had been lush only the day before now drooped pathetically. Yellow crime-scene tape stretched across the entire display.

She was about to step forward to get a closer look when she heard voices in the hall.

"Could the timing have been any worse?" Desmond moaned. "I'm coming up for review in another two weeks. Two weeks! Do you have any idea how a murder looks on a résumé?"

"As if a murder is something that can be scheduled," Courtney shot back angrily. "Penciled into someone's Filofax like...like 'Make a dentist appointment for a cleaning'!"

Desmond Farnaby and Courtney Conover. Mallory stepped closer to the doorway, hugging the wall so she couldn't be spotted from the corridor.

"That's so typical, Des," Courtney added. "It's all about you."

"Des"? Mallory thought, startled. What happened to "Mr. Farnaby"?

"I just know my history with Phil is going to come out," Desmond continued. "That man never seems to stop causing trouble for me. Even now, when he's dead."

My sentiments exactly, Mallory reflected, remembering that she'd had the exact same thought not long before. She took a few steps closer to the doorway, hoping to hear more before they walked away.

"But that was ages ago," Courtney insisted. "Besides, there's no way the police would ever link his murder with what's basically ancient history."

Courtney and Desmond were talking to each other with a sense of familiarity that Mallory hadn't picked up on before. She hadn't realized there was history between them.

Desmond also seemed to have a history with the murder victim. That suddenly made him a lot more interesting.

Mallory remained in her hiding spot, expecting the two of them to pass by. Instead, Desmond said, "We can talk about this later, Courtney. Right now, I have a hotel to run. And that includes getting the ballroom back into shape."

He strode into the ballroom and snapped on the lights.

"Mallory!" he cried, looking startled. "What are you doing here?"

"I, uh . . ."

"The police were very clear about keeping everyone away from the crime scene," he scolded. "I could get in trouble."

"I know, but—"

"Look at this place!" he exclaimed, putting his hands on his hips as he surveyed the ballroom. He already seemed to have forgotten all about her transgression. "That horrid yellow tape is plastered everywhere. I don't know why it's still up, when the cops have already spent ages collecting evidence. They made me turn off the waterfall, and I'm supposed to keep the door closed. I can practically hear the mildew growing! Do you have any idea how much it hurts to see my beautiful hotel in this state? And I'm not even going to mention what it's doing to our guests' morale!"

Mallory supposed she shouldn't have been surprised that his take on the situation was the same as it had been the day before, when he'd instantly morphed into Mr. Clean.

"You wouldn't believe how many guests have already checked out," he lamented. "Or how many cancellations we've had. With CNN carrying the story, even our international clients are steering clear of the Polynesian Princess. Thank you, Ted Turner, for helping bad news spread faster than ever!"

"You can't blame people for being upset about a murder," she commented, irritated by his self-centered attitude. "Even people who didn't know Phil."

"Right," he sniffed. "The people who *did* know him aren't upset at all."

Desmond's openness about his feelings concerning the murder victim emboldened her. "I heard there was some bad blood between you and Phil."

She expected him to be happy he'd found someone who would listen to him vent. Instead, a look of shock crossed his face.

"How did you know about that?"

Mallory did some fast thinking. "I believe one of the other journalists mentioned it."

"Not that it's a secret or anything," he added hastily. "A lot of people in the tourism business know that Phil and I were in business together."

It's news to me, she thought. "The hotel business?"

Desmond shook his head. "About twenty years ago, Phil and I tried to cash in on the incredible tourism boom that was sweeping over central Florida. We opened a fabulous tourist attraction: a haunted house called Crypt Castle."

Frankly, Mallory couldn't picture Desmond getting involved in something so whimsical. Somehow, it didn't fit with the crisply ironed shirts and the bow ties. She couldn't imagine Phil in the haunted house business, either.

Still, she supposed business was business. If something looked like a good investment, there would be no reason for anyone not to pursue it.

"It was fabulous," he continued proudly. "The special effects were enough to scare the pants off anybody. Screeching ghouls, trapdoors that opened unexpectedly, rattling chains... It was state of the art in the haunted house industry."

"What happened to it?"

"It failed." Sighing, he added, "It turns out that being an entrepreneur may look easy, but it's not. There are too many factors that go into making a business a success. Most of them impossible to control."

Mallory hoped he'd list a few, but he'd drawn his mouth into a thin straight line. She almost got the feeling he was being careful not to say something he might regret.

"I guess the tourism industry is a pretty small world," she observed casually. "I understand that Phil's ex-wife tried her hand at entrepreneurship, too."

"On a considerably smaller scale," Desmond noted huffily. "Opening an ice-cream stand is hardly the same thing as operating a major attraction. Patrice's venture was small-time. Crypt Castle, on the other hand, was something special. It was tremendous, for one thing. It sprawled over more than ten acres, including outbuildings that housed little extras, like the Dungeon of Death and the Ghosts 'n' Ghouls Gift Shop. Families could spend an entire day there. We had a refreshment stand, a playground with a giant skull kids could crawl through, and two huge parking lots.

"And the main building, the haunted house, was fabulous. We had room after room with all kinds of creepy special effects, not to mention live actors and a terrific sound system. We had a wall that breathed, a heartbeat that throbbed beneath the bed in the master bedroom, cobwebs that changed shape and turned into ghouls...."

"It does sound amazing," Mallory commented. "I'm surprised it didn't make it."

Desmond shrugged. "Like I said, there are a million things that can go wrong. In the end, I decided to go into something more reliable, like the hotel business. Of course, there are a million things that can go wrong there, too, and they usually do. But at least it's not your head on the chopping block all the time. Even more important, there's definitely something to be said for getting a weekly paycheck."

"There certainly is," she agreed.

So Phil once had business interests here in the Orlando area, she thought, mentally filing away what Desmond had told her about the defunct haunted house. That, she decided, is a part of the murder victim's past that warrants further investigation.

"What about Patrice?" she asked. "What happened to her business?"

"Frankly, I don't remember. She might have sold it to somebody else who wanted to swirl ice cream into cones all day. Or maybe a developer bought it, knocked it down, and crammed a hundred condos on the land."

"Where is she these days? Still in Orlando?" Realizing she didn't want to sound as if she was giving him the third degree, she added, "I wonder what kind of job somebody gets after giving up on the ice-cream business."

"Oh, she's long gone," Desmond replied. "She got out of here a couple of years after the divorce. She went up to Chicago, I think. Of course, that was ages ago. Lord knows where she is now."

Too bad, Mallory thought. Picking her brain might have been helpful.

Suddenly Desmond sighed. "I should really get back to work," he said, glancing around the ballroom as if the mere sight of it was almost too distressing to bear. "I just wanted to check and see if the cops had taken down this horrid crime-scene tape yet. I can't wait to turn this jewel of a ballroom back into an active part of the hotel. I've got a twenty-fifth-anniversary party scheduled for Saturday night and a Sweet Sixteen on Sunday. Keep your fingers crossed that they won't end up canceling, too, just like everybody else."

As she headed back to her room, Mallory pondered what Desmond had told her. He certainly made no bones about his dislike for Phil Diamond. Still, he seemed so matter-of-fact about their failed business venture, it was hard to believe that seeking revenge had ever been on his agenda.

Yet there was no reason for him to have been completely honest with her concerning either his past interactions with Phil Diamond or his current feelings about the man. And she had seen him destroy evidence with her own eyes. While his actions could have simply been the result of his fastidiousness, it was equally possible he'd been trying to cover something up.

She knew that if she wanted to get her name off Detective Martinez's list of suspects, she would have to do whatever she could to find out. In the meantime, however, the gnawing in the pit of her stomach reminded her that she was about to face something that was almost as traumatic as finding Phil Diamond's body floating at the base of the Gitgit Waterfall: her first date in more than twenty years.

9

"I can't think of anything that excites a greater sense
of childlike wonder than to be in a country
where you are ignorant of almost everything."
—Bill Bryson

Ten minutes later, Mallory stood in front of her hotel room closet, taking deep breaths in a fruitless attempt to calm herself.

Why on earth did I ever agree to let Wade come with me tonight? she thought. None of the clothes she'd brought seemed appropriate. The pink linen blouse that had looked perfectly fine at home suddenly struck her as boring. Her silky black shirt not only seemed too bare, she suddenly remembered that it was a little tight around the arms.

It occurred to her that her main problem was that she had no idea about the proper dress code for an evening of yo-ho-ho'ing with a shipload of pirates.

Or maybe it wasn't the pirates' opinion that she was concerned about.

With a defeated sigh, she reached for her dependable beige linen go-everywhere dress, reminding herself that its primary virtue was that it could be dressed up or down with the right jewelry. She had just slipped it on and was studying her upper arms in the mirror, agonizing over whether they were too plump to be seen in public, when her cell phone trilled.

Great, she thought, making a mad dash for her purse. Somehow Wade got hold of my cell phone number and he's calling to cancel. He finally realized he has absolutely no interest in spending an entire evening with a boring, middle-aged woman who hasn't been called upon to hold up her end of a serious adult conversation in months. *Especially* a serious adult conversation with a member of the opposite sex.

So she was surprised that her home number was flashing on the screen.

"Jordan?" she answered breathlessly, afraid that something was wrong. "Amanda? Is everything okay?"

"Of course," her daughter returned calmly. "Everything is fine, Mother. It's you I'm worried about. Are you all right?"

"Of course I'm all right," Mallory replied.

She remembered that it was her life, and not her children's, that was suddenly in turmoil. Yet she hoped her daughter had been so tuned in to her own personal crisis that she hadn't bothered to tune in to any news media.

Trying to sound casual, she added, "Why wouldn't I be?"

"Because you're in a brand-new place, doing a brand-new job," Amanda replied matter-of-factly. "Because you don't know a soul down in Florida. Because you're staying at a hotel all by yourself, sleeping alone in a strange bed. Because this is practically the first time you've left Rivington since Daddy died."

Even though she was greatly relieved that her daughter clearly didn't know a thing about Phil Diamond's murder, Amanda's list of Five Good Reasons to Feel Anxious still gave Mallory pause. Each one was completely true. Yet out of all of them, the only one that made her stop and think was the last.

And the sole reason was that her daughter had called her at the exact moment she'd been agonizing over what to wear on something that sounded an awful lot like a date. For the first time since before her wedding day, she'd been getting ready to spend an entire evening with a man who wasn't either her husband, a co-worker, or a dentist about to perform a particularly long procedure on her. And trying to come up with ways to look good while doing it.

"I'm fine," Mallory assured her daughter. "Orlando is like a big playground. You couldn't get into trouble if you tried."

"How about the other journalists on the trip?" Amanda asked. "Are you getting along with them?"

"All the writers are very nice." Except for the one who's very dead, she thought. But since Amanda obviously hadn't heard about it, she certainly wasn't going to be the one to give her one more thing to worry about. At least not unless she found out about it in the news, like her editor had. "And we're in very good hands," she continued. "A lovely young woman from the Florida Tourism Board has been taking good care of us. So has the general manager of the hotel."

"That's a relief," Amanda replied. "I've been so worried about you being down there all alone."

"How about you?" Mallory asked, a bit irritated by her daughter's concern over her ability to function on her own. "Any new developments?"

"Yes, as a matter of fact. Today I had a long conversation with Mr. James. Do you remember him? He was my favorite history teacher in high school. We had a long talk about my future. I really wanted his input, since he's someone who knows me well."

"What was his advice?"

"To follow in Daddy's footsteps. Mr. James feels I have the verbal skills and the mental agility required to be an excellent lawyer."

"Then you've made your decision—and you're ready to go back to school?" Mallory asked hopefully.

"Not yet. Tomorrow I'm going to see if I can track down my Girl Scout leader. I seem to remember that one year I sold more cookies than anyone in our troop's history."

Which clearly puts you in the running to be the next Bill Gates, Mallory thought.

Aloud, she said, "How is Jordan doing?"

Amanda sighed. "What does it take to get that boy off the couch?"

"Remind him that tomorrow is recycling day," she suggested. "Dragging the pail out to the street is about the only exercise he gets these days."

"I will. But tell me more about this press trip," Amanda urged. "Do all the writers do everything together, like on one of those European tours that covers eight countries in fifteen days?"

"Actually, we're all interested in seeing different things," Mallory explained, still peering at her arms in the mirror. "But Courtney—she's the woman from the tourist board—came with me to the *Titanic* museum. And one of the other writers who specializes in travel for senior citizens tagged along when I went to a reptile preserve called Gatorland."

"I'm so glad you're making new friends!" Amanda sounded like the proud mother of a kindergartner. "What about meals? Please don't tell me you're eating alone tonight."

"Actually," Mallory replied, doing her best to sound nonchalant, "I'm going to a dinner show with a ... a new friend."

"A friend?" Amanda sounded suspicious. Or at least

confused. "What do you mean? Is this someone you met in Florida?"

"It's one of the other journalists."

"How nice! What magazine does she write for?"

"It's not a she."

After a long silence, Amanda croaked, "You have a *date*?"

"It's not exactly a date," Mallory insisted. "Like I said, I'm simply having dinner with one of the other writers on the trip. We're just friends."

The silence at the other end of the line seemed to last an eternity. Mallory was beginning to wonder if the capricious technology behind cell phones had failed.

But then Amanda said, "Mother, I think that's wonderful. That you're spending time with a man, I mean."

The girl was full of surprises. "You do?"

"Yes, I do. It's important for you to make all kinds of new friends—including male friends. Platonic relationships with members of the opposite sex can play a very important role in building a person's self-esteem."

Mallory was contemplating whether or not to say that she wasn't so sure Wade belonged in the platonic category when Amanda instructed, "Now, I want you to do your best to have a good time tonight. And remember: You're a very interesting person with a lot of worthwhile things to say. You can do this. There's absolutely no reason to be nervous."

Just hearing the word *nervous* sent Mallory into a tizzy. She was suddenly back to obsessing over the presentability of her arms, her collection of inappropriate outfits, a platonic relationship versus the almost unimaginable alternative. . . . By the time she hung up, she was completely convinced she'd made a mistake in agreeing to have dinner with Wade, even if scores of pirates would be serving as her chaperones.

But it was too late. There was nothing for her to do

but try to have a good time. Even if it did mean she would actually be following her daughter's advice.

*   *   *

As Mallory strolled through the front door of the Pirate's Dinner Adventure with Wade at her side, she told herself she'd been silly to think of the evening ahead as a date. How could it be anything that serious when the restaurant's male employees wore shirts with puffed sleeves and a wooden treasure chest brimming over with gold doubloons was protected by nothing more ominous than a big DO NOT TOUCH sign?

As soon as they exchanged their vouchers for purple tickets, a wench wearing a flimsy off-the-shoulder blouse and too much eyeliner approached them.

"Step over here, please," she instructed, making it clear they had no choice. "We're going to take a photo of you with Captain Morgan."

"Captain Morgan?" Wade repeated as they shuffled into position next to a life-size statue of a grinning pirate. "Shouldn't he be home making rum?"

"Stand closer," the pirate who doubled as a photographer insisted. "No, not closer to Captain Morgan. Closer to each other." He frowned. "Why don't you try putting your arms around each other so you look like a couple?"

Mallory opened her mouth to explain that they weren't a couple. But this pirate didn't look as if he'd be interested. Not with a long line of people waiting to be photographed standing next to a shiny, fake-looking pirate who appeared to have been manufactured in the same factory as Ronald McDonald.

"These guys are pirates," Wade said, draping one arm around her shoulders and the other around Captain Morgan. "We'd be wise to do whatever they say."

He pulled her close enough that they undoubtedly looked like a bona fide couple. It's not a date, it's not a date, she repeated in her head over and over again. Still, she could feel her cheeks burning. She only hoped the lighting wasn't good enough to capture how red her face was undoubtedly turning.

After the requisite photo op, Mallory and Wade wandered through the spacious room that all the guests had been corralled into. Wenches were serving up hors d'oeuvres, bartenders were pouring dangerously large drinks, and face painters and tarot card readers were trying to lure children into spending a little more of their parents' money. The various shops lining the walls made the interior look like a Caribbean town, although the fact that there was a huge bar in the center instead of a village square detracted from the effect somewhat. A dock that jutted far out into the room looked as if it doubled as a stage.

"This part of the evening is called the King's Festival," Mallory explained. "I read that in the brochure."

"The king is clearly a capitalist," Wade noted, glancing around. "Face painting, a fortune-teller ... and look! There's Johnny Depp!"

He pointed to a life-size cardboard cutout of Johnny Depp wearing his Jack Sparrow costume. It was a shameless salute to the *Pirates of the Caribbean* movies, one more vehicle that perpetuated the image of pirates as a bunch of fun-loving, rum-drinking, stunt-performing dudes who occasionally indulged in a bit of harmless pillaging and plundering. The two-dimensional pirate stood outside a shop that sold the usual assortment of pirate paraphernalia: shot glasses emblazoned with pictures of pirates, plastic skull-and-crossbones refrigerator magnets, and eye patches, bandannas, swords, pistols, and everything else a person would need to launch a career in the lucrative pirate industry.

"Look at this place!" Wade exclaimed. "It reminds me of the last bar mitzvah I went to."

"Except for the three bars," Mallory commented.

"Right. There were at least six at the bar mitzvah."

She laughed. This is fun, she thought. *He's* fun.

Once they'd waited in line for appetizers and bought rum-based drinks at the bar, Wade asked breezily, "So, tell me, Ms. Marlowe, how did such a talented investigative reporter ever get involved in travel writing?"

Mallory stiffened. His tone was definitely flirtatious, she decided. She was relieved that one of the pirates on staff chose that particular moment to leap onto the dock and grab a microphone.

"I am Frederick the Town Crier," he boomed, "and tonight is special, because Princess Anita is visiting the citizens of Port Santa Cruz de Timucuan. . . ."

"I didn't realize they had such outstanding sound systems in the 1600s," Wade whispered.

"But we must beware of Captain Sebastian the Black," Frederick continued. "He is the cruelest of pirates and has vowed to kidnap her. . . ."

Mallory was relieved that there was little opportunity for conversation as, one by one, the rest of the cast members joined Frederick onstage. Princess Anita was dressed in a long dress that resembled a wedding gown. Since she was wearing white, she was clearly one of the good guys. As for the redheaded wench who sashayed onto the stage as if she owned the joint, she wore a black leather bustier and a red skirt that was split up the front. Her risqué outfit made it clear she was one of the bad guys.

A third woman in the cast, a gypsy who looked an awful lot like Marisa Tomei, magically emerged from a trunk that only seconds before had appeared empty. After making a few dramatic hand gestures, she nimbly ascended a rope that just happened to be close by and began performing graceful stunts on high. This was obviously one gypsy who had used her gold doubloons to pay for gymnastics lessons.

"She can dance in the sky!" the narrator said admiringly.

And not an ounce of cellulite, Mallory thought with at least as much awe.

She glanced over at Wade, slightly embarrassed, hoping he wasn't having a dreadful time. But he seemed enthralled by the gypsy's performance. Or else he was just a good sport.

Mallory relaxed and focused on enjoying the show—that is, until Frederick announced with chagrin that Princess Anita had been captured and hauled onto Sebastian the Black's pirate ship. That was when it became clear that the paying guests had no choice but to attempt to free her.

"When you came in, you were given a colored ticket," Frederick reminded them. "When your color is called, follow the pirate who's dressed in that color into the theater."

When it was time for the purple team to assemble, Mallory and Wade joined all the others who shared the same ticket color, lining up like schoolchildren coming in from the playground. They stood in front of a hunky pirate wearing purple pants, a purple vest that revealed an extremely muscular chest, and the same style headband the Teenage Mutant Ninja Turtles wore.

"I didn't realize we were going to have to rescue a damsel in distress," Wade commented as they shuffled into the theater. "If I had, I would have worn my bulletproof eye patch."

"And to think I left my can of Mace in my room," she added.

But her cynicism faded as soon as she entered a tremendous theater the size of a warehouse. Long tables and chairs that were set up on tiers created a theater in the round. In the center, floating in a pool of water, was a spectacular life-size pirate ship. According to the notes

Mallory had scribbled down from her guidebooks, the ship was a replica of a Spanish galleon that was forty-six feet long and eighteen feet wide, with forty-foot masts and tremendous white sails. It was outfitted with ropes, a ladder, and wooden trunks that she suspected would all play a role in the production. The same went for the water, which looked deep enough to keep any pirates who happened to tumble into it from getting hurt.

"My name is Saxon," the purple pirate announced once they were seated. "Whenever I perform a daring feat, cheer for me. Now, let's give it a try!"

Mallory did her best to cheer enthusiastically. She didn't want the purple team to look weak in front of all the other colors. She apparently did a good job, because Saxon immediately came over to her.

"What's your name?" he asked loudly enough for her purple teammates to hear.

"Uh, Mallory."

She was about to say something about her mother teaching her never to talk to pirates when he said, "I'm selecting you to be the flag-waver, Mallory. Whenever the purple team cheers for me, your job is to stand up and wave the purple pirate flag."

Mallory cast Wade a look of helplessness. But he just laughed as Saxon handed her a large purple flag attached to a wooden pole.

"I thought this was supposed to be fun," she moaned.

Wade shrugged. "That's what happens when you're the designated flag-waver. It's all about the responsibility."

For the next hour and a half, Mallory allowed herself to get lost in the production that played out on the deck of the huge pirate ship. She whooped and hollered with the rest of the purple team, leaping up from her meal to wave the flag every few minutes. The constant interruptions seemed a small price to pay for supporting Saxon, their own personal pirate, as he climbed the ropes, swung from the masts, and wielded his sword against Yellow, Blue, Orange, and all the other pirates on the ship. When it was time to rescue Princess Anita, Saxon dragged Wade out of his seat, insisting that he join the other able-bodied purple males who, like him, were strong, healthy, and at least four years old.

"Now it's your turn!" Mallory cried jubilantly. "See that? I'm not the only one whose special talents are needed to save Princess Anita."

"Yeah, but you didn't have to dress funny," Wade said as he reluctantly put on the three-cornered hat Saxon had just handed him.

The evening ended with the entire cast bursting into song, waving imaginary beer steins as they sang, "What do you do with a drunken sailor, what do you do with a drunken sailor...." Mallory and Wade sang along in voices that were at least as loud as their purple team-mates'.

"Thanks for coming with me," Mallory said as they filed out.

"I'm just glad we managed to hold on to both our wallets and our lives," Wade replied. "Most people who've had encounters with pirates aren't lucky enough to make the same claim."

"And we actually had fun. At least I did."

"I did, too, although you and I hardly had a chance to say a word to each other. Aside from a couple of 'yo-ho-ho's,' of course."

"That's because Saxon immediately recognized my natural talent for flag-waving." Mallory sighed. "But I guess it's time to become a landlubber again. We're invited to stay for the so-called Buccaneer Bash, but I really should get back to the hotel. It's probably a good idea for me to make some sense of all those notes I wrote in the dark."

"I have a better idea," Wade said. "I know a quiet place where there are no pirates and no wenches, although I believe there's plenty of rum. It's a nice, relaxing spot to sit and have a drink."

"You mean a place like that actually exists around here?" she asked. "I didn't think Orlando was zoned for anything that grown-up."

She was hedging, trying to decide whether or not to say yes. Part of her wondered if this nice, quiet place was his hotel room. Another part of her replayed her daughter's instructions about enjoying herself tonight. As far as she could recall, Amanda hadn't said anything specific about exactly how to accomplish that.

"The place I'm thinking of is the bar at the Peabody Hotel," Wade explained. "I went there this afternoon to see if it was a place I should write about in my article. It's right next door to the Orlando Convention Center, only a few blocks from here. And if I remember correctly, its claim to fame is a fountain with real, live ducks, even though it's indoors."

Frankly, it sounded like the perfect place to recover from all those carousing pirates. Besides, the idea of going back to an empty hotel room sounded dreadful.

"Show me the way," Mallory said.

• • •

Wade's description of the bar at the Peabody Hotel turned out to be accurate. It was peaceful, all right, at least compared to the visual and aural mayhem outside on the streets of Orlando. In fact, it seemed as if its designers had made a conscious effort not to include anything that would attract children.

The bar was crowded with what looked like conventioneers. Enough people were talking to one another, standing around in groups or clustered together in the comfortable wicker-and-wood chairs, that it seemed like one big party. Water streamed down a marble fountain along the back wall, a considerably more dignified version of the waterfalls back at the Polynesian Princess. A baby grand piano played background music by itself, its keys actually pumping up and down.

In the center was the fountain Wade had promised, an octagonal ring of marble. Real, live ducks lounged along the edge. The hotel had even named its restaurant Dux in their honor.

"Better?" Wade asked once they'd gotten drinks at the bar and sat down on opposite sides of a small round table in the corner.

"Much better." Mallory glanced around, noticing that most of the other people wore name tags. "Even if it is filled with people who are involved in . . . does that really say 'Eastern Fats and Oils'?"

"So it does." He leaned back in his chair and sipped his drink. He'd ordered a martini, which struck Mallory as a truly grown-up drink. She wished she'd thought of it before she'd ordered a whiskey sour.

"So, what's your angle for your article?" Wade asked.

"I'm trying to find if the old Florida survived Disneyfication," she explained. "I'm visiting all the old-style attractions I can find. You know, the type that were popular in the fifties and sixties. Alligator farms, snack bars shaped like the foods that are sold there, that kind of thing."

"You mean kitsch Florida. The Florida of the pink plastic flamingo."

Mallory laughed. "You got it. At least, that's a big part of it."

"You know, *kitsch* is actually a German word that originally referred to art that copied another style—badly," Wade explained. "But over the years, it came to mean bad taste in general. The term is generally used in a fun way, meaning something that's so tacky it's fun.

Things like paintings of kittens on black velvet or...or Elvis salt and pepper shakers."

"Lava lamps," Mallory volunteered. "Inflatable chairs."

"Coconuts with faces glued on."

"Ketchup dispensers shaped like tomatoes."

"And we can't forget places," Wade added. "Theme parks like Storyland or Santa Claus Village. Or even the Accounting Hall of Fame."

Mallory blinked. "Does that really exist?"

"It certainly does. It's on the Ohio State University campus in Columbus, along with the Insurance Hall of Fame and the Agricultural Drainage Hall of Fame. Then there's the world's largest chest of drawers in High Point, North Carolina. Smokey the Bear's burial place in the Capitan National Forest in New Mexico. And Carhenge in Nebraska. It's a replica of Stonehenge made out of junked cars that have all been painted the same shade of gray."

"How do you know these things?" Mallory asked, laughing.

Wade shrugged. "My head is filled with useless trivia. I guess that's one of the reasons I love publishing a lifestyle magazine. It gives me a chance to put all my otherwise worthless knowledge of pop culture to good use."

She was enjoying herself so much that she was actually disappointed when her cell phone trilled.

"I'm sorry, I'd better take this," she said, checking the phone number on the screen. "It's one of my children—probably my daughter."

"By all means."

"Mother?" Amanda asked anxiously before Mallory had even had a chance to say hello.

"Hello, Amanda," she answered, turning away. "Is everything all right?"

"Of course everything is all right. I'm calling to see how your evening went."

Mallory hoped she wasn't blushing as she said to Wade, "Excuse me, I'm going to take this someplace quieter."

"Mother, don't tell me you're still out with that man!" Amanda exclaimed.

"As a matter of fact, I am," Mallory replied, weaving through the crowd and out of the bar.

"But it's so late!"

Mallory glanced at her watch. To be perfectly honest, she'd lost track of the time. "It's not even eleven o'clock."

"That's late for someone like you to be out."

The whiskey sour seemed to have gone to her head, because she shot back, "Do you mean someone like me who's old or someone like me who's dull?"

"Neither. I mean someone who's having dinner with a man for the first time in ages."

"It turns out it's not that different from riding a bicycle," Mallory replied. "It all comes back to you."

Amanda sighed as if she was finding that trying to deal with an irrational person on a rational level was a complete waste of time.

"Amanda, I'm having a really nice time," Mallory told her daughter patiently. "Wade and I went to a pirate theme dinner that I thought would be silly but actually turned out to be fun. And now we're at a lovely bar in a big hotel, having a drink—"

"For heaven's sake, Mother, when I told you to have a good time, I didn't mean for you to have *that* good a time!"

"Good night, Amanda," Mallory said pointedly. "I'll talk to you soon."

"Mother, don't you think—"

"Good *night*, Amanda."

"Everything all right?" Wade asked when she returned. She sighed. "Yes, aside from overly concerned children who find it hard to accept the fact that their mother has a life of her own."

"Funny, I have a similar problem with my kids," Wade said, chuckling. "Tell me about yours."

Mallory smiled. "I'm absolutely crazy about them. Even though a lot of the time, they drive me absolutely crazy."

"They sound great."

"They are. Amanda is twenty. She's a junior at Sarah Lawrence. And she has a good head on her shoulders, at least most of the time." Rolling her eyes, Mallory added, "At the moment, she's in agony, trying to decide between business school and law school. I don't know which one of us is headed for a nervous breakdown faster, her or me."

"If she's as grounded as you say, I'm sure she'll make the right decision. And either way, she'll make enough money to support you in your old age."

Mallory laughed. "I sure hope so. Because right now, it doesn't look as if her brother is about to make a significant contribution to his mother's pension fund. Jordan—he's eighteen—went off to Colgate in September. But he came home after a few weeks, convinced it wasn't the right place for him.

"But he's a good kid. I think he's just a little confused right now." Wistfully, she added, "I think we all are."

"How long has it been?" Wade asked gently.

"Six months. It happened last summer. David was standing on the balcony of a hotel and somehow he must have leaned too far over the railing. It was one of those freak accidents you read about in the paper. The kind that always seem to happen to other people."

Wade reached over and gently laid his hand on her arm. "I can't imagine what you must have gone through. What you still must be going through."

"It's been rough," Mallory admitted. "I keep thinking

that if only I'd had a chance to prepare for it. If he'd been sick, or had had some sort of health problems, it would have been easier." She swallowed hard. "Instead, one day a cop just showed up at the house, looking as if he'd rather be anywhere else in the world.

"I was in shock for weeks afterward," she continued. "To be honest, I hardly remember any of it. But there's one thing I do remember, because it struck me as one of the strangest things: doing a dead man's laundry."

When she saw the startled look on Wade's face, she quickly said, "I'm sorry. I know that probably sounds bizarre. What I mean is that the first time I did laundry after David died, the hamper had his clothes in it as well as Jordan's and mine. His socks, his T-shirts...so I washed them. I knew I'd be throwing them away, but somehow following through on my usual routine just seemed like the right thing to do. It was almost as if David's laundry deserved to be treated just like any other laundry."

Mallory glanced at Wade, suddenly self-conscious. "I'm so sorry. I'm sure you regret even asking me in the first place and right now are trying to think of a polite way to——"

"Not at all," he insisted. "I'm sorry you had such a tough time. But it's oddly reassuring to hear that I'm not the only one who's had to fight to keep from falling apart."

"Your divorce?"

He nodded. "Fortunately, my kids are grown, so I think it's been a lot easier on them. Jennifer is twenty-four. She lives in Vancouver and does something with computers. Don't ask me what. And Lindsey is twenty-one. She's graduating from the University of Toronto in the spring. As for the marriage, it's not as if I couldn't see what was happening. Even though I didn't admit it to myself practically until I was signing the divorce papers, deep down I knew it was coming.

"What I didn't anticipate was how much it would hurt to lose such a big piece of my life all at once," he continued. "I lost the house, since Laura and I agreed to sell it. I lost a lot of my friends, too, since many of them were the husbands of women Laura had become friends with. I also lost the day-to-day companionship I'd come to rely on. Someone to have dinner with, to celebrate holidays with, even to go on vacation with. Suddenly, it was all gone. There I was, alone at age fifty, living in a new place, and faced with the challenge of creating a brand-new life for myself."

"You seem to have come a long way," Mallory observed.

"I hope so. It's been a year. At first, I did what any self-respecting middle-aged male would do: I threw myself into my work." Wade paused to sip his drink. "But, little by little, I found a new way to do things. I make a point of having lunch or dinner with each of my kids at least once a week. I became active in a couple of professional organizations I belong to. I've thought of doing volunteer work, too. I just haven't decided yet which way to go with that."

"I have a feeling you'll figure it out," Mallory commented. "And not just the volunteer work. All of it."

"Me, too." His blue eyes burned into hers with alarming intensity as he added, "In fact, I think I'm finally starting to get the hang of being single again."

• • •

"I really had fun tonight," Mallory told Wade sincerely as they strolled through the lobby of the Polynesian Princess shortly before midnight.

"That's because you're such a pushover for a man with an eye patch and a wooden leg," Wade joked.

Shyly, Mallory said, "I don't think that's it."

"I had a good time, too," he said.

He put his hand on her arm, as if to stop her. When she did, he turned her so she was facing him.

"Mallory, I never expected to meet someone like you on a press trip," he said earnestly. "Actually, I never expected to meet someone like you at all."

"I didn't, either," she replied in a hoarse voice.

For a fleeting moment, he looked as if he was going to lean over and kiss her. Instinctively, Mallory took a step backward, then made a show of glancing at her watch.

"Goodness, is it really this late?" she said with forced heartiness. "I'd better get some sleep. I've got another full day ahead of me tomorrow."

When she finally dared to glance up at him, she saw a look of disappointment flicker across his face.

"In that case, we should probably just say good night," he said, "instead of me pretending that it's chivalry that's motivating me to offer to walk you to your room."

She opened her mouth, waiting for a hundred excuses or explanations or apologies to come rushing out. Instead, she simply said, "Good night, Wade. And thank you for a really lovely evening."

Even though she wasn't about to win the award for Date of the Year, she floated all the way to her room. She couldn't remember the last time she'd felt this way.

She let herself in quietly, figuring most of the other hotel guests were nestled all snug in their beds. She could hardly wait until she was, too. But it wasn't because she was tired. In fact, she had a feeling she wasn't going to fall asleep for a very long time. Not when she was looking forward to replaying the entire evening in her head, trying to decipher the meaning of each moment, like a teenage girl who'd just come home from her very first high school dance.

When she noticed the red light on the phone next to her bed was blinking, her first thought was that it was Wade, calling to say good night. Then a more practical voice said it was more likely that either Jordan or Amanda had left her a message.

She kicked off her high heels, perched on the edge of the bed, and pressed the Listen To Messages button. Then felt all the blood in her body turn to ice when she realized she had been wrong on all three counts.

"Ms. Marlowe, it's Detective Martinez. Please give me a call as soon as you get this message. I'd like you come down to the station as soon as possible. There's something related to the murder of Phil Diamond that I want you to see."

10

"The real voyage of discovery consists
not in seeing new landscapes,
but in having new eyes."
—Marcel Proust

With trembling hands Mallory dialed the number Detective Martinez had left. Her heart was in her throat as she waited for the desk sergeant to put her through.

"Detective Martinez."

"Detective, it's Mallory Marlowe," she said, trying to sound calm. "You left me a message?"

"I'm sending a car over to your hotel, Ms. Marlowe. We found something in the victim's room that we think may be relevant to the investigation."

"What is it?" she asked anxiously. "I can't imagine what Phil would have had in his room that had anything to do with me. I barely knew the man."

"The car will be there shortly. If you don't mind, wait in the lobby, near the front door."

She felt dazed as she hung up. So many questions were spinning around in her head. What had they found? Was it something that tied her even further to Phil

Diamond...or worse yet, to his murder? Was she now a bona fide suspect? Would she be spending the night at the police station...maybe even in a jail cell? Should she contact her children so someone knew where she was, or would a late-night call saying she was on her way to the Orlando police station only frighten them?

She thought about calling Wade, but quickly rejected the idea. She had no desire to let him see her in a state of such confusion and uncertainty. Not when she had so enjoyed having him get to know the relaxed, confident version of herself, one that had become so unfamiliar in the last six months that even she barely recognized her.

Grimly, she recalled that only a few hours before she'd agonized over what to wear for an evening with pirates. Now she found herself trying to decide what to wear to a police station—especially when her worst fear was that she'd be spending some serious time there. Maybe even several nights, although that thought was simply too horrible to entertain.

She finally changed into flat, comfortable shoes, pants, a loose-fitting shirt, and a sweater. She checked her purse to make sure she had ID, some cash, and basic creature comforts, like tissues and lip balm. Then she waited in front of the hotel, trying to remember the last time she'd felt so alone.

At least the car that pulled up a few minutes later wasn't a police car. Being driven to the station in the middle of the night was bad enough. Doing so in a vehicle that would make everyone in the hotel think she was a criminal would have made it unbearable.

She hoped the uniformed officer driving her to the station would be a good source of information. Instead, he was as close-mouthed as Detective Martinez had been on the phone, supplying only terse answers to her questions and claiming he didn't know what this was about.

The police station was a stark structure that stood

seven or eight stories high, looming above the buildings that surrounded it. The tall, narrow windows slit into the light-colored brick facade reminded Mallory of the bars on a cell door. As the driver pulled up in front, she saw that beyond the semicircular walkway that curved along the front was a courtyard. Rather than looking like a friendly place to relax, however, it was outfitted with uncomfortable-looking concrete benches and a few trees that appeared pathetically meager compared to most of the landscaping here in the Sunshine State.

Mallory suspected that even in broad daylight the building looked grim. In the middle of the night, it reminded her of something out of a horror movie.

"This way," the driver instructed her gruffly after opening the car door for her and then leading her up a few steps and through a glass door.

Once inside, she blinked as she struggled to adjust to the harsh fluorescent light. A uniformed cop peered at them over a high counter. Centered behind him on the wall was a huge circular seal. ORLANDO POLICE, it read. COURAGE, PRIDE, COMMITMENT.

"Martinez upstairs?" the driver asked.

"He's waiting for you," the desk sergeant replied.

Mallory felt dazed as she trudged up some stairs and along a corridor. She would have expected a police station to be bustling at all hours. Instead, the place was like a ghost town.

Unfortunately, the one ghost she wasn't in a hurry to see was sitting at a large metal table. It was the only piece of furniture in a room she would have preferred to think of as a conference room but which was probably called an interrogation room. He looked as alert as if it was one in the afternoon instead of one in the morning.

"Thanks for coming in, Ms. Marlowe," Detective Martinez greeted her.

As if I had a choice, she thought dolefully.

"What did you want to show me?" she asked, trying to sound as if being summoned to the police station in the middle of the night hadn't rattled her in the least.

"Please sit."

She would have preferred to stand, since she hoped she wouldn't be staying long. But it was clear that Detective Martinez had every intention of conducting this meeting on his own terms. Stiffly, she lowered herself onto a cold metal chair, the only other seat in the room.

"We found this envelope in Phil Diamond's hotel room." He held up a plain brown mailing envelope with no writing on the outside.

A wave of relief washed over her. She didn't know what she'd been expecting, but certainly it was something more dramatic than an envelope. A gun, perhaps. Or a severed body part, even.

But when he reached into the envelope, all he pulled out was a pile of newspaper clippings. She exhaled loudly, relieved by the sight of something so harmless. He spread them out on the table, reminding her of a Las Vegas dealer slapping cards on a green felt table.

Her relief vanished as soon as she read the headlines.

DAVID MARLOWE WINS LANDMARK REAL ESTATE CASE, the large letters on the first one screamed.

ATTORNEY WINS INSURANCE FRAUD CASE, read the second headline. Underneath was a grainy black-and-white photo of her late husband.

DAVID MARLOWE PREDICTS CHANGES IN BANKRUPTCY LAW WILL CAUSE UPHEAVAL, a third clipping read.

And finally, DAVID MARLOWE DIES AT AGE 48.

Mallory could hear a strange whooshing sound in her brain that made it difficult to comprehend what she was seeing. But even in her fog, she knew what she was looking at. Newspaper clippings about her husband. There were dozens of articles, and from their headlines, she could see that they spanned two entire decades. According to Martinez, the police had found them in the murder victim's hotel room.

"Ms. Marlowe?" Detective Martinez prompted.

"I—I don't know what to say," she stuttered. Her throat was so dry she was barely able to get the words out.

"We were particularly interested in these." Detective Martinez pulled a few clippings from the bottom.

The headlines on these articles made her gasp.

MALLORY MARLOWE PROMOTED TO SENIOR REPORTER.

RIVINGTON RECORD REPORTER WINS WESTCHESTER COUNTY JOURNALISM AWARD.

Mallory's hands were shaking as she reached for the third article. It wasn't that she needed to look at it more closely to see what it said. It was the fact that she remembered it so well that she wanted to make sure it really was what she thought it was.

This one was different from the others in that it was printed on an 8½-by-11-inch piece of white paper. That meant that someone, probably Phil, had gotten it off the Internet.

PICKING UP THE PIECES AND MOVING AHEAD, the headline read. Underneath was a photo of her taken by one of the freelance photographers who worked for the *Rivington Record*.

This article had come out only a few weeks earlier. It was about women in their thirties and forties who became widows, a feature about the challenges of adjusting to a whole new life at a relatively young age.

The fact that it was so recent—and that the topic was something so personal—made her dizzy.

"I thought you said you didn't know the victim, Ms. Marlowe." The sound of Detective Martinez's voice hit her like a splash of cold water. His eyes burning into hers, he added, "You told me that Sunday was the first time you'd met him."

"It's the truth!" Mallory insisted. She hated the desperation she could hear in her voice. "That *is* the first time I met him!"

"Phil Diamond was obviously quite interested in you." The detective stared at her for another few seconds. "Your husband, too."

Mallory suddenly remembered the conversation she'd had with Wade at lunch the day before. He had surprised her by how much he knew about her, all because he'd taken a few minutes to look her up on the Internet.

"Maybe he was just doing some routine research on me," she suggested. "The Florida Tourism Board gave all the journalists a list of the other writers who were coming on this press trip, along with the names of the publications they work for. One of the other people on the trip made a point of finding out something about each of us. He told me he Googled us."

"Googling a name is one thing," Detective Martinez countered. "These articles about your husband were cut out of the actual newspapers. East Coast newspapers. Yet Phil Diamond lived in Los Angeles, which means he would have had to go out of his way big-time to get a hold of these. It's also important that they date all the way back to the late 1980s. Ms. Marlowe, all of this tells me he's been compiling information about you and your husband for years. He must have had some reason to do so."

Mallory's stomach lurched. What if Detective Martinez was right and Phil Diamond had been keeping tabs on David and her, clipping every article he could find and neatly filing them all away? For a moment, she was glad he was dead. If he had intended to do her family harm, he was no longer in a position to do so.

Instead of comforting her, however, that thought raised another question. "But why would he have been saving all those articles for such a long time? It's not as if he was communicating with us."

"Did he ever contact your husband?"

"No!" she replied vehemently.

"How do you know?"

"Because . . . because David would have told me."

Yet even as she said the words, she knew how weak they sounded. And how feeble the argument behind them was. Of course David didn't tell her every single detail about his life. He especially didn't tell her everything about his law practice. If he had known Phil Diamond— or at least known *of* him—it was perfectly plausible that he had never mentioned it to her simply because it had never occurred to him that there was any reason to do so.

Or perhaps because he hadn't wanted her to know.

And now both of them were dead.

The idea that David might have been involved with the murder victim was chilling. What was even worse, she quickly realized, was that having newspaper clippings about her and her husband turn up in a murder victim's hotel room automatically tied her to said victim.

Ironically, this was turning out to be one of those situations in which she desperately craved the chance to talk to David. How she longed to pick up the phone and have him clear up this disaster that had suddenly fallen from the sky. Once, looking to him for help had been an everyday occurrence. Now, of course, it was impossible.

Detective Martinez scooped up the clippings and slid them back into the envelope.

"Ms. Marlowe," he said icily, "I can't help feeling that you're not being completely straight with me. In fact, the further along I get with my investigation, the more your name seems to be coming up."

"Detective Martinez, I swear I never even heard Phil Diamond's name before Sunday," Mallory insisted. "And I certainly had no reason to do him any harm! You've got to believe me!"

The look on his face told her that her protestations had

absolutely no effect on him. She was tempted to ask if she should be talking to a lawyer. But she felt as if merely posing the question would incriminate her even further.

"Just make sure you don't leave Orlando, Ms. Marlowe," he continued in the same somber tone. "I have a feeling I'll be talking to you again."

It was after one by the time she rode back to the hotel with the same taciturn driver. The streets of Orlando were eerily empty and the dark windows of the houses they passed reminded her of unseeing eyes.

In contrast, the garish lights and brilliantly colored flowers of the Polynesian Princess were a welcome sight.

Home, she thought with relief as she leaped out of the backseat and slammed the car door behind her. But it wasn't her *real* home, the one she really longed for.

Suddenly, she realized, even the concept of home seemed up for question.

She rode up the elevator in a daze, recounting the overwhelming events of the night. Up to this point, she'd been trying to find out everything she could about Phil Diamond. But suddenly someone else was in the picture. David. Her husband and the father of her two children. The man with whom she had shared a bed, a bathroom, a checking account, a last name, and over twenty years of her life.

She had assumed that after all that, she knew him pretty well. Yet she had just learned there were still a few things she had yet to find out.

11

"It is impossible to travel faster than the speed of light,
and certainly not desirable, as one's hat keeps blowing off."
—Woody Allen

After her late-night ordeal at the police station,
Mallory expected to fall into a deep sleep the moment she collapsed into bed. Instead, she spent the
rest of the night wrestling with the sheets as she desperately tried to make sense of what Detective Martinez had
shown her.

Why had Phil Diamond been collecting newspaper articles about David? What did it mean? Was Phil a deranged stalker...or had there been some connection
between him and her husband that she hadn't known
about? The more she struggled to make sense of it all, the
more dead ends she hit.

Mallory was actually relieved when the glowing red
numbers on the digital clock beside her bed read 7:00.
She stumbled into the shower, making the water as hot as
she dared in the hopes that the steam would clear her
head. When that didn't work, she headed downstairs to
the Tiki Tiki Tearoom.

"Coffee," she instructed the waitress even before she'd sat down. "Please."

She'd just taken the first few swallows and was feeling the caffeine start to kick in when she heard someone croak, "Rough night?"

Glancing up, she saw Annabelle Gatch hovering next to the table. Even though it was early, Annabelle's clothes were rumpled, and a good portion of her black hair had already escaped from the plastic clip that held the rest of it in a crooked bun.

"It looks like you and I are the only early birds this morning," Annabelle chirped.

Mallory didn't remember her being quite this cheerful before. Or maybe she was finding her fellow journalist particularly irritating this morning because even with the caffeine boost, her head still felt as if it was swathed in bubble wrap.

She decided to pretend she was up at this hour for a good reason instead of because her high level of anxiety made sleep impossible. "I thought I'd get an early start."

Annabelle plopped down in the chair across from her and grabbed a menu. "Where are you headed today?"

"The Ripley's museum." She couldn't bring herself to call it by its real name, the Ripley's Believe It or Not! Orlando Odditorium. "It opens at nine."

"Maybe I'll go with you. I've been meaning to check it out for my readers to see if it's worth what they charge. You don't mind, do you?"

"Not at all," Mallory replied.

She was lying, of course. Her first thought had been, *How on earth can I get out of this?* Even under the best of circumstances, spending an entire morning with a professional penny pincher wasn't exactly appealing. Given the way she was feeling today, she didn't know how she'd manage to remain civil.

But she quickly realized that an outing like this might

provide her with an opportunity to find out more about Phil. The world of travel writing was turning out to be much smaller than she ever would have thought. Since Annabelle seemed fairly seasoned, it was possible she had some information about the murder victim that could prove useful.

"Why don't we meet in the lobby just before nine?" Mallory suggested after they'd finished breakfast.

"Fine," Annabelle agreed. "That'll give me enough time to get in touch with Courtney. I'm not going unless I get a voucher. And you'll drive, right?"

"Of course." Skinflint Hint #483, Mallory thought wryly: Whenever you go somewhere by car, make sure someone else drives so you don't have to pay for gas.

• • •

The Odditorium was close by, less than half a mile away on International Drive. The attraction was housed in a large white building with a red tile roof that gave it a Spanish look. Yet the attractive architecture was secondary to the fact that the entire structure had deliberately been built on a slant, to make it look as if it was sinking into the ground.

Predictably, Annabelle gasped when she saw the cost of the tickets. "Wow! I'm going to have to pay close attention to see if the admission price is worth it for my readers."

Why should today be different from any other day? Mallory thought cynically.

Aloud, she said, "If you don't mind, I need to stop in the ladies' room. I'll just be a minute."

"No problem. I'll wait here." Glancing at the large metal horse positioned right outside the rest rooms, Annabelle commented, "Look at that. It says that Lucky, a life-size model of a prize-winning racehorse, was made from over four hundred pounds of iron horseshoes. I don't think that's particularly hard to believe, do you? Even though it says BELIEVE IT OR NOT!"

How did I allow myself to get roped into this? Mallory thought, wondering how she was ever going to survive an entire morning of listening to Annabelle complain. It would have been hard enough under normal circumstances, but given the fog that still engulfed her brain, even the simplest tasks seemed more difficult than usual. She decided to try focusing on the museum and the fact that this morning's outing gave her an opportunity to pump Annabelle for information about Phil.

Ever since the cops had found those newspaper clippings in the victim's hotel room, the stakes had gotten higher than ever. Not only had their appearance brought David into the scenario, they had also fueled Detective Martinez's suspicions that she had played a part in Phil Diamond's death.

The fact that Annabelle seemed to have met Phil before they got here meant that she might be a good source of information about the man. And given the comments she'd made about him at the group's introductory lunch—especially her crack about how anyone who'd ever spent any time with him at all knew what a jerk he could be—she seemed to know him pretty well.

Mallory was surprised to find that even the ladies' room was part of the museum. The oddities on display directly related to the bathroom theme—fortunately, with some semblance of taste. The poster on the door, for example, claimed that in 1994, in Vilnius, Lithuania, thirty tons of old money was recycled into bathroom tissue. The blown-up cartoon illustrating this mind-boggling feat included toilet paper dotted with dollar signs.

But they probably don't use the dollar sign in Lithuania, Mallory thought. Then she hoped she wasn't becoming as contrary as Annabelle.

Right inside the museum was the desk that had actually belonged to Robert Ripley, the man behind the Believe It or Not! phenomenon. Sitting at it—or at least giving the appearance of sitting at it—was a hologram of an actor portraying the famous cartoonist.

"Clever, huh?" Mallory commented, taking out her notebook and jotting down a couple of sentences.

"Sure," Annabelle grumbled. "Especially since it means they don't have to pay a *real* actor."

The exhibits continued with more displays about the creator of the popular series. Mallory copied down all the pertinent facts: that Robert Ripley created over 56,500 of the cartoons for his newspaper column in the *New York Globe,* that he worked from 6 A.M. to noon every day for thirty years, that he visited 198 countries looking for oddities.

A black-and-white video showed a funeral that took place in China in 1932, as well as actual footage of some of the tribes Ripley visited. Next came glass cases containing some of his finds, including a horrifying mask that was supposedly made of human skin and a shrunken head from the Jivaro Indians of Ecuador. Unfortunately, the shrunken head was wearing a long straight black wig that made it look like an American Girl doll.

Most of the displays, however, were simply blown-up reproductions of Ripley's cartoons. And the next room was filled with optical illusions, fun house mirrors, and a hologram of a huge jewel that visitors were invited to steal.

"So far, this is pretty cheesy," Annabelle grumbled. "Given what they charge, there's no way I can recommend this place to my readers." She scribbled some notes in a small spiral notebook she'd whipped out of her purse. Mallory couldn't help noticing a big orange sticker on the front that said, CHEAP-O CHUCK'S, 19 CENTS.

"Frankly, tourists can find this kind of thing in other places, for less money," Annabelle went on in the same disgruntled tone. "As far as I'm concerned, this place should be called the Rip-Off Believe It or Not Museum."

Mallory was less inclined to be critical, especially since she thought the hokey displays were kind of fun.

"I think children would enjoy it," she commented, annoyed by Annabelle's negative attitude, which was turning out to be even more pervasive than her miserliness. "A lot of adults, too. This place brings me back to my family's trips to Florida when I was a kid. In fact, I'm kind of glad that an attraction that relies so strongly on people's imaginations still exists."

She felt vindicated when the displays in the next room turned out to be an improvement over what they'd seen so far: artifacts Ripley had brought back from his travels, like blowpipes from Borneo from the 1930s and a Maori canoe paddle.

Not far beyond, however, she and Annabelle came across some truly grotesque items, the kind of thing that only prepubescent boys were likely to get a kick out of. In fact, Mallory could hardly bring herself to look at the Siamese piglets that had been born stuck together or the alligator whose head was impaled with a pitchfork.

"This stuff is gross!" Annabelle announced. "I mean, can I really advise my budget-conscious readers to pay good money to see a two-headed calf? Or look at this so-called Fiji mermaid. It says right on the display that it's a fake, nothing more than a monkey and a fish sewn together."

"The Fiji mermaid is actually famous," Mallory commented. "P. T. Barnum had one in his American Museum in New York during the 1860s. It really brought in the crowds."

"In that case, he was right about a sucker being born

every minute," Annabelle replied tartly. "And I want to make sure my readers aren't among them."

The statue of Robert Earl Hughes, who weighed 1,069 pounds and died at age twenty-one, didn't do much to change their minds. Neither did the model of Thomas Wedders, a circus sideshow entertainer who had a nose seven and a half inches long.

Mallory and Annabelle agreed to skip the exhibit that highlighted the methods of torture employed by various cultures. It wasn't until they wandered a bit farther that they came across the types of exhibits Mallory had been expecting, items that were unusual, entertaining, and truly worthy of the claim "believe it or not!" In the center of the room was a 1907 Silver Ghost Rolls-Royce constructed from more than one million wooden matchsticks. Hanging on the walls were a reproduction of the *Mona Lisa* made out of bread and a portrait of Lincoln made from Lincoln pennies.

"Now, this is something I can write about," Annabelle announced.

"Definitely old Florida," Mallory agreed.

They wandered over to a rickshaw from China that was made entirely from jade. According to the sign in front of it, it weighed almost a ton. Since it was designed to be carried by small men, Mallory wondered if chiropractic treatments had been invented in China, just like spaghetti, paper, and gunpowder.

"Speaking of Florida," Mallory said casually, realizing she was running out of time to pump Annabelle for information, "did you know that Phil Diamond was originally from Florida?"

"I think I heard something about that," Annabelle replied vaguely, staring at the gigantic jade wheel with more intensity than it deserved.

"I understand the police still haven't identified the

killer," Mallory added, making another attempt to draw Annabelle into a conversation about the murder victim.

"Not yet. Hey, look at this bedpan collection!" She stopped in front of dozens of bedpans attractively arranged in a geometric pattern on a high white wall. "It says here that Stella Downing of Fort Hunter, New York, spent sixty-six years collecting them. Where would somebody store all these bedpans? Maybe in an out-house?"

Mallory obviously wasn't making much progress with her investigation. She tried to think of another way of gracefully turning the conversation to Phil as she and Annabelle studied a vampire killing kit from the mid-1800s. Neatly packaged inside the box were vials that according to their labels contained "flour of garlic" and "herbe-gris." The kit also included a cross and a silver stake big enough to drive through the heart of the vampire in question.

But she just couldn't focus. Maybe it was because of her sleepless night—or maybe it was because she was simply too distracted by the huge portrait of Vincent van Gogh made from postcards of his paintings or the chunk of the Berlin Wall.

And then she and Annabelle walked through one more doorway . . . and stumbled onto a display of frightening-looking spears. It was impossible not to notice how closely they resembled the one that had been used in Phil Diamond's murder.

Mallory was staring at them, transfixed, wondering whether or not to point out the obvious, when she heard a strange noise that almost sounded like someone was choking. Turning, she saw it had come from Annabelle. In fact, tears were streaming down her cheeks.

"Annabelle!" Mallory cried. "Are you all right?"

She just nodded.

"Are you sure?"

Annabelle nodded once again. Yet after only two or three bobs of her head, she stopped and began shaking her head from side to side.

Mallory put her arm around Annabelle's shoulders protectively. "It's these silly spears, isn't it? This is hitting a little too close to home."

Annabelle nodded again, this time sniffling loudly.

"You're really traumatized by what happened to Phil, aren't you? It was a shock for all of us."

"Th-that's not it," Annabelle said. "I—I mean, it is, but there's more to it."

Mallory sharply drew in her breath. Trying not to show how anxious she was to hear what was coming next, she reached into her pocket with her free hand, pulled out a tissue, and handed it to Annabelle. And here she'd believed that now that her children were grown, her days of pulling tissues out of her pocket like a magician were over.

"Is it because of the horrible way he ended up, drowned at the bottom of a fake waterfall?" she asked.

Annabelle shook her head again, this time more vehemently.

Mallory was still puzzling over Annabelle's extreme reaction when the other woman blew her nose loudly and wailed, "It's because I was in love with him, damn it!"

Mallory blinked, struggling to digest what she'd just heard.

Boy, if that isn't the biggest "believe it or not" in the joint! she thought.

But this was a time for diplomacy, not honesty. So, aloud, she said, "You know what? I think it's time for an early lunch."

• • •

Annabelle was sobbing into her third tissue as Mallory pulled into the parking lot of the first restaurant she spotted, Race Rock. The good news was that it was only a few doors down from Ripley's. The bad news was that it was a theme restaurant built around the race car concept.

Maybe a little whimsy will lighten Annabelle's mood, she rationalized, not knowing where else to take her weeping companion.

The building was round, its exterior decorated in the same bold black-and-white check pattern as a NASCAR flag. A short stretch of road ran along one side of the round building. Parked on it was a big blue car with oversized wheels, appropriately stenciled with the nickname Big Foot.

As they walked through the main entrance, she saw that race cars hung from the ceiling. Mallory took a moment to appreciate the fact that Florida wasn't in earthquake territory.

Inside the cavernous building were more race cars, displayed on platforms high in the air. The distinctive decor also included motorcycles in glass cases, along with life-size mannequins decked out in racing outfits. Race-car drivers apparently favored bright colors like orange and yellow, with matching helmets. It was a look that reminded Mallory of Jordan's early childhood obsession with the Power Rangers.

Once they were seated, Annabelle continued sniffing. She also seemed reluctant to make eye contact. She looked at the floor, the menu, the car races on the huge screen next to their table, anywhere but at Mallory.

"Would you like a drink?" Mallory suggested.

"I usually just have water in restaurants," Annabelle replied. "It's an easy way of keeping the cost down. Not only in terms of the drink itself, but also the tax and tip."

Oh, dear, Mallory thought. The budget thing, even at a time like this.

Annabelle let out another loud sniffle. "But maybe I'll splurge this one time and treat myself to a Diet Coke."

"I was thinking of something a little stronger," Mallory said. "Something that might make you feel better." She scanned the menu. "How about a Race-A-Rita?"

"You mean alcohol?" Annabelle seemed shocked. "I don't usually drink at lunch. Not when restaurants charge such exorbitant amounts for—wow! Will you look at these prices?"

"It's on me," Mallory insisted, resisting the urge to roll her eyes. "In fact, I'll join you."

She scanned the menu, struggling to make sense of the unusual combinations of alcohol, fruit juices, and even some ingredients that had no place in alcoholic beverages, such as ice cream, bananas, and chocolate syrup.

"How about an Oil Slick?" she finally proposed. It was just beer with a fancy name, but she figured that was less likely to get Annabelle loopy than one of the restaurant's more creative concoctions. It also happened to be one of the cheapest drinks on the menu, which meant her tightwad of a dining companion wouldn't have such a hard time allowing herself to indulge.

"I guess I'll have one of those Race-A-Ritas," Annabelle finally decided.

"Let's order some food, too," Mallory suggested. The last thing she wanted was to end up with a luncheon companion who was slumped on the table, sobbing into her glass over her lost love.

Fortunately, their waiter came by almost immediately.

"A Race-A-Rita for my friend, and I'll try a Barney's Purple Passion." Mallory hoped Annabelle wouldn't notice that the drink she'd ordered for herself had no alcohol mixed in with the raspberries and ice cream.

"Would you like those in a fuel can?" the waiter asked matter-of-factly, glancing up from his pad.

Mallory blinked. "Excuse me?"

"You can get your drinks in a fuel can with the Race Rock logo," he explained, pointing to the fine print on the menu. "Or for an extra charge, you can get it in a twenty-two-ounce logo collector pub glass."

"I think we'll both stick with a regular glass," Mallory told him. "And we'd like some appetizers. How about an order of the Chicken Dragsters and some Nitro Wings... easy on the High Octane Nitro Sauce?"

Mallory had come to this bizarre place with the goal of calming Annabelle down—and perhaps even finding out more about the man who had not only been murdered but also had some mysterious connection to her dead husband. Yet now that she was here, she couldn't stop the newly uncovered writer's voice in her head from narrating the experience.

Race Rock offers travelers a chance to feast on foods with a race-track theme—or at least race-track-themed names—in a truly unique environment. Where else can a vacationer dine on Nitro Wings dipped in a High Octane sauce while watching racing footage on a tremendous screen, enjoying the rrr-rrr *sound that's unique to this popular pastime?*

"Sorry about all this," Annabelle suddenly said, gesturing at the clump of damp tissues wadded up in one hand. "I don't usually get so emotional about things."

"I don't blame you," Mallory insisted, her thoughts returning to the assignment at hand. "Not when you had such a close relationship with Phil."

All of a sudden, instead of seeing an irritating travel writer who was obsessed with pinching pennies, Mallory saw Annabelle as a woman in pain. True, it was difficult to imagine any woman falling in love with an oaf like Phil, but there was probably no greater mystery on earth than the reason one person was attracted to another. Couples had their own secret life, one that no one else was privy to. Even attempting to comprehend it was usually a waste of time.

Fortunately, the waiter brought their drinks quickly.

He seemed to have had some experience with tourists who were at the end of their rope and had become desperate for alcoholic beverages served in tall curvy glasses that resembled hurricane lamps—even if it was still way before noon.

As she stirred her purple foamy drink, Mallory commented, "I have to admit, I had no idea you and Phil were...a couple."

She hoped she'd used the correct term. She braced herself for a confession of unrequited love. Or worse yet, a heartbreaking report that Annabelle and Phil's relationship had consisted of nothing more than a series of one-night stands in travel destinations all around the globe, everywhere from Albuquerque to Zanzibar, which Annabelle had interpreted as love and Phil had seen as one of the perks of travel writing, along with free shampoo and gift baskets.

So Mallory was relieved that Annabelle nodded. She opened her mouth as if she was about to speak, but instead leaned over and took a long, slow sip of her bright-orange Race-A-Rita. In fact, by the time she came up for air, a full third of the gigantic hurricane lamp was empty except for a thin film of foam around the glass.

"It started about five years ago," she began. "I'd just gotten into writing travel articles. I think I was on my third or fourth press trip—"

"What did you do before you got into travel writing?" Mallory asked. She couldn't resist learning everything she could about Annabelle Gatch's history while her guard was down and her blood alcohol level was climbing.

"I was a technical writer. I wrote pamphlets on how to program your VCR or change the message on your answering machine."

No wonder no one can figure out how to do those things, Mallory thought.

"Anyway, I was in the BVI—"

She blinked. "I'm sorry, the *what*?"

"The BVI," Annabelle repeated. "The British Virgin Islands."

"Got it."

Annabelle took another impressively long sip of her drink, wiping out another third. Mallory glanced around the restaurant, hoping their waiter would materialize so she could order Annabelle another before she started making embarrassing slurping sounds.

"There were five journalists on that trip," Annabelle continued, "along with the usual escort. This one happened to be from the PR firm that represented the BVI's Tourism Board."

A faraway look had come into her eyes and her voice sounded uncharacteristically dreamy. Whether that was due to her trip down memory lane or the fact that she'd just downed enough alcohol to incapacitate a sailor, Mallory couldn't say. Still, she pushed the plate of chicken wings closer to Annabelle, hoping she'd take the hint and add a little solid food to all the tequila sloshing around in her stomach.

"I barely noticed him at first," Annabelle continued. "In fact," she added with a smile, "believe it or not, I actually thought he was kind of obnoxious."

Imagine that, Mallory thought wryly.

"At least, until the third night," Annabelle went on. "That was Calypso Night. The hotel we were staying at, the Tortoise Island Resort, had set up a table right on the beach for just the six of us. All around us were tiki torches that were stuck into the sand. We had a whole team of waiters, who brought us one course after another. I can't tell you how beautiful it was. Or how romantic. Sitting on the beach under a sky filled with stars and a big, bright moon..."

Mallory could picture the entire scene. In fact, she

could practically hear the waves pounding on the shore and experience the grittiness of a grain of sand that had found its way into her appetizer.

"Anyway, somehow I ended up sitting next to Phil, even though I'd kind of been avoiding him up until then," Annabelle went on. "And for the first time, we talked. I mean, we *really* talked. Not only about the past, but also about our hopes and dreams for the future. And before long, we both realized there was a real connection between us. That we were meant to be together. It was almost as if we were soul mates."

Somehow, Mallory was having a difficult time picturing boorish Phil as anyone's soul mate. Unless, of course, he thought that playing that role would result in a payoff—namely, one that took advantage of the fact that hotels changed the sheets every day. Yet given Annabelle's sincerity, she had no choice but to concede that there was at least a possibility that the man had had another side to him.

"That was probably the most amazing night of my life," Annabelle said wistfully. "After dinner, all the other writers went off to their rooms. But Phil and I walked along the beach, holding hands." She sighed. "It was incredibly romantic. It was also the beginning of something wonderful. That same night, Phil and I made love for the very first time. It happened on the terrace outside his room, overlooking the Caribbean Sea."

I hope that terrace wasn't also overlooking the kitchen, Mallory thought. Or else that's a night the hired help is still talking about, too.

"We made love three times," Annabelle told her.

Too much information! Mallory thought, wincing.

Annabelle didn't seem to notice. "Phil and I connected in a way I'd never connected with anyone else before," she continued in the same dreamy voice. "Neither of us slept a wink that night. We were too busy getting to know each other. For me, it was as if I'd been in a deep sleep and I'd just woken up for the first time in my life.

"But we knew our relationship would never work in the real world," Annabelle continued, her voice hardening. "Not when I had my life in Baltimore and he had his far away in Los Angeles."

Just like Wade and me, Mallory thought. She quickly reprimanded herself for being as silly and starry-eyed as Annabelle.

"So we decided that we'd simply do our best to go on the same press trips," Annabelle concluded. "And that's what we've done ever since. We always pretended we didn't know each other well because we didn't want to embarrass anyone else on the trip. But for us, each travel junket was another secret rendezvous. Phil and I have made love in Barbados, Madrid, Namibia, New Dehli, Boston, the Canary Islands, and Fallbrook."

"Fallbrook?"

"Fallbrook, California. The avocado capital of the world."

Pretty convenient, Mallory thought cynically, especially for a man like Phil. Not only was he accumulating frequent flyer miles, at the same time he was racking up another type of benefit that also began with the letter *F*.

Annabelle leaned forward and slurped up the rest of her drink. Instead of making her even more intoxicated, however, for some unfathomable reason, reaching the bottom of a hurricane glass the size of a tornado seemed to sober her up.

"But ever since Sunday, I've been in a panic." For the first time since they'd sat down, she sounded like her old crusty self. "I can't help worrying about what will happen if the police find out."

"You mean you didn't tell Detective Martinez about it?" Mallory asked, startled.

Annabelle snorted. "Why would I? The fact that Phil

and I were intimate is bound to make me a suspect." She narrowed her eyes. "And of course I didn't kill him. Why would I? I was in love with him, for heaven's sake! I'm the last person in the world who would have wanted him dead!"

"Of course," Mallory agreed.

Yet she was thinking the exact opposite. Annabelle's admission that she and Phil had been enjoying a lot more than free HBO in their hotel rooms hardly absolved her of guilt. In fact, as far as Mallory was concerned, it shot her way to the top of the suspect list.

As Annabelle had admitted herself, the police almost always began a murder investigation by focusing on the murder victim's significant other. And Mallory saw no reason why she shouldn't do the same.

12

"Travel is the frivolous part of serious lives,
and the serious part of frivolous ones."
—Anne Sophie Swetchine

Mallory was still pondering the unlikely pairing of
Phil Diamond and Annabelle Gatch later that
day as she drove to Kissimmee, a town just south
of Orlando on the map.

The more I learn about the other travel writers, she
marveled, the more amazed I am. It turns out you really
can't judge a book by its cover.

At the moment, however, she had other things to concentrate on besides the intrigues of her fellow travelers
and how they might relate to Phil's murder. On the
agenda were two stores that she sensed would turn out to
do a pretty good job of capturing the old Florida.

She pulled up in front of Orange World, a gift shop
and produce store on Highway 192. When she'd stumbled across it while doing research on the web, she'd
known immediately that it would be perfect for her article. For one thing, it had opened in 1973, meaning its
roots were in the golden days of Florida tourism. Yet

probably even more important was the fact that the building was designed to look like the piece of fruit that had inspired its name—at least its top half. The bright-orange, dome-shaped structure epitomized kitsch—especially Florida kitsch.

How wonderful that this building survived, she thought as she snapped a few photos.

Outside were bins filled with brilliantly colored oranges, grapefruits, and even tangelos. Mallory had never dreamed that so many different varieties of citrus fruits existed. Unable to resist a little shopping, she grabbed a plastic basket and picked out a bag of oranges. Each one was perfect, making them look as if someone had painted them with a coat of orange enamel.

Inside the shop, she found the usual tourist paraphernalia, the T-shirts and baseball caps and pens that were available pretty much everywhere. She was much more interested in the grocery section, which was stocked with local specialties produced by Florida-based companies. Mallory filled a basket for Amanda with several flavors of coconut patties and jellied citrus fruit squares that were made right in Orlando. For Jordan, she chose a chocolate alligator called a ChocoGator, which was packed in a box with so-called Gummie Gators. Personally, she found both types of candy creepy, but that was exactly why she thought her son would get a kick out of them. After a long debate, she tossed a jar of guava jelly into her basket, figuring she'd give it to Trevor.

Her second stop was a store that was farther along the same road. Shell World, which had opened a few years after Orange World, occupied a whopping twelve thousand square feet. Before going inside, she took photos of the Volkswagen covered in seashells and the golf cart with the same motif, both parked outside. For no apparent reason, a statue of a pirate guarded the door. Mallory looked for a treasure chest—one filled with seashells, of course—but there was none.

Inside, Shell World was all that its name promised. Aisle after aisle was jampacked with merchandise that was a tribute to the seashell. Seashell wind chimes, seashell night-lights, seashell necklaces, seashell tissue boxes, seashell boxes, seashell wreathes, even a curtain made of shells, which could be purchased with or without a palm tree design created by different colored shells.

The store's inventory also extended to any and every other item that was even vaguely related to the sea: plastic lobsters, mermaid snow globes, rubber sharks. There were also aisles containing nothing but seashells in their natural state, in case shoppers became so inspired they wanted to go home and cover various parts of their homes or possessions with shells.

Mallory wandered through the Seashell Museum, which featured exhibits of different types of starfish, sand dollars, and other unusual sea creatures. "Reticulated cowrie helmet," she wrote in her notebook. "Video on deep-sea diving."

While at first she'd been horrified by the store's seashell-themed wares, as she snaked through the aisles on her way out, she kept stumbling across items that caught her fancy. A seashell night-light for the bathroom, shell earrings for Amanda, one of the rubber sharks for Jordan, even though she had no idea what he'd use it for. She also bought a few shell-covered boxes, soap dishes, and necklaces for purposes that had yet to be determined.

I'd better get out of here before I buy enough shells to cover my Subaru back home, she thought.

As she came out of Shell World, blinking in the bright sunlight, she glanced around, wondering if Highway 192 had any other treasures left over from the old Florida days. Her heart began to beat faster when she spotted a building right across the street that she hadn't noticed when she'd arrived.

It was shaped like a giant ice-cream cone.

Patrice, she thought. Phil Diamond's ex-wife.

She knew that Patrice was no longer in the ice-cream business. But she couldn't resist checking this place out on the off chance that the person who worked there might know something about her.

Mallory hurried into her PT Cruiser, got back on the road, and made the first U-turn she could. As she pulled into the parking lot, she saw that the ice-cream shop's window was cut out of the "cone" and giant swirls of what was supposed to be soft-serve vanilla ice cream formed the roof.

Mallory was afraid the stand would be manned by a sixteen-year-old whose idea of ancient history was Bill Clinton's presidency. Instead, a woman who was at least Mallory's age stood at the counter, hunched over a magazine. She was wearing an orange halter top made of fabric that looked wet and slippery, and a pair of denim shorts that were daringly short. Her hair, dyed an unnatural shade of red that still managed to look flattering, was piled up on her head and held in place with half a dozen silver barrettes.

"What can I get you, hon?" the woman asked. She barely glanced up from an article that, according to the headline, promised "amazing weight loss secrets" that enabled someone to lose ten pounds in one week while eating chocolate cake.

"I'll have a vanilla cone," Mallory replied without even bothering to check the short menu posted along the back wall.

"Yeah, that's pretty much what everybody has," the woman replied with a knowing smile. "Power of suggestion, you know? Small or large?"

"Uh, small."

"Ever hear of subliminal messages?" the woman asked as she stood at the gleaming silver soft-serve machine, expertly filling a normal-size cone with a tower of ice cream. "It's a technique people in advertising use all the time. See, they sneak secret messages into the ads you see on TV. In magazines, too. Like in a vodka ad, the swirls in the ice cubes spell out 'Buy Stoli Now!' That's how they brainwash you. Anyway, I swear that's what this giant ice-cream cone over my head does. It makes people order vanilla."

Or maybe people simply like vanilla, Mallory thought. But she wasn't about to argue. Not when she was hoping to get more than just ice cream from this woman.

"This is a great building," she said, taking her first few licks while she waited for her change.

"No kidding," the woman said with pride. "This place is a classic."

"I'm actually pretty interested in this kind of thing. Old Florida, I mean." Mallory swiped at her cone with her tongue, forestalling a nasty drip in the nick of time. "I'm a travel writer, and I'm writing an article about whether the old Florida still exists. I'm focusing on places just like this that recapture the feeling of the past."

"Then I guess you've already been to Shell World and Orange World," the woman commented, handing over a pile of coins.

"I just came from both. But I'd love to include something about these ice-cream stands that are actually shaped like ice cream." She paused. "There's somebody in particular I'm trying to get in touch with. I understand there's a woman who had a place like this about twenty years ago, back in the late 1980s. I don't suppose there's any chance you'd have ever run into her . . . ?"

"I might have," the woman said. "The tourism business is a pretty small world, at least around here."

Just like the travel-writing world, Mallory thought.

"What's her name?" she asked.

"Patrice Diamond. At least, that was her married name. She's gotten divorced since we lost touch, so I don't know what name—"

"Sure, I know Patrice. At least I used to. I haven't talked to her in ages, though."

Mallory tried not to let her excitement show. "Is her ice-cream stand still around?"

"Nah. They knocked it down. I think they put up a KFC instead."

"That's too bad. But what about Patrice? I understand she left Florida a long time ago."

The woman cast her an odd look. "Why would you think that?"

Mallory blinked. How about because that's what Desmond Farnaby explicitly told me? she thought.

"You mean she's still in the area?" she asked.

"Sure is. You could probably find her in the phone book. Of course, she's using her maiden name these days. It's Hammond."

"Patrice Hammond," Mallory repeated. "Thanks."

"Hey, anytime. And enjoy that ice cream." With a shrug, she added, "Who knows how long this place will survive before somebody puts some fast-food joint on the property—all in the name of progress."

• • •

Energized by the possibility of having found a new lead, Mallory wolfed down the rest of her ice-cream cone as she drove along the highway, then pulled into the first parking lot she spotted. After digging out her notebook and a pen, she dialed Information. Sure enough, within seconds an automated voice recited a local number that belonged to a Patrice Hammond.

She dialed that number next.

"Patrice?" Mallory asked when a woman answered.

"You got her. Who's this?"

Mallory did some fast thinking. She hadn't expected to get Patrice on the phone this easily, so she hadn't planned out what to say.

"My name is Mallory Marlowe."

As she paused to think of what her next sentence should be, Patrice said, "If you're selling something, I'm not interested."

"Actually," Mallory said haltingly, "I'm the person who found your ex-husband's body a couple of days ago."

While she hadn't intended to be quite that blunt, her simple statement seemed to have the desired effect.

"Go on," Patrice said, her tone wary.

"I should explain that I didn't actually know him," she went on, speaking quickly. "I'm down here in Florida for the same press trip he was on. It's my first, since I just started writing travel pieces for a magazine. I actually live in New York. Well, outside of New York. Anyway, what really matters is that the police have this ridiculous idea that I might have had something to do with his murder."

She stopped talking, hoping that what she'd said so far would be enough to keep Patrice from hanging up on her. As she was debating whether or not to add anything about the clippings about her and her deceased husband that had turned up in Phil's hotel room, Patrice asked, "What do you want from *me*?"

"I'm not sure," Mallory replied honestly. "I'm simply trying to find out whatever I can about the man, since I'm suddenly in the horrible position of having to convince the police I had nothing to do with him, either dead or alive." She could hardly believe her life had taken her to a place in which she would actually utter the phrase *dead or alive*.

"I don't know how helpful I can be." Patrice's voice

had softened. "I mean, I haven't seen the guy in, what, more than a decade?"

"It's not his recent past I'm interested in," Mallory told her. "I can't help wondering if maybe some of the stuff he was into in the past could have led to his murder." She let out an exasperated sigh. "Look, it's kind of hard to go into all this on the phone. Is there any chance you'd be willing to meet with me? Even for half an hour? Just tell me where and when, and I'll accommodate your schedule."

"I could do that," Patrice agreed. With a hoarse laugh, she added, "It's funny: No matter how much time goes by, women never get tired of bad-mouthing their ex. How about Thursday afternoon, on the late side? Like around four?"

"Perfect."

"Where are you staying?"

"The Polynesian Princess Hotel on International Drive."

"Of course." Patrice laughed. Once again, there was a definite undertone of bitterness. "The place where Phil finally got what he deserved, right?"

Mallory made a note to add Patrice's name to the list of people who had apparently felt the exact same way about Phil Diamond.

"I could meet you at the McDonald's on Sand Lake Road, right off International," Patrice suggested. "Do you know where that is?"

"I'll find it."

"Just ask anybody where the world's largest McDonald's is," Patrice said. "They'll know."

Somehow, it seemed fitting to Mallory that she meet with Phil's ex-wife in a McDonald's that held the distinction of being the largest in the world. Everything in Orlando was the biggest, the best, or at least the weirdest.

Why should something as mundane as a fast-food restaurant be any different?

But she knew perfectly well that it wasn't the meeting place that mattered. It was the information Patrice would hopefully have about her ex—information that Mallory hoped would lead her closer to the man's murderer and farther away from Detective Martinez's list of persons of interest.

13

"If you reject the food, ignore the customs,
fear the religion and avoid the people,
you might better stay at home."
—James A. Michener

Mallory actually felt optimistic as she headed back to the hotel. She was finally making progress with her investigation. Tracking down Patrice—and getting her to agree to talk to her—represented a major step in unraveling the details of Phil Diamond's past. She was still hopeful that understanding everything he had done and everyone he had angered while doing it would enable her to reconstruct the emotions and events that had led to his murder.

She was about to go back to her room to luxuriate in this rare wave of good feeling when she suddenly remembered that today was Annabelle's birthday.

Oh, my gosh! she thought guiltily. Here I spent the entire morning with her and not once did it occur to me to wish her a happy birthday.

The likelihood that no one else had remembered, either, only made her feel worse. Spending one's birthday alone struck her as terribly sad, especially since turning forty was a major milestone in any woman's life. On top of that, this particular woman had just lost the love of her life—because he was murdered, no less. She wracked her brain, trying to come up with a way to acknowledge the occasion without looking as if she had forgotten about it until the very last minute.

She realized she was holding the solution to the problem in her hand.

Mallory thought of calling first, but decided that birthdays were all about surprises. And if Annabelle had gone out to celebrate, Mallory decided as she rode up the elevator, she would simply try again later.

She rapped on Annabelle's door, braced for the possibility that no one would answer. Instead, it opened almost immediately.

"Mallory!" Annabelle exclaimed, her eyes widening. "I thought you were Room Service."

Annabelle was dressed in the fluffy white bathrobe the hotel provided and a pair of dark socks. She would have looked as if she was enjoying an evening by herself if her eyes hadn't been rimmed in red. The television, which was tuned to CNN, blared from the other side of the room.

"I hope you don't mind me dropping by unannounced," Mallory said, realizing that calling first wouldn't have been a bad idea, after all. "I have a birthday present for you." She handed Annabelle one of her purchases from Shell World, wrapped in a cloud of white tissue paper.

A look of astonishment crossed Annabelle's face. "You remembered?"

"Of course."

"Come in." Annabelle still looked stunned as she studied the small gift. "Wow. That was really thoughtful, Mallory."

"It's not much," she said quickly. "Just a token."

Annabelle switched off the TV with the remote and sat down on the edge of the bed. "Can I open it now?"

"Please do."

The vehemence with which Annabelle tore off the paper reminded Mallory of Jordan when he was five years old. She half expected the woman's face to droop with disappointment when she saw what the present was. Instead, she simply looked confused by the tiny square box that was covered with seashells. She opened it, as if she thought there might be something inside, then snapped it shut again when she saw it was empty.

"I know it's tiny," Mallory said apologetically, "but I suppose you could put jewelry in it. Small jewelry, anyway."

"Where on earth did you find something like this?"

"I went to a store called Shell World today. It was full of things that were either made out of shells or decorated with them. Shell night-lights, shell wind chimes, shell jewelry, you name it."

"It was very thoughtful of you," Annabelle assured her, placing the box on the night table. "Thanks a lot. I mean it."

"I was glad I found something that's unique to Florida," Mallory babbled. "That way, it'll always remind you of this—"

She stopped mid-sentence, having realized the implications of her statement just a few seconds too late. Of course Annabelle would never forget this trip. How could she, when the man with whom she'd been having an affair for years had been murdered?

"I'm sorry," she said. "I—I wasn't thinking."

"Don't worry about it."

"Anyway, happy birthday." She paused, trying to think of something else to say to get past the awkward moment. "That birthday cake Courtney promised never materialized, did it? I guess she forgot about it after everything that happened."

"It's okay," Annabelle insisted, her tone just a little too brusque. "I'm a big girl. I don't need a big celebration with a lot of people making a fuss over me."

As she spoke, her eyes drifted over to the round table in the corner. Mallory automatically looked in the same direction. Sitting on it was a tray that looked as if it had been delivered earlier by Room Service, littered with the remains of a dinner eaten alone in a hotel room. A white linen napkin smudged with lipstick was loosely folded along one side, and a few chicken bones stuck out from beneath the silver dome that was askew on the dinner plate. A small carafe containing only a quarter-inch of red wine stood next to an empty glass.

Sitting on the table next to the tray was a partially eaten piece of chocolate cake decorated with a single birthday candle.

Mallory pretended she hadn't noticed any of it. She averted her eyes and looked around the room, hoping to find something less embarrassing to focus on.

Her eyes lit on the top of the dresser, where she noticed something that was very small yet so shiny that it glinted. It took a moment or two for her to realize it was a ring.

Next to it was a black-and-white photograph in a silver frame. Even though it lay flat, she could see that the woman in the picture wore an old-fashioned white dress. Her dark hair was styled in a way that reminded Mallory of a 1940s Joan Crawford movie. Oddly enough, she was holding her hand toward the camera.

Annabelle's eyes traveled in the same direction as Mallory's. "Oh!" she squawked.

"What a pretty ring," Mallory commented, wanting to smooth over Annabelle's obvious embarrassment, even though she didn't understand what Annabelle was embarrassed about. "Mind if I take a closer look?"

"Be my guest," Annabelle said woodenly.

Glancing over at her, Mallory noticed that all the blood had drained from Annabelle's face. Still, she picked up the ring and examined it. The intricate filigree ring was set with a large diamond, with at least half a dozen small diamonds studding the delicate strands of gold that surrounded it.

"Wow, it's gorgeous," she commented. "Kind of old-fashioned, though. It's so ornate. Rings tend to be a bit plainer these days." She made a point of looking at Annabelle so she could gauge her reaction as she added, "Especially engagement rings."

There was a frantic look in Annabelle's eyes. "It was my grandmother's ring," she blurted out. "That's her in the photograph. This was taken on her wedding day, right before the ceremony."

Comparing the ring in her hand with the one in the picture, Mallory could see that they were indeed one and the same.

"This ring looks pretty valuable," she said, putting it back on the dresser.

"I suppose it is," Annabelle replied. "But what's even more important than its monetary value is the fact that it's a family heirloom."

"In that case, shouldn't you keep it in the safe? There's one in my closet and there must be one in yours."

"I have been," Annabelle said defensively. "I just took it out a minute ago to look at it."

"I'm kind of new to this travel thing," Mallory said in what she hoped was a conversational tone, "but wouldn't it be better to leave something that valuable at home? It would be so easy for it to get lost. Or stolen."

"I'm taking excellent care of it." As if to demonstrate, Annabelle strode over to the dresser, picked up the ring,

188 · Cynthia Baxter

and slid it on her finger. Mallory noted that she slipped it onto the ring finger of her left hand.

"Maybe I'm just cautious by nature," Mallory said, hoping she wasn't pushing too hard, "but I can't help wondering why you'd bring such a valuable ring on a trip like this."

"I just wanted to have it with me, that's all." Annabelle's voice sounded much higher than usual. "Today's my fortieth birthday, and... and it seemed like something it would be nice to wear. As a way of celebrating such an important occasion, I mean. I don't own that many valuable things. Or beautiful things, for that matter."

"Of course." Mallory smiled, wanting to make sure she hadn't generated any bad feeling. "My engagement ring is special to me, too. It's funny, I hardly ever wore it when I was married. But after my husband died, I put it on and just kept it on. It was as if I wanted to remember the beginning of our relationship once it had come to an end." Sadly, she added, "I finally took it off when I took off my wedding ring."

"Why did you take either of your rings off?" Annabelle asked. "Some women simply keep wearing them."

"I know they do," Mallory replied. "But for me, I guess it was a way of finally acknowledging that I wasn't actually married anymore. I had to find a way of letting go."

The two women remained silent for a long time.

"Well, I'd better get in the shower before the health department comes after me," Mallory joked to lighten the mood. "Again, happy birthday, Annabelle. I hope next year's is better."

As she rode the elevator to her floor, Mallory pondered the strange interaction with Annabelle.

Why on earth would she bring a ring like that on a press trip? Mallory thought. It doesn't make sense. Even if she was taking good care of it, there was a risk of losing it or having one of the hotel employees walk off with it. It's not as if she ever gets dressed up. Even on Sunday night, when she showed up in the ballroom for the reception, I don't recall her wearing it. . . .

Suddenly a lightbulb went on in her head.

Of course! The reason Annabelle brought an engagement ring on this trip is that she expected to get engaged!

Annabelle had known she'd be seeing Phil on this trip. Maybe she'd decided that it was time to change their haphazard relationship. After all, she was about to turn forty, an occasion that was enough to make any woman stop and take stock of her life. Perhaps she had hoped Phil would propose.

But why now? Mallory wondered. If they've been continuing on in the same way for years, why would Phil suddenly want to get married?

The fact that she couldn't come up with a single reason led her to another conclusion: Annabelle had planned to propose to Phil.

Or maybe she already had, Mallory thought. Maybe she popped the question on Sunday night, showing up for a rendezvous with that engagement ring in her purse.

If she had proposed marriage and if Phil had said yes, chances are she would have told everyone. What newly engaged woman wouldn't be so excited that she'd babble about it to anyone who'd listen?

But what if she had proposed marriage early on Sunday evening and Phil had said no? What if she'd taken it a step further, giving him an ultimatum? What if she'd said "We wed or I walk" and he'd chosen option B? Wouldn't she have reacted strongly, perhaps even by flying into a rage?

A rage fueled by so much anger and disappointment and frustration that she killed him?

14

"All that is gold does not glitter,
not all those who wander are lost."
—J.R.R. Tolkien

As Mallory slipped her card key into the door of her own hotel room, she was still pondering the possibility that Annabelle had killed Phil in a fit of fury. A love affair that went awry had certainly been the motivation for more than one murder. The fact that Annabelle had gone so far as to bring an engagement ring with her on this trip struck Mallory as a pretty fair indication that the woman was determined to take their relationship to the next level. Yet it wasn't difficult to imagine that Phil had seen their love affair in an entirely different way.

She tossed her purse on the bed and was contemplating taking her second shower of the day when she noticed the red light on her phone was blinking.

She froze, staring at the phone as if it was a ticking bomb.

No, she thought. What now?

Her heart was pounding so hard as she punched the

Listen To Messages button that she felt sick. She braced herself for the sound of Detective Martinez's voice. So when the male voice that had left the recorded message turned out not to be his, it took a few seconds for the meaning of the words to register.

"Hey, Mallory, it's Wade. It's almost five, and I just got back from a trying day of research. Got a massage, sat in a sauna, drank some complimentary champagne... tough life, huh? Anyway, I know it's a long shot, but I was wondering if you might be interested in getting together for dinner again tonight. Give me a call. I'm in Room 718. Later!"

She was so relieved that she wasn't being hounded by Martinez again that after she hung up, she forgot all about Wade's invitation. It wasn't until she was towel-drying her hair and her eyes wandered over to the phone that she remembered.

She was agonizing over whether or not to return his call when the phone rang again.

This time, she wasn't sure who she hoped was calling.

"Hello?" she answered uncertainly.

"Glad I caught you," Wade said casually. "I don't know if you got my earlier message, but I was wondering if you wanted to have dinner tonight. I found a place that may be kitsch enough for you to write about but still sounds as if it has decent food. It's called Bahama Breeze, and it's just down the block. If we can get past the steel drums and all the coconut that's undoubtedly sprinkled on everything on the menu, I think we might actually enjoy it."

She tried to think up an excuse. Then reminded herself there was no reason to.

"I'd love to," she replied.

Two nights in a row, she thought after they made plans to meet in the lobby a half hour later. She rationalized her decision by telling herself that checking out another theme restaurant was simply part of her research. As for having dinner with a man who bore the distinction of not being on her list of suspects, the prospect was positively refreshing.

• • •

Just as its name promised, Bahama Breeze embraced a Caribbean theme. The restaurant reminded Mallory of the estate house on a sugar plantation. The wooden building had a wraparound porch made of natural wood that segued into a deck. The outdoor seating area was illuminated by strings of white lights. Inside, banquettes upholstered in bright tropical colors lined the walls, and an energetic band played the requisite reggae tunes.

"Let's sit outside," she suggested eagerly. She found the idea of dining alfresco irresistible, given the fact that back home, January was undoubtedly inflicting its usual wrath.

"This place is confusing me," Wade commented once they'd been seated far enough away from the band that they could hear each other speak. "I thought I was in Florida. But all of a sudden, I feel like I'm in Aruba."

"Then they've done their job," Mallory replied. "Actually, this is the perfect sequel to last night's dinner. That one demonstrated the 'before,' when pirates ruled the Caribbean islands. This one shows the 'after,' how it is today."

"Right. Now that the Royal Caribbean cruise line rules them."

Mallory laughed. She realized she did that a lot when Wade was around. And that it was something she hadn't been doing enough before coming to Florida.

In fact, she was amazed at how much was changing. This trip was forcing her to do so many different things. Renting a car and finding her way in a new and unfamiliar place, making decisions about where to go and when to get there, recording her impressions so she'd be able to write an article that other people would look to for guidance . . . She felt as if she was doing new kinds of exercise that utilized muscles she hadn't even realized she had. But afterward, instead of feeling sore, she felt stronger and more energized.

Of course, she couldn't say the same for some of the other new things she was experiencing, like being interrogated by a homicide detective and taking late-night trips to the police station. But at the moment, thanks to the pulsating music and the festive lights and the congenial company, she felt as if she'd even find a way of solving that crisis.

"So what looks good?" Wade asked, skimming the menu. "Aside from the woman sitting opposite me, that is."

Alarm bells immediately began clanging in Mallory's head. He's flirting! she thought, the feeling of serenity she'd experienced only moments before slipping away. And now I'm supposed to come back with some equally flirtatious reply. . . .

"The signature drink sounds good," she mumbled, burying her face in the menu. "The Bahamarita."

Out of the corner of her eye, she saw Wade's expression change. Whether it became one of disappointment or amusement, she couldn't say.

"Kiwi, mango, strawberry . . . seems a little sweet for my tastes," he replied, letting her off the hook. "I think I'll try the Mojito Cubano. Rum with spearmint and lime sounds more to my liking."

After they'd ordered their drinks, he asked, "So how's your research going?"

"Surprisingly well," Mallory replied. "I must admit, I'm really getting a kick out of all the 'old Florida' attractions I've been visiting. I expected them to be cheesy, but they're turning out to be much more polished than I expected. And at least as much fun as the theme parks."

"Don't tell me. You actually enjoyed yesterday's trip to the alligator farm?"

She laughed. "Yes, as a matter of fact. I was really impressed by Gatorland. It's more a preserve than one of those tacky old tourist traps from the old days. They seem to take really good care of the animals. The *Titanic* exhibit was also a lot more tasteful than I expected—at least, aside from the giant iceberg that's on display."

"Talk about weapons of mass destruction," Wade commented.

"Exactly. I also visited the Ripley's Believe It or Not! Orlando Odditorium. That was fun, once you got past the creepy stuff, although much of it reminded me of a carnival. Funny mirrors, optical illusions, that kind of thing. Still, by the time I reached the end, I felt I'd gotten my money's worth."

"And don't forget the pirates," Wade teased. "No vacation is complete without a few pirates."

"That's what they say. And you're right: I enjoyed that, too."

"I'd like to think I had at least a little to do with it."

There he was, flirting again.

"What do you have on the schedule for tomorrow?" he asked.

"Would you believe a place called Dinosaur World? My plan is to go there late in the morning, since I have an errand to run first."

"Dinosaurs, huh? Sounds like you might need some protection. Would it be okay if I invited myself along?"

Mallory blinked. Dinner, even two nights in a row, was one thing. After all, she and Wade were both spending a few days in a place where they didn't know anyone besides the other writers on the trip. Everyone got hungry, and most people preferred to have someone to talk to in a restaurant. But offering to come along on a sightseeing expedition that was likely to consist of nothing more interesting than wandering around a park, looking at a bunch of fake dinosaurs...that was something else entirely.

In fact, it could only mean one thing: that this man was pursuing her. She didn't know whether to feel pleased or terrified.

"Sure, why not?" Mallory replied, trying to sound blasé. "I'd enjoy the company."

She was glad their waiter appeared just then, depositing tall frosty drinks in front of them. She took a sip, hoping hers was heavier on the mango and kiwi than it was on the alcohol.

"What about your research?" she asked.

"Actually, I'm having a better time than I thought I would," Wade said. "I mainly came down here because I wanted to get away for a few days. I didn't really think about where I was going—just where I *wasn't* going to be, which was Toronto in January. But I've come to realize that travel writers have a really good thing going. Spa treatments, fabulous meals, luxury hotels—and it's all comped. Not a bad way to make a living."

"This trip has been an eye-opening experience for me, too," Mallory agreed. "And most of it's been great—aside from Phil's murder, that is."

She decided not to admit that while finding Phil's dead body floating in a pool of water had been traumatic, it paled beside being considered a murder suspect by the homicide detective investigating the case. As far as she knew, Wade had no inkling of that.

In fact, she didn't think any of the other writers on the trip had any idea of what had gone on in her second interview with Detective Martinez the night of Phil's murder. Similarly, they knew nothing about the clippings about her and her husband that had turned up in his hotel room. The last thing she wanted was for that knowledge to spread—especially since she was trying to get whatever information she could out of them.

"Have you heard any more about the murder?" Wade asked, supporting her belief that he was still in the dark about her role in all this. "Since Sunday night, I mean?"

"No," Mallory lied. "But of course everyone's been talking about it. It turns out that both Annabelle and Frieda knew him fairly well. From going on other travel junkets with him, I mean."

"Do they have any theories about who might have killed him?"

Mallory hesitated, wondering if she should confide in him, after all. But she quickly decided she had nothing to gain.

"The one thing everyone seems to agree on is that Phil wasn't exactly a popular guy," she finally said.

Wade nodded. "His work ethic certainly didn't make him popular with me."

Mallory's ears immediately pricked up. "What do you mean? You make it sound as if you worked with him."

"Actually, he worked *for* me."

She just stared. This was the first she'd heard about Wade having any sort of past relationship with the murder victim.

"When was that?" she asked casually.

"A few years ago. Four, maybe five. I was managing editor at a magazine called *On the Road*. And I got royally screwed by Phil, if you'll excuse the expression."

"What happened?"

"I hired him to do a freelance assignment. It was a long one, a comprehensive piece on Route 66. You know, the highway that runs from Chicago to L.A. It's not marked on maps anymore, yet it still has a mystique about it. That's probably due at least in part to the old television show from the 1960s.

"Anyway, I gave Phil a long lead time. I seem to recall it was something like three months. Once the deadline started getting close, I tried to get in touch with him to make sure he was going to get it in on time. For weeks he didn't return my phone calls or respond to my e-mails. Then, once I finally did manage to get him on the phone, he swore up and down that he'd make his deadline." He shrugged. "At that point, I had no reason to doubt that he'd follow through."

"I take it that didn't happen?"

"Nope. The deadline rolled around and I still hadn't received a single word from him. I tried calling him, I tried e-mailing him, but he seemed to have disappeared off the face of the earth."

"So what did you do?"

"I stayed up all night, throwing together some piece of garbage that would fill the magazine's empty pages." Smiling coldly, he added, "Needless to say, after that, Phil Diamond never got another assignment from me."

"Who could blame you?" Mallory said.

But she was thinking something else entirely.

For the first time since Sunday night, Mallory found herself considering the appalling possibility that Wade had murdered Phil. Could past interactions between the two men have been Wade's motivation? It certainly seemed unlikely. Still, she wasn't prepared to rule out any possibility. Not when the list of suspects was so limited.

Aside from her shock over learning that Wade was one more person who had had a bad experience with Phil, her head was spinning for an entirely different reason. Here she'd let down her guard with Wade and had really started to like him. To trust him, too. Yet she suddenly realized she didn't know him at all—and that she couldn't rule out the possibility that there was a lot more to his past with Phil Diamond than he'd admitted to.

She was actually relieved when her cell phone began to trill.

"It's one of my kids," she said, glancing at the screen. "I'd better get this."

"Of course. Do you want privacy?"

She shook her head. "I won't be long."

"Hi, sweetie," she answered, using a name either one of her children would answer to.

"Hey, Mom. How's it going down in Florida?"

Jordan. She was surprised by how pleased she was to hear her son's voice. "It's going just fine," she replied. "How are things with you? Is everything okay?"

"Yeah. It's just ... I've been thinking. Having Amanda in my face for the past few days has got me doing a little soul searching of my own." Jokingly he added, "It's hard not to when you suddenly find yourself living with Dr. Phil."

Not another identity crisis, she thought with dismay.

"Mom, I've decided to go back to Colgate."

Mallory gasped. "That's great, Jordan! I'm so pleased. I really think returning to school in the fall is exactly what you should do."

"Actually, I was thinking of going back second semester," he said. "I called the admissions department to see what it would take to get reinstated. Classes start the week after next. I'm waiting to hear back."

"Honey, I couldn't be happier."

"Sounds like good news," Wade observed after she'd hung up.

"The best." She let out a loud sigh of relief. "I guess my son finally got tired of hanging around the house, doing nothing. Or maybe with his sister, Amanda, there, his days of leisure finally came to an end. I can imagine her writing up a list of rules and regulations and posting it on the refrigerator.

"Whatever's responsible for his change of heart, I

couldn't be more pleased. I know he's been having a rough time since his father died, but dropping out of school—dropping out of society—certainly isn't the answer. I'm glad he's finally got his sense of direction back."

Her cell phone trilled again. Mallory assumed Jordan was calling back to add a postscript to his announcement. She glanced at Wade apologetically, but he just shrugged.

"Yes, Jordan?" she answered her phone.

"Mallory? Trevor Pierce."

Busted, she thought, panicking. Now, *this* is a call I'd have preferred to take in private.

Actually, she would have preferred not to take it at all. But she'd been caught.

"Trevor! What a nice surprise." Catching Wade's eye, she mouthed the words *It's my editor*.

"Mallory, I expect my writers to act like professionals!" Trevor thundered. "When I call someone who's on assignment, I need to hear back as soon as possible. I've been leaving messages on your cell phone for two days. Don't you ever check them? Do you have any idea how irresponsible it is to disappear like that—especially given what I've been hearing in the news?"

She was about to apologize when he added, "Hell, Mallory, I've been worried sick about you!"

His earnestness caught her completely off guard. She wasn't surprised he was reading her the riot act. But sounding as if he was truly concerned about her well-being was something else entirely.

"I'm sorry, Trevor," she said sincerely. "I was trying not to worry you, but apparently I ended up doing the opposite."

"Just tell me that you're all right," he demanded.

"I'm fine."

"If you want to change your ticket and fly back up here—"

"No," she assured him. "I'm fine, Trevor. Really."

That, plus I've been warned not to leave the state, she thought ruefully.

"Let me know if there's anything at all I can do to help," Trevor persisted. "No magazine article is that important. For God's sake, Mallory, we're talking about a murder!"

"Honestly, Trevor," she insisted, "I can take care of myself."

While she wished she believed that claim herself, at the moment it was much more important to her that he believe it.

"I know you can," he said, all the fire suddenly gone from his voice. "It's just that it's hard for me to get past the fact I sent you down to a place where there's a killer on the loose."

And the police think it might even be me.

"Besides, you're all alone down there," Trevor added.

"Not exactly," she said, eyeing Wade. "There are other writers on the trip, after all."

"I know, but they're strangers."

That's not exactly true, either, she thought. But she wasn't about to go there.

"Tell you what," she said. "I promise to call you if I feel the least bit uncomfortable or if there are any new developments that seem important. . . . From now on, I'll do a much better job of staying in touch."

"Thank you, Mallory," Trevor replied, sounding relieved. "In that case, I'll let you get back to work."

"I guess you heard all that," Mallory said after she hung up, casting Wade an embarrassed glance as she tucked her cell phone back into her purse.

"I think the whole restaurant did," he replied with a smile. "It sounds like the guy is really worried about you." He hesitated before adding, "So tell me: Should I be worried about the competition?"

"Don't be silly," she replied. "Trevor's my boss."

"That didn't exactly sound like someone's boss," he said, sounding uncharacteristically grumpy.

Mallory could feel her cheeks burning. Not long before, she would have been flattered by the idea that Wade was jealous. Yet now that she'd learned he was one more person who had a grudge against the murder victim, she didn't know whether to feel pleased or threatened by his attentions.

Her confusion made her more determined than ever to uncover the mysteries of Phil Diamond's past. And while up until now she had felt she was blindly trying to feel her way through unknown territory, for a change she knew exactly what her next step would be.

15

"Life is either a daring adventure or nothing."
—Helen Keller

The Orlando Public Library, located downtown, was an imposing gray stone building that stood several stories high. A tremendous slab constructed of the same material jutted out like a marquee, sheltering the row of welcoming glass doors lining the front.

This place looks strong enough to withstand an attack from another galaxy, Mallory thought as she headed inside. She hoped its fortresslike appearance meant it was a safe haven for all forms of the printed word—including outdated newspaper articles.

Inside she found a tremendous entryway with high ceilings and white walls that almost made her feel as if she was still outdoors. Large, airy spaces stretched to the left and right. But she zeroed in on the woman sitting behind a reception desk.

"Can I help you?" the woman asked pleasantly.

"Where would I find old newspapers?" Mallory asked. "I'm interested in both the *Sentinel* and the *Observer*."

"From how far back?"

"I'm hoping you still have them from the nineteen-eighties."

"They're stored on microfilm on the fourth floor," the woman replied matter-of-factly. "We've archived both newspapers back to the early nineteen-seventies."

Yes! Mallory thought.

As she rode the elevator, she wished she were more confident about her library skills. Her goal, after all, was to learn whatever she could about Phil Diamond's past here in Orlando, mainly by tracking down all the articles that had been written about the attraction Phil and Desmond had once owned.

Mallory had been thinking about the murder victim's strong ties to this area ever since she'd found out that he was a former resident, and she was determined to find out if the seeds of his destruction had been planted long ago. She hoped she was up to the task of delving deeply enough to figure out what the scandal that had destroyed Phil's writing career was all about, as well as piecing together all the other information she'd gotten, to see if somehow the haunted house from years ago had come back to . . . well, to haunt him.

The elevator doors opened onto another large room. The walls were painted soothing shades of gray or blue, their calming effect augmented by gray carpeting. A line of a dozen or so microfilm machines stretched across the room. Alongside them stood rows of old-fashioned wooden card catalogs. Orange labels gave the years of the newspaper articles cataloged inside, beginning with 1971.

Mallory started with the *Orlando Observer,* the newspaper Phil Diamond had written for. The cards were filed alphabetically by subject, so she perused the H's.

"Haunted, haunted . . . Nothing in 1986," she muttered, switching to another cabinet. "Nothing in 1987 . . ."

204 · Cynthia Baxter

She hit pay dirt with 1988. "Haunted House," the listing read. " 'Diamond in the Rough' by Phil Diamond."

"Perfect," she whispered, her heartbeat quickening.

She was confused by the article's title, however: "Monster Mansion: An Unwelcome New Neighbor Comes to Town."

"Monster Mansion?" she said, talking to herself quietly. "That wasn't the name of Phil's haunted house." Nevertheless, she jotted down the date, April 12, along with the page number.

When she didn't find any other listings for that year or the following few years, she moved on to the *Orlando Sentinel* files. Under 1988, she found a card that read, "Haunted House—Monster Mansion," dated December 9.

"There's that strange name again," she muttered. "Monster Mansion."

When she moved on to the next year, she found another card that read, "Haunted House—Monster Mansion" that had appeared just a few months later. She realized that the only way she was going to make sense of this was by reading the actual articles. At least she hoped that would clear up the mystery.

Once the librarian helped her locate the corresponding tapes, Mallory threaded the microfilm machine with the tape that contained the first article. She had decided that reading them in chronological order would be the best way to piece together events that had occurred such a long time ago.

When Phil's name came up on the screen, she did a double take. Even though she'd expected to see it, there was something eerie about reading an article by someone she'd known, someone who was now dead— *a murder victim.* But she wasn't about to let that stop her.

MONSTER MANSION:
AN UNWELCOME NEW NEIGHBOR
COMES TO TOWN
"Diamond in the Rough"
by Phil Diamond

If there's one thing the world needs—aside from peace in the Middle East, an end to pollution, and calorie-free ice cream—it's another haunted house.

I'm being sarcastic, of course. I feel I need to be up front about this fact just in case anyone who's reading this just emerged from a lengthy coma and has therefore been deprived of the opportunity to read my column for a long time.

But let me modify that claim. It's not that the world doesn't need another haunted house, it's that the world doesn't need Monster Mansion, the new attraction that recently slithered onto the scene courtesy of aspiring entrepreneur Henry "Huck" Hollinger.

True, central Florida's tourist biz seems to offer unlimited possibilities to any guy who can convince a few investors to finance his latest get-rich-quick scheme. After all, the Yanks are coming in droves. So are tourists from California, the Midwest, Alaska, Hawaii, and yes, even places more foreign that any of those. They're all dragging their whining kids and their aging parents and their credit cards down here in search of a good time.

And they'll try anything once. Water parks, bumper cars, miniature golf, you name it. As long as it's got some tacky theme that includes waterfalls, fire, teenaged girls in skimpy costumes, and a gift shop—preferably all of the above—they'll converge on it in their rented cars, pay to park, pay to get in, pay to buy refreshments, and pay to acquire worthless souvenirs, all in the name of family fun.

To be honest, the attractions themselves don't have to be all that great. After all, we're not looking for repeat customers. We're looking for one-timers, those suckers who are born every minute. You know, the same ones who built P. T. Barnum's fortune.

But come on. We've always maintained *some* standards, haven't we? That's what I always thought— that is, until I got an invitation to visit Monster Mansion.

It's important to note here that I got in free. Free! And by the time I got out of there, I still didn't think it was worth the price of admission.

I went in with a spirit of adventure. Optimism, even. I thought, Okay, here's something new. Something different. Something that promises to be *fun*—at least according to the billboards Mr. Hollinger has been plastering all over town as if he was a graffiti artist from the Bronx who'd been reincarnated as a money-grubbing businessman.

The key to the inevitable failure of Monster Mansion lies in that last sentence. Can you find it? Five points if you can. Okay, here's the correct answer: money-grubbing. Because Huck Hollinger clearly put the bulk of his money into creating a buzz without remembering to use some of it to make his attraction worthwhile.

And that's where he went wrong. Monster Mansion, folks, is a waste of time. A rip-off. Bad for tourism, bad for central Florida. Because once all those tourists who routinely flood our area go home, we want them to tell their friends and neighbors that they enjoyed their time here. Not that they got swindled.

Okay, not everything about Monster Mansion is horrible. There's plenty of parking, for one thing. The gift shop is well lit. And it's air-conditioned—let's not forget that.

Unfortunately, that's where the list of positives ends. As for the list of negatives, it begins with tacky special effects and ends with lackluster actors wearing shoddy costumes that look like something their mothers ran up on their Singer sewing machines the night before. In between, there's a poor sound system that makes the ghouls sound as if they lisp, fog drifting out of fog machines we can see only too well, and ghosts whose wristwatches peek out of their white sleeves. Even worse is the confusion about which elements actually belong in a haunted house. Monsters? I thought they lived in laboratories, not haunted houses. Aren't those supposed to be reserved for ghosts, ghouls, and the occasional poltergeist?

The most terrifying moment comes at the ticket booth, when visitors are asked to fork over fifteen bucks apiece. If a horror show like that isn't enough to anger the spirits, I don't know what is.

It certainly angered me.

The air-conditioned library suddenly felt very warm as Mallory realized what she had just read. Phil's tourist attraction, Crypt Castle, had had competition. Monster Mansion. And he had used his newspaper column to denigrate it.

She wondered how many of his readers knew that Phil Diamond had invested in a haunted house of his own?

Whether or not his readers did, she had a feeling his boss did. And that she'd just found the root of the scandal that had cost him his job.

Eagerly, she tucked that reel back into its box and

pulled out the next one, which contained the first of the two *Sentinel* articles. She scrolled through the microfilm until she came across the article, which had appeared eight months after the first.

HAUNTED HOUSE CLOSES
ITS CREAKING DOORS
by Marilyn Benevito

Monster Mansion, the haunted house attraction on International Drive that opened just eight months ago, closed its doors on Monday. In a telephone interview, owner Henry "Huck" Hollinger said it was "one of the saddest days of my life."

The 12,000-square-foot haunted house was one of the most eye-catching attractions on International Drive. The structure, separated from street traffic by a massive vine-covered iron fence, had the appearance of a decaying Victorian mansion. The empty rocking chairs on the porch moved back and forth constantly, suggesting that they were inhabited by ghosts. Mournful moans, the rattling of chains, and other eerie sounds regularly emanated from the cemetery that ran along one side of the house. Even after hours, feeble lights in the attic windows flickered on and off, and white billows that looked like specters drifted up from the roof.

Yet despite these clever effects, Hollinger reported that for a variety of reasons, he and his backers were unable to keep the attraction viable. According to Hollinger, the building and its contents will be put up for auction.

It closed! Mallory thought, feeling as if she'd been hit in the stomach—hard. Monster Mansion went out of business mere months after it opened!

Her head was spinning as she considered the enormity of Phil's offense. He had invested in Crypt Castle, and when Huck Hollinger opened a competitive attraction, he used the poisonous power of his pen to condemn it—so harshly that it failed.

It took her a few seconds to remember that she still had one more article about haunted houses to read. This last one, which also ran in the *Sentinel*, was dated just a few months after the article about Monster Mansion closing. Her hands were actually trembling as she threaded the microfilm into the machine. She felt as if she was witnessing an accident, and even though she longed to look away, she had no choice but to watch the entire event.

ORLANDO-AREA ATTRACTION
FAILS TO ATTRACT
by Marilyn Benevito

Special to the *Sentinel*—Crypt Castle, a haunted house attraction located on West Irlo Bronson Memorial Highway in Kissimmee, announced yesterday that on Friday it will close permanently. The attraction, which featured live actors and special effects, was owned by *Orlando Observer* columnist Phil Diamond.

Crypt Castle was in direct competition with another Orlando haunted house, Monster Mansion. Monster Mansion closed its doors three months ago.

Phil Diamond could not be reached for comment.

Mallory reread the short article three times, wanting to make sure she hadn't missed anything. Because something was blatantly missing.

There was no mention of Desmond Farnaby.

Yet Desmond had told her himself that he and Phil had gone into business together, creating Crypt Castle.

Something else frustrated her: the fact that the brief article gave no information about *why* Crypt Castle had closed. Had the reason been technical difficulties with the special effects? An inability to find suitable actors? Financial failure due to lack of experience?

Or perhaps creative differences between the owners that might even have caused one of them, namely Desmond Farnaby, to bail?

Mallory's head buzzed with unanswered questions as she coiled the microfilm around the reel and stuck it back into its box. And she tried to focus on the questions she *had* been able to answer through her library research.

Important questions. Questions about the scandal that had destroyed Phil Diamond's career.

Yet while she now had a better idea of just how low Phil had been capable of sinking, she still didn't understand how his past transgressions might have been connected to his murder. Especially since two entire decades had passed since the haunted house fiasco.

I still need more information, she thought, frustrated. No matter how much I find out, there are still missing pieces. And while I'm learning about all the unethical things Phil did, I still have no idea which one of them enraged someone enough to kill him.

She was still contemplating the maze she couldn't find her way out of as she headed back to the elevator. As she did, she happened to glance to the side. She noticed the library's magazine section, tucked into another part of the fourth floor. The sight of all those magazines gave her an idea.

She scanned the collection until she located the G's. Just as she expected, displayed on a shelf just after *Good Housekeeping* was *Go, Seniors!*

While she didn't have a concrete reason for suspecting Frieda, the woman had expressed strong feelings about Phil. Strong negative feelings.

And Frieda had told her herself that she'd known Phil for a long time, perhaps even back when he'd owned Crypt Castle.

Could there be a connection? Mallory wondered as she flipped through the pages of the magazine. It was a long shot, she knew. But she figured she might as well take advantage of being in a library by checking into every angle she could think of.

She found the masthead, then skimmed the listing of names and titles, her eyes traveling downward past the publisher and the editor-in-chief. She stopped when she reached the managing editor, which she knew from her years at the *Rivington Record* was the title of the person responsible for running a newspaper or a magazine on a day-to-day basis.

"John Crane," she wrote in her notebook. Next to it, she copied the telephone number she found way at the bottom of the page, right after the address of the publication's editorial office.

Phil's distant past may have been filled with treachery, she told herself as she finally rode down the elevator, armed with enough new information to have made her trip to the library worthwhile. But so was his recent past.

And with someone that unethical, she thought, I have to consider every rotten thing he ever did as a possible reason for his murder.

16

"Travel is more than the seeing of sights;
it is a change that goes on, deep
and permanent, in the ideas of living."
—Miriam Beard

It was close to eleven by the time Mallory got back to the hotel. She'd almost forgotten about her plans to visit Dinosaur World—and she'd completely forgotten that she'd invited Wade to join her.

Ever since the evening before, when she'd learned about his past interactions with Phil, she couldn't help seeing him in a new light. But she also couldn't think of any way to get out of spending the afternoon with him.

She decided she'd simply have to make the best of it. After all, she didn't have much of a choice. Besides, as much as she hated to admit it, she really did enjoy his company. And even though she'd decided she couldn't completely rule him out as a suspect, she was still reluctant to believe he could be a murderer.

"Thanks for letting me tag along," he commented as they neared the interstate exit that according to their map was the closest to their destination. "If I get one more massage, I'm going to scream."

"You're making me jealous," Mallory replied. Just then, she spotted a T. rex looming up alongside I-4, baring its teeth menacingly. "Uh-oh. Either we just found Dinosaur World or we're in serious trouble."

"The big guy doesn't appear to be moving, so I think we're okay," Wade replied, peering out the car window. "It's only when one of them is chasing you that you have to worry."

After getting off the interstate, they drove along a quiet country lane. The route took them past a serene lake, a field in which cows peacefully grazed, and a row of trees gracefully draped with Spanish moss. Not only were they traveling to a more peaceful spot, they also seemed to be going back in time.

"This is definitely old Florida," Mallory commented. "Anytime I start feeling like I'm seven years old again, I know I've stumbled across something that's stored in my brain from my childhood trips."

"And this place definitely falls into the kitsch category," Wade added as they drove into the parking lot. "Big-time. It's perfect for your article."

She immediately understood what he was referring to. As they strolled toward the entrance to Dinosaur World, she snapped a few photos of the large archway made of fake gray stone, presumably to give it a prehistoric look. Three life-size dinosaurs were perched along the top and a long-necked dino wearing an unusually friendly expression stood in front. Edging the walkway were two bright red hatchlings peeking out of gigantic yellow eggs. As she drew closer, Mallory realized that the cute baby dinos were actually trash cans. Each one had a circle cut out of its chest for depositing garbage.

"Definitely kitsch," Mallory agreed as they passed through the archway and onto a wooden bridge that crossed over a meandering stream. "Although I guess anything involving dinosaurs is pretty much guaranteed to be kitsch, isn't it?"

Despite her cynicism, she had to admit that her surroundings couldn't have been more peaceful. The stream was set amidst what could only be described as lush foliage—although she realized that if she was ever going to make it as a travel writer, she was going to have to come up with some other phrase. The warm air was heavy with humidity, which added to the feeling that she was embarking upon an exotic adventure.

"Okay, now we're *really* in kitsch territory," Wade said as they approached the first building.

While the large yellow letters above the door spelled out the word *Welcome,* it was hard to feel welcome when the head of a huge gray dinosaur baring an inordinate number of pointed white teeth protruded out of the roof like a chimney. Two of his tremendous gnarled gray legs served as columns, although they appeared to have been dislodged from the rest of his body and strategically placed to provide maximum support for the roof. Whether the fluorescent lights stuck in the ceiling between them were meant to designate some other part of his anatomy wasn't clear.

Inside the building was a gift shop. Just as the store at Gatorland had sold alligators in every possible size, shape, form, and material, this one specialized in dino merchandise. There were plastic dinosaurs, cuddly stuffed dinosaurs, and dinosaurs that looked peeved over being trapped inside snow globes. But this shop's inventory also included other items that pertained to the planet back in the day, including gemstones, fossils, and jewelry made from some of the pretty rocks that had once been part of the earth's crust.

Inside the park, a concrete walkway wound through all the greenery. Every few feet, another dinosaur glowered at them from inside the woods. Fortunately, each terrifying animal was separated from the modern-day visitors by an informative plaque.

Mallory dutifully copied down the names of each one, meanwhile snapping pictures to help keep them all straight.

"Plant-eating Lystrosaurus," she wrote in her notebook, noticing how good she was getting at walking and writing at the same time. "Massopondylus. Liliensternus. Ceratosaurus. You know, I don't remember learning about any of these in school."

"Me, either," Wade said. "Of course, when I was a kid, these guys were still wandering the earth. Hey, here's a stegosaurus. That's one I remember hearing about."

Mallory noticed that of all the visitors, the ones who appeared to be having the most fun were those in the two- to three-year-old category. Still, she had to admit that strolling through the scenic park, with its hot steamy air and—well, the lush foliage—was extremely pleasant. The only sound was the chirping of birds and the din of the traffic on I-4. Maybe the experience wasn't exactly accurate, given the constant reminder that this was actually the twenty-first century, but it was still relaxing.

When Mallory and Wade happened upon a Coke machine, he said seriously, "Now, this has to be one of the originals. See the way it's housed in its own wooden hut?"

"Definitely authentic," Mallory agreed with mock seriousness, "although I can't help wondering how the dinosaurs managed to push the Diet Coke button, given how big their claws are."

"Hey, check out this turquoise guy." Wade stopped to admire a protoceratops that looked like an animal that would have hung out with the Smurfs. "He'd make a nice house pet. Undoubtedly add a bit of color to the place, too."

In a burst of creativity, Mallory scribbled a few lines that she hoped she'd actually be able to use in her article.

"The creatures that inhabit Dinosaur World don't move," she wrote. "They don't make unearthly sounds. They don't even have a particularly menacing look in their eyes.

"Yet even though the park doesn't provide an over-the-top Jurassic Park–style experience, visitors who make the one-hour drive from Orlando to Plant City can nevertheless have a pleasant outing. There's plenty to enjoy here—particularly for those who are looking for the old Florida. First, the grounds are spectacular. Second, while these dinos may not make the ground tremble, they are all spectacularly detailed models of some of the most fascinating animals that ever stomped across the planet...."

"Let's see what this is," Mallory suggested when they wandered past another building. It was made of fake stone, making it look as if it had been designed by *The Flintstones*'s cartoonist. Above the doorway was THE BONEYARD. Not surprisingly, the letters were made out of bones.

Ducking inside, she and Wade discovered an exhibit that allowed children to get an idea of what it would be like to dig for fossils. The interior was nothing more than a very large sandbox. However, brushing away the sand revealed what looked like dinosaur bones.

"Check out these rules," Wade said, reading a sign that was stuck in the sand. " 'Dig carefully. Don't throw sand on tools. Take turns.' Do you suppose professional paleontologists also have to be reminded how to behave on a dig?"

"I don't see any rules about stealing other people's discoveries and claiming they're yours," she countered.

Across from the Boneyard was a second sprawling building. This one also had the look that modern-day folk tended to associate with prehistoric times, even though real dinosaurs hadn't been big on architecture.

"What's in here?" Wade asked, poking his head through the doorway. "Hey, a movie. Let's watch."

They sat on a bench made of synthetic rock for fifteen minutes, enthralled by a video that contained interviews with paleontologists and footage of them working on-site.

"You've got to admit, dinosaurs really are fascinating," Mallory commented as they wandered out of the dark building and back into the bright light of midday. "And the kitsch aspect aside, this is a great way to learn about them."

"True, but time travel makes me hungry," Wade said. "Where do they sell the brontosaurus burgers?"

"There's no food for sale here." Mallory held up the tote bag she'd been carrying. "I read about that in one of my guidebooks, so I brought us a picnic lunch."

"Aha. So you're one of those people who's actually organized enough to read up on the places you're going to visit."

"This is all so new to me," she admitted. "The idea of traveling to a new place to write about it instead of just enjoying it, I mean. I'm trying really hard to get it right."

She was silent for a long time, thinking about how something as simple as getting into an argument with some fool on an airplane could create problems that no one could ever anticipate.

Dinosaur World's picnic area consisted of a large group of tables lined up like desks in a classroom. That was probably because so many of them were occupied by schoolchildren, and the folks who ran the park no doubt wanted them to feel at home. In fact, Mallory estimated that even taking the few teachers into account, the average age of the park's attendees that day was about eight.

"Putting together a picnic lunch was actually kind of

fun," Mallory said as she and Wade sat down at a corner table that was as far from any impending food fights as they could get. "I had a long consultation with the waitress at the Tiki Tiki Teahouse this morning. We planned out the whole menu, and then she packed it." She sighed. "I must say, I feel as if I've done more planning in the past week than I have in months."

"I hardly planned for this trip at all," Wade commented. "Coming to Florida was actually a last-minute decision."

The sudden change in his tone of voice prompted Mallory to glance up. She noticed he was avoiding making eye contact, so she bent her head over her tote bag and began unpacking the food.

"A little over a week ago," he continued in the same strained voice, "my ex called me up and dropped a bomb. She told me she was getting married again."

"That was fast." The comment slipped out before Mallory could stop herself.

"My sentiments exactly." Wade was silent as he watched her unwrap sandwiches and pop open cans of soda. "But then the other shoe dropped. She told me who she was marrying."

She raised her eyebrows but said nothing.

"Turns out her fiancé is one of my closest friends. *Was* one of my closest friends. In fact, the four of us—Laura and I, Jeff and Sarah—used to get together as couples all the time. We'd take turns making dinner, get theater tickets, go to concerts, that kind of thing.

"I was surprised when Jeff and Sarah separated around the same time Laura and I did. But I didn't have a chance to give it very much thought. I was too busy dealing with my own emotional roller coaster. All along, I just assumed it was a coincidence that both couples were splitting up so close together." His voice grew even thicker. "But last Monday, I suddenly put two and two together. I realized that Laura had been having an affair with Jeff while we were still married. That in the end, it was the real reason our marriage ended."

"But you don't know that for sure," Mallory observed quietly.

"I didn't until I came right out and asked her," Wade said warily. "The silence at the other end of the phone told me everything I needed to know."

"Oh, Wade," she said in a somber tone. "That's horrible."

She could imagine how hurt she would have been if she'd ever found out that David had been unfaithful. In fact, the very idea made her stomach tighten.

"And here I'd thought getting divorced was bad," he said with a sardonic smile. "Turns out it was nothing compared to finding out what an idiot I'd been."

For a long time, Wade just stared at his sandwich. The chirping of birds and the rumbling of truck engines suddenly seemed very loud.

Instinctively Mallory reached over and put her hand on his arm. "Look, the reason you came down here was to get away. So let's forget all about what we left behind and try to have as good a time as we can."

She tried not to think about the fact that she was hardly one to talk, as she was a long way from accomplishing that goal herself. In fact, she'd encountered even more problems in Florida than she ever had at home.

• • •

"That was fun," Wade said as they strolled out of the park later that afternoon. "Thanks for letting me tag along. And thanks for listening to me whine about my personal life."

"I didn't mind a bit. And I had fun, too." Mallory was glad they were walking side by side along the wooden bridge that led back to the parking lot. She could feel her cheeks burning, and she was hoping he wouldn't notice.

She stiffened when he suddenly stopped, placed his hand on her shoulder, and gently turned her so she was facing him.

"You know, Mallory, after all that's happened to me, I wouldn't think it would be possible for me to trust anyone ever again," he said earnestly. "But I trust you. And I trust what I think you and I could become, if we gave it a chance."

He leaned forward as if he was going to kiss her. Mallory was so caught up in the moment that she almost leaned forward, as well.

But something stopped her.

Instinctively she took a step away. *I don't really know this man,* she thought amidst the alarms going off in her head. *And it has nothing to do with David or the grieving process or the newness of being back in the world again.*

This man could have killed Phil.

"I'm sorry, Wade," she said, staring at his shoulder to avoid looking into his eyes. "I can't. I thought I was ready, but I'm not."

"Of course," he said earnestly, taking a step away himself. "I understand."

But you don't understand! a voice inside her head cried. *I thought you might be someone I could care about, too. At least I did at first. But now I don't know what to believe.*

Mallory felt overwhelmed by the fact that she didn't know what to believe about anyone. All her perceptions seemed to have been wrong. She'd thought Annabelle was a social zero, yet it turned out she'd been carrying on a secret love affair with Phil for years. Frieda had struck her as the quintessential sweet little old lady. But her age didn't keep her from taking the occasional stroll on the wild side.

Then there was Courtney. She had acted as if Desmond was a near-stranger, yet the two of them actually knew each other quite well. As for Desmond, it turned out his past life had been closely tied to Phil's, making her wonder if his current life might have been, too.

As for Wade, she didn't know what to think. She wasn't sure what she felt, either—except that she was wrong to have even entertained the idea that she might be ready to connect with a new man.

And that uncertainty paled beside her concerns about the role Wade might have played in Phil's murder.

Wade had just told her that coming to Orlando was a last-minute decision. But even that didn't lessen her suspicion. It would have been too easy for him to lie. Going on a trip with Phil Diamond, a man he'd harbored bad feelings against for years, could have been something he'd been plotting for a long time.

Or maybe it had been something he'd chosen to do impulsively. Perhaps seeing Phil's name on the list had made him decide to sign on for this press trip. Perhaps he'd even taken the assignment away from one of the writers on his staff, who'd already been packing his sunblock and his flip-flops.

People don't kill over a missed deadline, she told herself.

But maybe there was more to their history, something Wade hadn't told her.

She hated being this mistrustful. Yet she had to consider every possibility if she was going to find out who had really killed Phil Diamond.

Why did I ever think I was ready to take on a challenge as monumental as becoming a travel writer? she wondered, her head spinning as she and Wade walked back to the car in silence.

Amanda was right. For the past six months, she had

barely left Rivington. Even taking the train into the city for her job interview had been a big deal.

Too much, too soon, she thought. Maybe it was a cliché, but it suddenly seemed to define every single aspect of her life.

17

"One's destination is never a place
but a new way of looking at things."
—Henry Miller

As soon as she let herself into her hotel room, Mallory made a beeline for the round table in the corner, her cell phone in her hand. The last thing she wanted was to believe that Wade had killed Phil Diamond, which made her more determined than ever to find out who had.

She rifled through her purse until she found the name and phone number of Frieda Stein's editor at *Go Seniors!* magazine. Then she steadied her hand long enough to punch in the number.

"John Crane," a deep voice answered.

She took a deep breath before jumping in. "Mr. Crane, my name is Mallory Marlowe. I'm considering hiring Frieda Stein for a freelance project, and she gave me your name as a reference."

"Really?" John Crane sounded doubtful. "I don't recall Frieda saying anything to me about that."

Mallory was about to suggest a possible explanation

for her forgetfulness when he added, "But that's Frieda for you. The woman's a terrific writer and she has a real sense of fun. Frankly, that's a winning combination you don't come across every day. But occasionally she skips over some of the details." Chuckling, he added, "The workings of a creative mind, I suppose."

"It sounds as if you've been pleased with her work," Mallory observed.

"Very pleased," he replied. "In fact, I can't say enough about her. Have you seen her piece on skinny-dipping at Epcot?"

"Not yet. But I'm looking forward to—"

"Of course, her article created a bit of a problem for the Disney people." John paused. "It seems that quite a few of her readers decided they wanted to try a little skinny-dipping of their own. There's this one photograph that ran in one of the newspapers that shows... well, I won't go into that."

Please don't, Mallory thought.

"Anyway, Frieda has a long, successful writing career behind her," John continued. "She started out at a weekly in Brooklyn, then moved up the ladder, writing for bigger and better magazines and newspapers. In fact, I'd be hard-pressed to think of a publication she hasn't written for."

"I suppose writing for *Go, Seniors!* is something that's more suitable to her lifestyle at this point," Mallory commented, carefully measuring her words.

"If you're politely trying to say that *Go, Seniors!* isn't exactly *Condé Nast Traveler,* you're absolutely right. It's definitely a comedown. But Frieda is at a different stage of her life right now. I don't think she's as anxious to go running all over the world, staying at seven different hotels in a single week and getting facials at as many different spas."

"Can't blame her for that."

"You certainly can't. Especially given all that's happened to her over the past couple of years."

Mallory's ears pricked up. "Sometimes life throws more at us than we think we can handle."

"Isn't that the truth. I mean, losing her husband was enough of a shock. I don't know if she ever told you that poor Harry had a long bout with cancer. It was hard on everyone in the family. And not only emotionally. It was also a financial drain. After he died, poor Frieda faced a huge amount of debt. And so she was forced to come out of retirement and start working again."

Mallory remained silent, afraid of saying something that might discourage this knowledgeable source from continuing.

"I felt so bad for her." John sighed deeply. "In fact, I was almost as heartbroken as she was when her book deal fell apart. It would have been the one way she could make a lot of money without working her butt off, if you'll excuse the expression."

"She had a book deal?" Mallory asked. Quickly she added, "When we talked about this particular assignment, I don't recall her mentioning anything about writing a book."

"Not just one book," John said. "An entire series. With a good publisher, too. Far and Wide Press in New York."

"A travel series?"

"That's right. She was going to do a book on every destination you can think of, customizing it for the senior traveler. The books were going to describe hotels and tourist sights all over the world—not only in terms of what they offered, but also how wheelchair-accessible they were, how convenient the bathrooms were, how much walking was involved, whether or not they offered foods that were compatible with quirky digestive systems...in short, everything travelers who were getting on in years would want to know."

"That's a great idea," Mallory said sincerely.

"It is. And it was especially suited to someone like Frieda, because it wouldn't require doing that much actual travel. She could have taken existing guidebooks, contacted the places that were listed, and gotten all the information she needed over the phone or by e-mail. Thanks to digital photography, she could even have the spots she was writing about send her photos of their ramps and bathtubs and anything else she needed. The woman has been to so many places already that doing the books would have been a simple matter of expanding on information she already had in her head.

"Frieda saw the series as her ticket to fame and fortune," John went on. "And she deserved it. The lady has worked hard for decades, starting in a time when good jobs for women were few and far between. So were the paychecks. But she endured it all, and with a big smile on her face. I'm telling you, she's one of a kind."

"Mr. Crane," Mallory asked, trying to keep her voice light, "what killed the book project?"

He let out a contemptuous snort. "That idiot of a co-author Frieda had the bad luck to sign on with," he said bitterly. "The jerk basically wrecked the whole deal."

Mallory experienced a sinking feeling in her stomach. I'd bet a thousand dollars I could guess who that jerk was, she thought.

"Phil Diamond, right?" She held her breath as she waited for an answer.

"Who else?" John snapped. "The guy's too much of a fool to have realized it would have been *his* ticket to fame and fortune, too. He wouldn't have had to work any harder than Frieda. Making phone calls, customizing information that already existed, without even leaving his computer... but as usual, he just couldn't follow through. Phil spent his half of the advance without writing a word. They missed their first deadline, and lost the deal."

"That's terrible!"

"It gets worse, too. Not only did Frieda have to give back her half of the advance. She also had to pay back Phil's. Turns out there was some indecipherable legal mumbo jumbo in the contract that made it impossible for the responsibility to be placed where it really belonged."

Mallory's mind was racing. So Frieda had signed on to a fabulous book deal with Phil Diamond. Then, as a result of his incompetence, she had lost the opportunity to get on her feet financially, not to mention to let go of some of the more physically demanding aspects of her career.

"I had no idea," she said. "Mr. Crane, when did all this happen?"

"Just a few months ago." John let out another sigh, this one even deeper than the last. "The poor gal's still reeling from it. Not that she'd ever let on, of course. Not our Frieda. She's too much of a trouper for that. She's very strong. A real lady."

Undoubtedly strong, Mallory thought. As for being a real lady, that was less certain.

In fact, she could even imagine Frieda Stein's anger leading the hard-drinking party girl to do something as unladylike as commit murder.

• • •

After Mallory hung up, she sat still for a long time, mulling over what she'd just learned.

So it turns out Frieda is one more person on this press trip who had good reason to hate Phil Diamond, she thought. The fact that they were both travel writers had thrown them together—with disastrous results.

Just like Wade.

But Desmond had also had business interactions with Phil in the past, she reminded herself, struggling to figure out which of the many different parts of Phil's sketchy past might have led to his murder. Interactions that apparently hadn't lasted, since by the time Crypt Castle closed, it seemed he was no longer an owner.

But why wasn't he? she wondered. What had happened between Desmond and Phil all those years ago? Whatever it was, it seemed to be something Desmond didn't talk about openly. Had the two of them had a disagreement? Or had Desmond simply been smart enough to get out in time, recognizing long before Phil did that Crypt Castle was destined to fail?

Mallory knew she also had to take Annabelle's broken heart into consideration. The phrase *Hell hath no fury like a woman scorned* certainly hadn't remained popular for centuries without good reason.

As far as she was concerned, any one of them could have murdered Phil Diamond. They all had motive, means, and opportunity.

At the moment, however, all she wanted was to lie down for a few minutes and find a way to force all the thoughts that were racing around in her head to take a rest. While she felt she had no choice but to spend every possible moment investigating Phil's murder, she was suddenly overcome with exhaustion. She kicked off her shoes and went over to the inviting king-size bed, already anticipating how good it would feel to sink into the soft, comfortable mattress.

All I need is twenty minutes to recharge my batteries, she thought. Just like Frieda.

She glanced at the night table, wanting to check the time. Instead, her eyes were drawn to the framed photograph next to the clock.

"Oh, my God," she breathed, suddenly feeling as if all the wind had been knocked out of her.

Something was wrong with the picture of her family vacationing in Jamaica. *Very* wrong.

Someone had cut off everyone's head.

18

"A traveler without observation is
a bird without wings."
—Moslih Eddin Saadi

Mallory stared at the photograph, sickened by the sight but unable to take her eyes off it. All the heads in the photograph—hers, David's, Amanda's, and Jordan's—had been carefully cut out with a sharp object, leaving four gaping white circles.

Who did this? she thought, rage and disgust rising inside her with the force of a tidal wave. What twisted, horrible, desperate person would stoop to an act that's so—

It could only have been one person, she realized abruptly. Phil's murderer. Someone who was more than likely a member of their little group.

The fact that she still couldn't put a name to that individual only fueled her fury.

"Damn!" she cried, her voice catching. "What is going *on*?"

It was only after she'd slammed the photo facedown on the night table that she fully understood the implications of this freakish act of vandalism.

Oh, my God, she thought, her knees growing so weak that she sank onto the bed. This is a warning. The killer is sending me a message.

A message to mind my own business.

But the murder *is* my business! she thought, her head spinning. I *can't* stop trying to find out who killed Phil Diamond! Not as long as Detective Martinez thinks I'm connected to his death—and not as long as I'm haunted by the inexplicable appearance of those newspaper articles about David and me that the police found stashed in Phil's hotel room.

And then another thought crept into her brain, pushing its way inside and settling there like an unwanted visitor. *What if the real killer is scheming to implicate me even further?*

Mallory pressed her fingertips against her temples, as if by doing so she could force herself to think more clearly. She was scheduled to fly home on Friday morning, now just a day and a half away. That meant she had only thirty-six hours to figure out who had killed Phil before testing Martinez's mandate that she stay in Florida. She could practically hear a clock ticking in her head.

If there's any way I'm getting on that plane, she thought frantically, I have to keep going. I *must* find a way to figure out who killed Phil. Maybe I'll stumble upon some clue that will solve the puzzle. Maybe Patrice will fill in some of the missing pieces when I meet with her tomorrow.

Maybe the killer will slip up somehow, do or say something that will reveal his or her identity.

She forced herself to stand up again, refusing to succumb to the overwhelming urge to climb into bed, pull the covers over her head, and simply give up. She thought back to Sunday, when she'd arrived in Florida. Had it only been a few days earlier? It seemed like a lifetime ago. As she'd driven from the airport to the hotel, it had occurred to her that she'd been thinking of this press trip as a test. Back then, she'd rejected the idea.

But that was then. A lot had happened since.

She considered the possibility that this could be some sort of test, after all. Cosmic or religious or...or who knew what. And proving that she hadn't killed Phil could be part of it, a way of convincing herself that she could handle anything without David, no matter how horrific it might be.

What that's old saying? Mallory thought grimly. Something about how whatever doesn't kill you will make you stronger?

It definitely applied to her situation, she decided. Especially since, for all she knew, killing again could be precisely what Phil's murderer had in mind. Only this time, the plan would be to make *her* the victim.

• • •

Early the next morning, as Mallory climbed into her cheerful red PT Cruiser, she was wracked with ambivalence about having to spend the morning checking out another tourist attraction. She felt she should be spending every waking moment trying to find Phil's murderer.

But with no brilliant ideas about what to do next, she figured she might as well put some more time into trying to write a publishable article for *The Good Life*. That way, once this nightmare was over—and she kept telling herself it would be *soon*—she'd have the satisfaction of completing the job that had brought her to Florida in the first place.

She had to admit that she was also a little relieved to have the distraction. Of all the places in Florida she'd chosen to visit, Cypress Gardens interested her the most. From her childhood vacations, she remembered it as a cool, green oasis with endless flower beds and statuesque trees dripping with Spanish moss. She wondered if the park still featured the pretty young women in pastel-colored antebellum gowns who sat on the lawn waving, their skirts fanned out to form large circles around them.

What she remembered best about Cypress Gardens, however, was its spectacular water-ski show. She could still picture the daredevils who formed human pyramids while skimming the water at breathtaking speeds and the attractive young women doing kicks and splits midair.

As she trekked across the immense parking lot toward the ticket booth, Mallory could hardly believe this was the same place that had lodged itself in her memory so firmly. Everything was on such a large scale compared to what she could recall. Even the name had become grander. These days, the attraction was called Cypress Gardens Adventure Park.

At the entrance, a huge brick walkway led to a visitors' center housed in a building-size white dome—something she didn't remember at all from her childhood. After exchanging her voucher for a ticket, she wandered inside and found herself trapped in a fake-looking village that was vaguely reminiscent of a small town in New England. Its touristy stores included a candle emporium and a Christmas shop, while its restaurants had overly cute names like Backwater Bill's BBQ and Aunt Julie's Country Kitchen. Mallory was relieved that at least its creators had resisted the temptation to spell *country* with a *K*. Even so, the precious architecture, with buildings that looked like quaint country cottages, gave Jubilee Junction the look of a poor man's version of Disney World's Main Street.

Farther along the walkway, a country singer with very red lips and very big hair sang her heart out inside a gazebo, backed by three men who looked as if they'd raided Johnny Cash's closet. Yet there were very few people to listen.

In fact, what struck Mallory most was how empty the

park was. Only a few elderly couples ambled around the shops, and a pair of young mothers pushing toddlers in strollers drifted toward an area that according to her map contained the rides. True, today was a weekday, and a few ominous-looking clouds had been gathering in the sky since early that morning. Still, she hoped this simply happened to be an unusually quiet day for what to her was an important Florida landmark.

Her map listed a dozen different sections, each with a different theme. A good third of the park was devoted to rides, a water park, and a so-called Adventure Arcade. But the others, thankfully, still conformed to the botanical garden theme.

Mallory began with the bird aviary, where streetwise birds with riotously colored plumage worked the small cluster of visitors with impressive professionalism. A glass butterfly house, aptly named Wings of Wonder, proved to be a warm, damp haven for butterflies, waterfalls, flowers, and lawn furniture. Next she wandered through the meticulously maintained Plantation Gardens, where nary a weed was permitted to linger. She was pleased that the trees near Lake Eloise were decorated with Spanish moss, just as she remembered, with huge clumps hanging from their boughs like tinsel.

At the center of the park was the Topiary Trail, which took her past gigantic bushes that had been pruned to form animals like a big green duck and a green seal balancing a ball on its nose. Some of them were studded with flowers, making the tremendous cardinal bright red and giving the peacock a brilliant blue body and splashing its tail with turquoise spots. As she strolled through each section, she jotted down every adjective she could think of, once again agonizing over the lack of a synonym for *lush foliage*.

But it was the water-ski show—listed in the schedule

as the Ski Show Spectacular—that she looked forward to the most. She followed the other stragglers who made their way toward the impressive amphitheater that had clearly been built in the decades since she'd last been here. The massive building consisted of two dozen tiered rows of seats and a huge blue overhang designed to shield the audience from the sun. Today, she realized woefully, it might end up keeping the rain off them.

Nevertheless, Mallory sat toward the front, not wanting to miss a single moment. She remained braced for the possibility that despite its name, the "spectacular" would fail to live up to her memories.

Not only did the show live up to them, it was practically an exact duplicate, replicating every element that was stored in her memory bank. A sleek motorboat towed three young men with Olympic-caliber muscles up a sloping platform at high speed. Then they flew into the air and did amazing flips and twists before landing squarely back onto the water's surface. A man and a woman did a waterskiing version of ice dancing, complete with hot pink and turquoise costumes and graceful arm movements. The Aquamaids, three pretty blond women who looked as if they'd been kidnapped from a high school cheerleading team, danced in unison. The grand finale was the human pyramid, with three men on the bottom, two women forming the second tier, and a third woman on top waving an American flag.

Cypress Gardens may have gotten a lot glitzier, Mallory thought as she snapped one picture after another, but thank goodness the water-ski show has stayed the same. This really is a piece of old Florida, preserved exactly as it was half a century ago.

Even though the show served as a welcome distraction, as soon as it was over she was forced to confront the disturbing reality of her situation once again. She drifted toward the Botanical Gardens that covered the back end of the park, lost in thought.

I'm supposed to leave tomorrow, she reminded herself, her mood darkening so much that she was only vaguely aware that the brick path she was following was now meandering through dense plantings with a distinctly tropical feel. If I want to get on that plane, I now have less than twenty-four hours to figure out who killed Phil.

At this point, she saw Phil's ex-wife as her last hope for finding out who could have wanted the man dead badly enough to actually carry out the dirty deed. If Patrice didn't come up with any helpful information, Mallory didn't know where she would turn.

She suddenly stopped, realizing that she wasn't taking notes or even paying attention to her surroundings. The fact that she had an article to write—on top of everything else she had to worry about—bordered on the ridiculous. Yet she couldn't neglect her responsibility to Trevor.

She noticed for the first time that there was no one else around in this section of the park. She also realized it was getting dark. Glancing upward, she saw that the gray clouds that had been hovering in the sky all day were quickly growing thicker, darker, and considerably more threatening. In fact, she realized she'd be wise to speed up her tour if she wanted to reach her car or at least the safety of a building by the time torrential rains began to fall.

She walked on at a brisk pace, pausing only momentarily to take notes. She jotted down a few lines describing the contrast between the manicured gardens that abruptly emerged just beyond wild, junglelike areas. Then she scribbled a sentence about the jarring juxtaposition of the natural-looking swamplands and the carefully crafted wooden bridges that crossed over the stream gently meandering alongside the path.

She paused when she reached a giant banyan tree, with hundreds of woody roots hanging down from branches that gave it an eerie look. She snapped some pictures and was about to move on when she heard what sounded like three or four footsteps in quick succession, as if someone was running.

So I'm not alone, after all, she thought.

Instinctively, she turned. She expected to see someone approaching behind her—one of the young mothers pushing a stroller, perhaps, or a park employee scurrying to shelter before the skies exploded.

But she saw no one. And the only sound was the rustling of leaves as the storm continued to move in.

As she continued on, a feeling of uneasiness weighed her down.

Someone is following me, she thought, her mouth growing uncomfortably dry. And I'm stuck out here in this isolated woodsy area, with no one else around...

Nonsense, she immediately scolded herself. It's just the wind.

Yet she knew perfectly well that while the wind was capable of setting the leaves on bushes and trees whispering among themselves, it rarely mimicked the sound of footsteps.

She quickened her pace, aware that her heart was now pounding thunderously in her chest. When real thunder rumbled above and lightning flashed in the sky, she jumped. A single fat raindrop fell on her shoulder, almost as if it was warning her of what was to come.

Once again, she was certain she heard footsteps behind her.

Closer, this time.

"Hello?" she called in a hoarse voice, stopping and turning abruptly.

Again, silence. But she was certain she saw movement

among the trees. A shadow. Or maybe the silhouette of a person determined to stay out of sight.

But she definitely saw someone.

"Who's there?" she demanded, her voice tinged with panic.

Oh, my God, Mallory thought. There really is someone following me. I have to get out of here!

Frantically, she glanced around, looking for a quick way out. Or at least someone to help her.

Once again, she heard a thumping behind her. Closer, this time. Whoever was following her was just a few feet away.

She let out a frightened, high-pitched cry and broke into a run. As she did, she heard a branch snap and the thud of footsteps against dirt.

At this point, she was afraid to turn around. There wasn't time. Not if she wanted to get away.

Another drop of rain fell, this one splashing against her foot. Surprised, she let out another cry. Then one more drop fell, this time on her neck. Then another. And another.

When she heard an entirely different type of sound amidst the plopping of raindrops, it took her a moment to identify it. A wave of relief swept over her as she realized it was a whirring sound. Something mechanical, like an engine.

A tram emblazoned with CYPRESS GARDENS ADVENTURE PARK on the side suddenly emerged on the brick path, snaking around the bend just ahead.

"Get in!" the young man sitting at the steering wheel yelled. "It's going to start pouring any second!"

"Thank you!" Mallory cried, jogging over and climbing in. She'd barely gotten under cover before the few warning drops gave way to sheeting rain.

"Just in time, huh?" the young man called, grinning at her over his shoulder.

If you only knew, she thought, watching the impenetrable tangle of vegetation she'd left behind disappear into the distance.

• • •

The thunderstorm ended long before Mallory got back to the hotel, giving way to a clear, blue sky and a bright, cheerful sun. Yet while the rainstorm had passed, the uneasy feeling from being followed in a deserted area of the park still lingered.

Once again, she looked forward to going back to her hotel room and locking the door. Yet as she stepped out of the elevator, she spotted a cleaning cart halfway down the hall.

Oh, dear, she thought. She hoped she wouldn't be a victim of that syndrome that seemed to plague her wherever she went: coming back to her hotel room at an off hour to discover the maid was in the middle of cleaning it. Not now, when she still felt so shaky.

She was relieved to see that she'd lucked out. The cart was parked farther down, two rooms away. The fact that the door was open meant she was busy working in that room, not Mallory's.

She was about to slip her key card into the lock when she heard a familiar voice call, "Mallory?"

She turned and saw Courtney striding down the hall.

"I'm so glad I caught up with you," the younger woman said. "I wanted to tell you that the tourist board has set up a special event for all of you tonight. We really wanted to send you guys off with a bang, so we've been knocking ourselves out to come up with something really amazing."

Assuming I'm going home, Mallory thought grimly.

"I didn't want to say anything until it was a hundred percent definite," Courtney continued, "but we've finally got it locked in." Her big green eyes were even brighter than usual as she added, "We're having dinner at Horror House tonight. In case it's not obvious, it's a haunted house."

"I'm game," Mallory replied, thinking about the irony of yet another haunted house tourist attraction playing a role in her life.

Automatically her mind began clicking away. She wondered if she'd be able to see enough of the attraction to include it in her article. She'd read about Horror House in the guidebooks, and it sounded perfect. But when she'd looked for more information on the web, all she'd found was an outdated website and a few blogs lamenting its imminent demise. It seemed to serve as one more example of the mysterious phenomenon that kept any haunted house attraction from surviving here in tourist heaven.

"I thought it was closing," Mallory commented.

"Oh, no!" Courtney looked shocked by the very notion. "It's a bit out of the way, and so a lot of visitors to the Orlando area never bother to make the trip. But I've heard that a bunch of new backers just came into the picture and they're going to start running a shuttle bus from some of the big hotels."

"Good idea," Mallory observed.

"In fact, that's one of the reasons the attraction is so excited about hosting us tonight. The new owners are really into getting coverage in the media. They seem to appreciate its value a lot more than the people who were making those kinds of decisions in the past. They're going all out for you guys. Cocktails, dinner, entertainment with special effects and costumes, all with a haunted house theme."

"It sounds fabulous," Mallory said sincerely. "Thanks for setting it up."

"No problem!" Courtney was beaming. "The plan is for everyone to meet there at seven. Some of the others won't be coming directly from the hotel. I believe Wade drove up to the Gulf Coast to look at a couple of resort hotels, and Annabelle is trying to spend an entire day at Sea World without spending a dime.... Anyway, I'll print out directions and slip them under your door."

"What fun! Should I go dressed as a ghost or a ghoul?"

Courtney giggled. "Oh, no! They'll take care of everything. It's going to be awesome!"

Just then, the maid came out of the room down the hall, carrying a bucket of cleaning supplies. She was a tiny woman, probably in her forties, with black hair and a demure demeanor.

"Hello," Mallory said, smiling.

Courtney echoed her greeting.

The maid returned the smile as she shuffled by, pushing the cart. "Hello," she said, nodding at them both. "Hello, Ms. Marlowe," she added, glancing at Courtney.

That's odd, Mallory thought. First of all, she clearly has Courtney confused with me, even though we don't look anything alike and we're not even close to being in the same age bracket. But the second aspect of their interaction struck Mallory as even odder. Why does the maid know my name at all? she wondered.

She must have overheard me talking to Desmond, she decided, although still puzzled. He must have called me by my name. And since Courtney and I are part of the same group, she probably mixed the two of us up.

Still, the maid's confusion over Courtney's identity combined with Mallory's certainty that someone had been following her at Cypress Gardens left her with a bad feeling. At this point, she no longer knew whether she was merely making mountains out of molehills—or if some of those mountains looming up ahead might turn out to be dangerous.

19

"The wise man travels to discover himself."
—James Russell Lowell

Mallory was gripped with anxiety as she drove to her meeting with Phil's ex-wife, Patrice. She clutched the steering wheel tightly, her sweaty palms causing her hands to slip every time she made a turn.

Even the fact that their rendezvous was taking place at a McDonald's that was billed as the world's largest didn't help. She supposed it might turn out to be one more place she could write about. But that was little consolation, given the fact that she was scheduled to leave Florida tomorrow, even though she didn't expect Detective Martinez to give her the go-ahead.

As she veered off International Drive onto Sand Lake Road, there was no mistaking which building was the one she was looking for. It had to be the one with an entire wall splashed with gigantic French fries at least three or four stories high. She was worried that merely looking at the garish mural was enough to send her cholesterol level skyrocketing.

As soon as she pulled open the restaurant's glass door, Mallory's ears were assaulted with nerve-twitching bleeps, clanks, chinka-chinkas, and other electronic noises, all of which aggravated her jumpiness. The culprit, she saw, was an impressively long row of arcade games. In addition, lights flashed and children screeched as they careened down giant slides. There was visual noise, as well, from the bright colors of the plastic chairs to the life-size jungle animals painted on the walls.

I don't know if it's the world's largest McDonald's, she thought, but it's got to be the world's most stimulating. I just hope the menu includes McValium.

Bracing herself against sensory overload, she walked the length of the restaurant, keeping an eye out for a woman who looked desperate enough to have once been married to Phil Diamond. Even though she didn't spot anyone who fit that description, her quick tour gave her a chance to check out what amounted to modern-day kitsch as interpreted by a mega-corporation.

The video arcade, which easily had more than fifty different games, comprised only one section. There was also a beach area, a circus area, a Sea World area, and of course the jungle area, with each different environment created primarily by brilliantly colored murals that could well have been painted by the same artist who had created the giant French fries. The restaurant also featured tubes and slides and an amazing collection of other playground equipment that hopefully enabled grease-and-sugar-addicted children to work off some of the calories they'd just consumed.

Even the menu went far beyond the tried and true. Naturally, the usual Big Macs and McNuggets were available. But the so-called Bistro Gourmet sold paninis, pizza, and soup, and a pasta station specialized in dishes like sun-dried tomato pasta with shrimp. Some of it almost sounded like real food.

The desserts were also a few notches above McFlurries. This burger joint had a glass display case that looked as if it had been stolen out of a bakery. So did the luscious-looking cakes with equally luscious-sounding names: Peanut Butter Explosion, Chocolate Corruption, Banana Split Pie. She could only imagine what the nutritional information for *those* looked like.

Mallory bought herself a cup of coffee, unimpressed by the use of the word *gourmet* to describe it in a McDonald's. She knew the last thing she needed was caffeine, but at least it gave her an excuse to sit down. She purposely chose a table that gave her a good view of the entire restaurant. It happened to be near a large, shiny replica of the Moon Man, a character she recognized from TV commercials. Even though he was sitting at a life-size piano, he was only a statue, not a robot, so he remained mercifully silent.

She sat up straighter when she spotted a woman striding through the restaurant purposefully, checking the faces of everyone she passed. She was tall and thin, an enviable combination that elevated her skintight jeans and white T-shirt with its deep-cut V-neck to high-fashion status. Her hair, primarily black but generously streaked with silver, curved under her jawline, accenting her sharp features and her dark brown eyes. A turquoise-and-silver cuff bracelet encircled her wrist, and she wore no fewer than three rings that similarly shrieked Southwest. A pair of silver earrings peeked out from beneath her black-and-silver pageboy.

Her face registered recognition as soon as she spotted Mallory.

"You must be Mallory, since you're the only person in here without a kid," she said breathlessly, sliding into the seat opposite hers. "Sorry I'm late. I got tied up at work." Rolling her eyes, she added, "As usual."

"Are you still in the ice-cream business?" Mallory

asked, still trying to overcome her shock over how different the real ex-wife was turning out to be from the version she had imagined.

A look of confusion flitted across Patrice's face. "Oh, that. Heavens, no. That was ages ago. Another life entirely. These days I'm into flowers."

"Growing them?"

"Decorating with them, actually. I work for a florist who does arrangements for big blow-out events. Weddings, huge birthday parties, business meetings at convention hotels, that kind of thing. It turns out I have a flair for creating fabulous bouquets, even though it's not exactly the kind of thing a little girl decides she wants to do when she grows up." Laughing self-consciously, she added, "Then again, hardly anything in my life has fallen into that category."

Mallory was surprised at how much she actually liked Patrice. It was difficult to believe she'd ever been married to a boor like Phil. Then again, it sounded as if Patrice was just as surprised.

"I'm sorry if I keep staring," Mallory said. "It's just that—well, you're not exactly what I expected."

"Did you think I'd be a female version of Phil? Someone who was spouting obscenities or obnoxious remarks like one of those unfortunate people with Tourette's?"

"I guess I did," Mallory admitted.

Patrice shrugged. "All I can say is that I was young once. Young and foolish. And Phil, believe it or not, had a certain charm back in the day. He actually knew how to turn it on when he felt it would serve his purposes."

"How long were you two married?"

"Seven years. But it took me about seven days to figure out what I'd gotten myself into." She shook her head slowly. "I guess I kept waiting around to see if things would get any better. Can I help it if it took me a really long time to figure out that wasn't going to happen?"

"No children?"

"No. Phil didn't strike me as someone with very strong fathering skills. After the divorce, I never remarried, never had kids...I've never even gotten a cat." Patrice laughed uneasily. "Maybe that's why I've focused on flowers. They're living things but they keep their mouths shut."

Barely pausing to take a breath, she asked, "So what can I tell you about my dearly departed ex? You mentioned on the phone that the police consider you a possible suspect. Frankly, you don't look like a murderer to me. Then again, I completely understand how anyone who's ever had any dealings at all with Phil could be driven to violence. I must admit, it's something that I thought about on more than one occasion."

"I barely knew the man," Mallory insisted. "Like I said when I called you, he and I came down to Orlando on a press trip with three other journalists. I've been a travel writer for exactly one week. This is my very first press trip, and I spent maybe an hour and a half in the man's company. No matter how much of a creep he was, that wouldn't have been enough time for me or anyone else in my position to have developed a strong enough dislike for him to feel compelled to kill him."

"So you're trying to find out if something—or someone—from his past was responsible?"

"Exactly. Whoever wanted him dead was carrying a grudge. And what I've learned is that almost everyone who has anything to do with this press trip had some kind of negative interactions with Phil somewhere along the line."

"Like I'm surprised," Patrice commented dryly.

"Some of them happened only recently." Mallory paused, wondering if she should mention Phil's long-term affair with Annabelle. She decided against it, reasoning that there were some things an ex-wife would never be happy to hear, no matter how long she'd been an ex. "And some happened as long as a couple of decades ago, back when he still lived here in Florida."

"Sounds about right," Patrice said. "Phil was one of those people who made enemies wherever he went. He was about as sensitive as a herd of buffalo."

"So it seems. But I can't help being curious about Phil's business venture. The one he started back when he was still writing for the *Observer*."

"Ah, yes. Crypt Castle." Patrice picked up the plastic salt shaker and toyed with it, feigning fascination with the back-and-forth motion instead of making eye contact. "That place was haunted, all right. In ways that had nothing to do with ghosts and goblins."

Mallory's ears pricked up. "What do you mean?"

"Everything that surrounded it seemed to be tainted. And it practically started on day one."

"Maybe you could take me back to the beginning," Mallory suggested.

Patrice sighed, as if she was about to tell a long and difficult tale. "In the late eighties, Phil decided to go into business with a guy named Desmond Farnaby."

"I know him," Mallory interjected. "He's the general manager at the hotel where I'm staying."

"I heard he went into the hotel business," Patrice said, nodding. "Anyway, this guy Farnaby had originally planned to open a haunted house with another man, Henry Hollinger, who everybody called Huck. But the two men apparently had creative differences, and their business relationship fell apart.

"When Phil heard about it, he pounced. He didn't even care that Hollinger went ahead with his plans and opened Monster Mansion, which was inevitably going to be in direct competition with Phil's attraction. Phil worked on Farnaby, convincing him that the two of them would make a great team. Of course, Farnaby was the creative one. He had all the ideas, many of which I suspect he stole from his former partner. I believe he came up with most of the financing, too."

"So Phil and Desmond Farnaby operated Crypt Castle together?"

Patrice smiled grimly. "For a while. At least until Phil ripped off the poor guy. It turned out Phil was dipping into the company funds for his own purposes."

Just as he had with Frieda, Mallory thought. But she kept silent.

"Phil had a way of getting the best of people," Patrice went on. "He always managed to come out on top. The haunted house was just starting to take off when Farnaby was forced out. Thanks to Phil, the poor guy's dreams of becoming a successful entrepreneur went up in smoke. That was when he got himself a regular job."

Mallory nodded. She had known about the partnership between Phil and Desmond, of course. And she'd known that Desmond had gotten out of the haunted house business. But up until now, she hadn't known about the circumstances—or the bad feeling it had undoubtedly left behind. Patrice's tale also explained why Desmond hadn't been mentioned in the *Sentinel* articles she'd found at the library.

"At first, Crypt Castle was a success," Patrice continued. "But then the facility started having flooding problems. A couple of rooms suffered major water damage, the parking lot turned to mud.... Phil brought in an engineer, who figured out that the land Crypt Castle was built on was too swampy to support the structure. It wouldn't surprise me if that was discovered *before* the Castle was built, and Phil had been paying off some government inspector. But whether he had or not, he was suddenly faced with a major problem. Even though his haunted house was starting to take off, he kept having to close it so he could dry it out.

"There was only one solution: rebuilding part of the facility on another piece of land. The good news was that there was a huge empty lot right next door. The bad news was that the owner wouldn't sell it to him.

"So in the end, they both failed," Patrice concluded. "First Hollinger's haunted house, then Phil's. But the really sad part is what happened to Huck Hollinger after his business went under."

"What happened?" Mallory asked, wide-eyed.

Patrice grimaced. "I thought you might not know anything about that part. So I brought this along." She reached into her purse and pulled out a yellowing newspaper clipping stored in a sandwich-size Ziploc bag.

HENRY "HUCK" HOLLINGER, ORLANDO BUSINESSMAN,
DEAD AT 33

She began to read.

Orlando native Henry "Huck" Hollinger, who is perhaps best known for creating Monster Mansion, a haunted house attraction, was found dead at his home earlier today. According to police, Mr. Hollinger committed suicide....

"Hollinger killed himself?" Mallory cried.

"Like I said," Patrice replied solemnly, "everything about that whole haunted house episode was bad news."

"Did he commit suicide because his business failed?"

"I'm afraid so."

Mallory was silent as she skimmed the rest of the obituary. Born in Ocala...settled in Orlando after college... sold insurance and encyclopedias before investing his life savings in an innovative tourist attraction...incorporated special effects and live actors to provide visitors with a spooky yet fun experience...

There was nothing new here. In fact, she was about to hand the obituary back to Patrice when her eyes lit on the last line.

"He is survived by his wife, Lynn, and his daughter, Courtney."

Courtney? she thought.

Mallory's head was suddenly buzzing even louder than the clinks and bleeps from all the electronics surrounding her. Of course, Courtney was a common name. There were undoubtedly thousands of Courtneys in Florida.

It was probably just a coincidence that she happened to know one of them ... wasn't it?

Yet the uncomfortable gnawing in her stomach told her that this was more than a coincidence. Especially when she checked the date of the obituary. She did a quick calculation and realized that Courtney Conover could indeed be Hollinger's daughter.

Up to this point, it hadn't even occurred to Mallory to connect Courtney with Phil. And she certainly hadn't connected her to Huck Hollinger, Phil's business rival. The main reason, of course, was that Courtney had a different last name.

But she found herself remembering Courtney's endless prattling about her wedding that day they'd gone to the *Titanic* exhibit together. Which meant her married name could be Conover while her maiden name had been Hollinger....

Which would mean that her father was the man Phil Diamond had destroyed.

Mallory struggled to make sense of all the bits and pieces of information floating around in her head. If she understood this correctly, not only was Courtney one more person who had ties to Phil Diamond, those ties were very close ... and very painful. Twenty years earlier, when she was just a little girl, Phil's damning review of the attraction that Courtney's father had sunk both his dreams and his life savings into had brought about its demise. As a result, her father had committed suicide.

And then Mallory had an even more chilling thought. It could also explain why the maid had thought Courtney was Mallory Marlowe. Courtney must have told the maid that it was her name in order to gain entrance to Mallory's hotel room, using the maid's master key so she could cut off the heads in the family photo next to the bed.

Which meant Courtney had murdered Phil and was trying to scare Mallory away from her attempts at finding the killer.

"Are you okay?" Patrice asked, interrupting her ruminations.

Mallory glanced up, blinking in confusion. "I—I had no idea Huck Hollinger had a daughter named Courtney."

Patrice frowned. "I vaguely remember something about the daughter. It seems as if this all happened so long ago...."

I bet it doesn't seem that way to Courtney, Mallory thought. In fact, she remembered the young woman's extreme reaction at the *Titanic* exhibit. She'd actually begun to cry, saying, "It's so sad! Wives lost their husbands, children lost their fathers...."

Courtney's own personal experience, to a T.

"Patrice," she asked in a low, even voice, "you said that Phil's business failed because he couldn't expand. I believe you mentioned that the person who owned the land next door refused to sell it to him."

"That's right."

"Why wouldn't he sell? Didn't Phil offer him a reasonable amount for it?"

"It had nothing to do with money. At least not in the immediate sense. In fact, the landowner was itching to sell his land to Phil. He even went so far as to shake hands on the deal. But then his lawyer talked him out of it."

The word *lawyer* made Mallory's blood run cold. "Lawyer?" she repeated. The word came out as a hoarse whisper.

"That's right. Apparently the guy's lawyer advised him to hang on to his land, told him to think of it as a long-term investment, something whose value was guaranteed to skyrocket over the next few years. So in the end, Phil blamed the lawyer for Crypt Castle's failure.

"That lawyer was right, of course," Patrice continued. "That was exactly what happened. Just a few years later, the landowner got ten times what Phil had offered him." With a little laugh, she added, "Figures it would take a slick New York City attorney to see the writing on the wall."

"Patrice," Mallory asked hesitantly, "do you happen to remember the lawyer's name?"

"Sorry." She shook her head. "My memory's not that good."

"Would you at least recognize it if you heard it?"

"Try me."

Mallory hesitated. "David Marlowe?"

Patrice was silent for a few seconds. And then she nodded. "That sounds right."

Mallory felt as if someone had just punched her in the stomach. She now understood why Phil had been hoarding clippings about David for the past twenty years—and why he had gone to the trouble of looking her up on the Internet once he learned someone with the same last name who lived in the New York area would be joining the press trip.

It also explained the nasty-sounding comment he'd made on the very first day, the one about how the two of them would "definitely have the chance to get to know each other a lot better."

"Anyway," Patrice continued, not noticing how strongly Mallory was reacting to her casual recounting of what to her probably seemed like ancient history, "around that same time, Phil also lost his column. Shortly after Hollinger opened Monster Mansion, Phil wrote a scathing article about it. After Hollinger killed himself, a reporter at the *Sentinel* found out that Phil was the owner of Crypt Castle. At that point, his true motive behind bashing the competition in the *Observer* became clear.

"Of course, Phil was immediately fired for using his column in such an unethical way. It would have been bad enough if people had figured out he'd used his visibility to hurt his business competitor, but the fact that the result was that his competitor killed himself over his business's failure was too much for people to swallow.

"Word traveled to a lot of other newspapers about what he'd done. Suddenly Phil couldn't get a job writing menus." With a wry smile, Patrice added, "And to think it was all a misunderstanding."

Mallory's stomach lurched. She felt as if she was falling in slow motion, and that each time she thought she'd reached the bottom, it turned out there was even farther to fall. "What kind of misunderstanding?"

"About the real reason Hollinger's business failed."

"What do you mean?"

"It had nothing to do with Phil's column. I mean, my ex had a following, but he wasn't exactly Oprah. Besides, most of his audience lived locally. They weren't the people who were going to make or break a tourist attraction."

"So you're saying it wasn't Phil's fault that Huck Hollinger's haunted house failed?"

"Nope. It was Huck's accountant."

Mallory shook her head fast, as if that might help break up some of the cloudiness that had settled around her brain. "I'm not following this."

"The accountant was embezzling funds. Basically, he took the money and ran. Disappeared. I don't think anybody ever heard from him again. There were all kinds of rumors about him moving to some Caribbean island and changing his name, but it was nothing but speculation. But that's the real reason Huck Hollinger lost everything."

Would Courtney have known that? Mallory wondered. After all, when all this happened, she was just a little girl. . . .

"Tell me more about this lawyer," Mallory suddenly blurted out. "David Marlowe."

"Why are you so interested in him?" Patrice asked. And then her expression turned into one of horror. "Oh, my God. Didn't you say on the phone that your last name is Marlowe? Don't tell me you're—"

"That's right," Mallory said somberly. "David Marlowe is—was—my husband."

"Divorced?"

She shook her head. "David died six months ago."

"Sorry," Patrice said, sounding sincere. "What was it, a heart attack?"

"Actually, everyone thought it was an accident," Mallory replied, trying to keep her voice light. "Including me. That is, until the cops found twenty years' worth of newspaper clippings about David in Phil's hotel room."

"Oh, no," Patrice said breathlessly.

Mallory searched her face for some sign that this conversation wasn't going where she thought it was going. "Please don't tell me you agree there could have been something else going on between Phil and my husband."

Patrice held out her hands helplessly. "Look, I don't know what really happened. I mean, it's not as if I have a crystal ball or anything. . . ."

"Just tell me what you think," Mallory said evenly.

"You knew Phil Diamond better than practically anybody."

Patrice drew in her breath sharply. "The haunted house wasn't the only business Phil ever invested in. Even though he liked writing—and he loved traveling—he always figured that sooner or later he'd find a way to make it big. He always had one get-rich scheme or another going. In fact, he had two other major business failures after the Crypt Castle fiasco."

"Go on," Mallory prompted, anxious to see where Patrice was going with this and dreading the moment she'd find out.

"Look," Patrice said, "it's possible none of this had anything to do with your husband. But a few months ago, I heard through the grapevine that Phil had come up with another idea for a business, one he was sure was going to make him wealthy." She swallowed hard. "But according to what I was told, it turned out the same lawyer he was so sure ruined everything for him the first time happened to get involved again. For the second time, Phil thought the guy was getting in his way." She hesitated. "I heard he even went up to New York to try to talk to him."

"No!" Mallory gasped.

"Phil was a blamer," Patrice said, shrugging. "Whenever anything went wrong, he had a million reasons why it wasn't his fault. It was always somebody else's doing. In this case, that somebody happened to be this New York lawyer."

"Can you tell me more precisely when all this happened?" Mallory asked, her heart in her throat.

"It was last summer, in late June. I remember because it was right around the time of our wedding anniversary. Not that I still celebrated. In fact, I usually tried to do something nice for myself every year to make up for the huge mistake I'd made marrying Phil in the first place."

Mallory's head was spinning so hard she barely listened to what Patrice was saying.

My God, she thought. Phil was in New York around the same time David fell from that balcony. It's possible it wasn't an accident. If events unfolded the way Patrice is saying they did...

"Are you all right?" Patrice asked a second time, interrupting her thoughts.

"Not really," Mallory said.

And from the way she felt, she suspected she never would be again.

20

"The journey not the arrival matters."
—T. S. Eliot

Mallory's head was swimming as she drove out of the McDonald's parking lot. She didn't know what shocked her more: the possibility that Phil Diamond had murdered David or her newfound conviction that the person who had killed Phil was the sweet young newlywed she hadn't even considered a serious suspect.

At the moment, making sure Phil's murderer was caught was her highest priority. But she couldn't simply go running to Detective Martinez, claiming that she'd magically morphed into Jessica Fletcher of *Murder She Wrote* fame and, using her superhuman investigative skills, had solved a crime that had even been beyond the capabilities of the Orlando Police Department.

But I have no other choice, she told herself. Maybe if I can get him to just sit down and hear me out ...

Besides, she didn't know what else to try.

When she stopped at a red light, she pulled her cell

phone out of her purse and punched in Martinez's number.

"Come on," she muttered. "Answer the phone. Answer the—"

"This is Detective Martinez of Orlando Homicide," his robotic voice droned. "Please leave your message at the tone."

Mallory let out a frustrated sigh. But as soon as she heard the beep, she began babbling. "Detective Martinez, this is Mallory Marlowe. I've come across some interesting information that's related to Phil Diamond's murder. *Important* information. I believe it even points to his killer. Please call me back as soon as you get this message. Thanks. Oh, my cell phone number is nine-one-seven..."

What now? she thought as the light turned green.

But she already knew that at this point, there was nothing else she could do. As she continued along International Drive, she decided to proceed as if nothing had changed. She would go back to the hotel, shower and change, and go to the reception.

Even though she was now convinced that her hostess for the evening was a cold-blooded killer.

• • •

Very frightening, Mallory thought as she pulled up in front of Horror House later that evening.

From the outside, the attraction looked like an abandoned house with a sagging front porch, peeling paint, and dark windows bordered by crooked shutters. A small cemetery was conveniently located along the side, and the only landscaping consisted of tall, leafless trees with spindly branches. In short, it looked like the perfect place for tourists with strong hearts and good imaginations to have the living daylights scared out of them.

Yet not another soul appeared around. In fact, as

Mallory pulled her PT Cruiser into the parking lot, she puzzled over the fact that hers was the only car in sight.

There must be some other place to park, maybe in back, she thought. I guess I missed the sign.

Deciding that one parking spot was as good as another, she pulled up right in front, then headed toward the house. But the fact that there were still no signs of life made her wonder if somehow she'd gotten the time wrong.

I'm nearly positive Courtney said to come at seven, Mallory thought as she pulled open the heavy wooden door, noticing the brass knocker was in the shape of a skull. In that case, I'm not really that early. It's only ten minutes to—

"*Hoh-hoh-hoh-hoh-hoh!*" A deep throaty laugh that sounded decidedly evil interrupted her thoughts. It also made her jump.

Okay, special effects, she thought, steadying herself. This *is* a haunted house, after all.

She stepped inside and found herself in a dark hallway. Even though a tremendous crystal chandelier hung from the ceiling, its hundreds of tiny bulbs emitted only the dimmest light. Looming up in front of her was a grand staircase, its dark red carpeting badly faded. The elegant wooden banister that ran up along both sides had more than a few broken balusters, and cobwebs were draped everywhere.

They're *fake* cobwebs, Mallory reminded herself, nervously clutching her purse against her side. Everything in this place is fake. It was created for tourists. It's *supposed* to look creepy.

Hanging on the walls were half a dozen huge portraits, imposing oil paintings of stern-looking men and women. They were all dressed in severe Victorian garb with high necklines and somber colors. She took a few steps into the room and discovered that as she moved, their eyes moved, too, as if the subjects of the portraits were watching her.

Clever, she thought, hoping that taking an analytical approach would diminish her uneasiness.

She was beginning to wonder where everybody else was—or if the others had already arrived and were gathering in some other part of the building.

"Hello?" Mallory called. "Is anybody—*e-e-ek!*"

She let out the screech as a female cadaver with long, wild gray hair suddenly careened toward her from out of the darkness. The dead woman's clothes had rotted to tatters that flew from side to side. The ersatz corpse came to a standstill inches from where Mallory stood, so that its decaying face was right in front of her. Its crooked grin revealed brown, uneven teeth and its dark, unseeing eyes bulged out of their sockets.

"Ugh!" Mallory cried, jumping backward.

It's not real, she reminded herself, pushing it out of her way. The only reason you got scared is that it came flying out of nowhere.

You'd think that at least they'd turn off the special effects until we all get inside, she thought, taking a few deep breaths to calm the jackhammer pounding of her heart.

Through the silence of the house, she heard the sound of a woman weeping.

So there *is* somebody else in here, she thought.

She listened more closely, trying to figure out who it could be. Annabelle? Frieda? Maybe even Courtney?

She followed the sound, wandering down a long corridor, toward the partially open door at the end.

"Frieda?" she called. "Is that you?"

As she neared the end of the hallway, she saw that the room up ahead was furnished with Victorian-style furniture. A gold brocade couch stood in the center and an ornate writing table with carved legs was pushed into one corner. Heavy dark green velvet drapes smothered the windows, preventing even the faintest ray of light from penetrating the darkness. An elaborately decorated tiered wedding cake sat on a small round table covered in white linen.

She stepped inside the room, then froze when she saw where the sound was coming from. It was a woman, all right. The hologram of a woman, to be more precise, dressed in a lace wedding gown that was splattered with red. Lying on the ground beside her was a man wearing a tuxedo, presumably the groom. A huge knife was stuck in his chest, and what looked like real blood gushed from the wound.

"Agh-h-h!" Mallory cried involuntarily.

It's *fake,* she told herself again. Everything in this place is fake.

She knew that reminding herself of that simple fact should have gone a long way in calming her down. But for some reason, taking a commonsense approach wasn't helping as much as it should have.

She backtracked, wanting to get away from the macabre scene. This time, she tried a different route, still hoping to stumble upon a cheerful party room where she'd find Wade and the other travel writers sipping champagne.

Heading in the other direction required going up a wooden staircase.

At least this one doesn't have cobwebs all over it, she thought.

Instead, right in front was a big sign that read HOLD ON TO THE HANDRAIL! THESE STEPS ARE ALIVE!

What on earth could that mean? she wondered.

Still, she did as she was told. Clutching the wooden handrail, she began to climb, surprised by how creaky the stairs were.

Special effects, she reminded herself once again. The creepy noise must be what the sign refers to.

Yet she'd gone up only two steps when they all started to move, the right side of each step moving backward, the left side moving forward, as if they were all split in half.

"Yikes!" she cried, grasping the handrail more tightly to keep from falling.

They've got to be kidding! Mallory thought, struggling to keep her balance. Who ever came up with this idea? Aren't there any lawyers in this state?

She was getting tired of navigating her way through a house whose special effects were not only getting irritating but had also started to get downright dangerous.

Besides, she still hadn't seen any other signs of life.

The uneasy feeling that had first crept up on her when she'd driven into the parking lot had escalated.

Something is very wrong, she thought.

She turned, planning to backtrack out of the house, when a sudden movement caught her eye. Glancing to the right, she saw that someone had lurched into the doorway.

Courtney.

Mallory's first reaction was relief. So there *was* someone else here in the house with her.

But her relief faded fast when she saw that Courtney was holding a gun. Unlike the other frightening effects in this haunted house, it looked very, very real.

And it was pointed right at her.

21

"Tourists don't know where they've been,
travelers don't know where they're going."
—Paul Theroux

Hello, Courtney," Mallory said, trying to sound as if chatting with someone who was pointing a gun at her was something that happened every day. "I was beginning to wonder if anyone else was going to show up for the reception you were nice enough to plan—"

"Don't try to sweet-talk me," Courtney shot back angrily. She held the gun a little higher, as if wanting to make sure Mallory had noticed it.

I have to get out of here, Mallory thought. She looked around and realized she and Courtney were standing on an ornately carved wooden balcony that overlooked a tremendous room. Peering over the side, she saw that it was a mirrored ballroom that was filled with couples in formal attire waltzing to music that was just out of tune enough to sound eerie.

"Help me!" she called down to them. "Help!"

Not a single one responded. Sheepishly she realized

that it wasn't a case of them being rude—or even of not hearing her. Like everything else in this place, they were fake. Nothing but holograms.

Courtney laughed. "Surely you didn't think anyone would help you," she said coldly. "Why would I have arranged to kill you here, of all places, if I thought there'd be somebody around?"

"But someone's going to show up sooner or later," Mallory insisted. "What about the other writers? Frieda and Annabelle and...and..."

"Trust me, no one's coming. I wasn't stupid enough to tell anyone else to meet us here tonight. It's just you and me."

"But what about other tourists?" Mallory asked, her desperation reflected in her breathy voice. "You told me yourself this place was staying open."

"Ha! I lied!" Courtney replied smugly. "It's been closed for more than a week. Fortunately, the electricity won't be turned off until tomorrow and I know where all the switches are, thanks to the fact that I checked this place out earlier today. I got the security guard to let me. It's amazing what an ID from the tourism board can get you."

Mallory felt like a fool for having believed the woman who had murdered Phil about *anything*.

Especially since Courtney clearly had no qualms about killing again.

Mallory realized her best chance for getting out of this situation alive was keeping Courtney talking. She could remember having read that it was important to make an attacker understand that you were a real live person, to decrease the chances of them doing something terrible to you.

"I know who you are, Courtney." Mallory struggled to sound calm and matter-of-fact, as if explaining herself at gunpoint was something that happened every day. "I know you're Huck Hollinger's daughter and that Conover is your married name."

"You're a clever lady," Courtney sneered. "I underestimated you, Mallory, at least at first. To think that when I met you, I thought you were just some boring soccer mom from the suburbs, moonlighting as a travel writer.

"But I'm a clever lady, too. So clever that I know exactly what you've been doing." She tightened her grip on the gun. "In fact, I've had my eye on you ever since Des came to me and said you'd been pumping him for information. Of course, it took him a while to figure out what you were up to, so he ended up telling you way too much. When he finally noticed that you seemed unusually interested in Phil Diamond's history, he tried to throw you off track by telling you Phil's ex had left Orlando and moved to Chicago. The last thing he wanted was for you to find Patrice, since he knew as well as I did that she was undoubtedly still bitter enough about the divorce to spill her guts to anyone who'd listen.

"Which is exactly what you did," she continued. "You listened plenty, right? Probably asked lots of questions, too."

"But... how did you..." Mallory sputtered.

"Don't think for a minute that the parking lot at McDonald's isn't big enough to be a great place to watch somebody's comings and goings," Courtney replied, narrowing her eyes. "Especially when they include a clandestine meeting with a blabbermouth like Patrice."

Mallory wracked her brain for something to say that would explain away what she'd been doing. But Courtney had her cornered. At gunpoint.

And to think that at my interview for this job, my biggest fear about travel writing was that I might have to visit a nudist colony, Mallory thought woefully. A few flopping body parts would be a breeze compared to this.

"But to be honest," she said, desperate to keep

Courtney's mouth moving so that hopefully her trigger finger wouldn't, "there's a lot I didn't find out. I'm wondering if you'd be willing to indulge me by filling in the blanks."

When Courtney remained silent, simply staring at her with the same cold look in her eyes, Mallory added, "You know, Courtney, I never doubted for a moment that Phil Diamond deserved to die. He was a crude, nasty, despicable man. Everyone who knew him seems to agree that it's amazing one of his countless enemies didn't bump him off sooner."

"My sentiments exactly." Courtney tossed her head triumphantly. "I'm fully aware that I actually did everyone a favor."

"You definitely did," Mallory agreed. "And I'm sure any jury in the world that hears about all the horrible things Phil did will agree. But they might not feel the same way about the death of an innocent bystander like me. If I were you, I'd stop at one murder. Any decent lawyer will be able to get you off by arguing that killing Phil was a public service. But two murders . . . now you're talking about a pattern. I don't think a jury would be quite as forgiving—"

"Quiet!" Courtney barked. Narrowing her eyes, she added, "Don't think I don't know what you're doing."

"What am I doing?" Mallory asked, all innocence.

"You're trying to distract me. And . . . and you're trying to talk me out of killing you. But it's too late, Mallory. I can't let you go free. Not when you're the only person who's figured out what I've done."

"Okay, I understand," Mallory said, holding out her hands with her palms toward Courtney. "But I still think I deserve an explanation. In the past few days, I found out about all the nasty things Phil did to everyone on this trip. He strung poor Annabelle along for years, having a secret affair with her and from the looks of things breaking her heart when she told him she wanted more. He spoiled a book deal for Frieda that would have been her ticket to a comfortable retirement. He nearly ruined a magazine Wade was working at." She was exaggerating, at least in terms of that last claim, but she hoped Courtney wouldn't figure it out. "And Desmond. He ripped him off and ruined his chances to be an entrepreneur...."

"That's nothing," Courtney insisted sharply. "None of it compares with what that bastard did to me and my family."

Keep her talking, Mallory thought. As long as she's talking, she's not shooting.

"What did he do, exactly?" she asked. "Tell me everything."

"Phil Diamond ruined my father," Courtney hissed. "He wrote an article in that stupid column of his in the *Observer*. He did it because my father was a competitor. And the next thing anyone knew, Monster Mansion was forced to close. My father was so distraught he killed himself. He killed himself, Mallory! Do you have any idea what that does to a little girl? And then my mother went into a deep depression. She couldn't even take care of me. I had to go live with her sister, Beth, and my aunt's husband, Desmond."

Mallory gasped. "Desmond raised you?"

"That's right. He's my uncle. But for the past twenty years, he's played the role of my father. A role he never wanted, by the way, but which he took on because he was responsible and caring and...and even though he and my real father had had a bitter split over the business, he knew what he had a moral obligation to do.

"I never got to know either of my parents," Courtney said bitterly. "And while Beth and Desmond did the best they could, they hadn't planned on having any kids. For one thing, they didn't have the money to give me the things I needed. When I went to college, I had to pay my own way. I was completely on my own financially, which meant I had to work all four years. While the other kids had time to study and even do fun things like going to parties and football games, I had to work—sometimes two jobs. That's why I worked at that radio station and that public relations firm I told you about. It wasn't because I wanted the experience. It was because I needed a way to feed myself!

"When I learned that Phil was coming back to Florida for the press trip, I begged to be put in charge of it," Courtney continued. "I hoped that once and for all, being in the same place as that monster would give me a chance to get the revenge I've always longed for. I told Des that I planned to kill Phil, and he tried to talk me out of it. When he saw he couldn't, he agreed to help me however he could, without getting directly involved."

That explains why he was trying to clean up the crime scene, Mallory thought. He used the fact that he was the general manager of the hotel as an excuse, saying he didn't want to upset his guests. But in reality, his main concern was protecting Courtney, the niece he had raised since she was five years old.

"I've had to live with what Phil did to my entire family since I was just a little girl," Courtney concluded, spitting out her words. "I was only five years old, but I knew exactly what happened."

"But that's the point!" Mallory cried. "Courtney, you *were* just a little girl—a little girl who was too small to be told the truth. The fact is, Phil didn't ruin your father's business. Your father's accountant did. He's the one responsible for your father's business going under."

"You're lying!" Courtney exclaimed. "You're just saying anything you can think of because you want to keep me from using this gun!"

"That's not true!" Mallory shot back. "I mean, you're

right that I don't want you to use that gun. But I'm not lying, Courtney. Phil's ex-wife, Patrice, told me everything."

"I'll never believe you, Mallory," Courtney declared.

"But you have to! It's the truth! Look, if you'd like, I can put you in touch with Patrice. She has no reason to lie. Besides, she was *there*! She was still married to Phil back then!"

"It's too late for all that."

Courtney took a step closer, a cruel glint in her eyes. Mallory glanced from side to side, desperately searching for something to throw in Courtney's path.

Without hesitation, she reached for the suit of armor standing in the corner and pushed it toward Courtney.

"*Wha-a-a!*" Courtney yelled in surprise.

The unexpected attack by Sir Lancelot gave Mallory the few seconds she needed to escape. She rushed past Courtney as the younger woman wrestled with the tin man, who, from the looks of things, was a lot heavier than Mallory had realized.

She raced across the balcony and down the flight of stairs, this time holding the handrail tightly to keep from teetering. She reached the bottom safely, then looked around, trying to guess which way was out.

But the interior of the house was so dark and there were so many hallways and doors that she didn't know which way to go. She chose a corridor that she thought looked familiar. She'd gone only a few feet before she realized she hadn't been here before. But she could hear footsteps hurrying down the stairs, a sign that Courtney wasn't far behind.

At the end of the corridor, she found herself in a room containing more than twenty funhouse mirrors arranged in a big circle. Rather than being fastened to the walls, they were freestanding, each one in its own Victorian frame. One mirror made her arms and legs look wavy, another made her look short and fat. But what concerned her most was that the room was a dead end.

The footsteps were getting closer. Mallory slid behind one of the mirrors, trying to stifle her gasping breaths.

She heard Courtney run into the room, then stop dead in her tracks.

"I know you're in here!" she shrieked.

I have to distract her, Mallory thought desperately.

She flung her purse into the middle of the room, knowing it would be reflected in every one of the mirrors. But what she didn't expect was the deafening, horrifying blast of a gunshot.

Then more noises followed: the tinkling of glass being shattered, then sliding onto the floor with a shushing that almost sounded like a waterfall, followed by a loud crash.

"Damn!" Courtney cried, no doubt having realized that what she'd just shot was nothing more threatening than a leather Stone Mountain pocketbook and a fun-house mirror.

But Mallory took advantage of Courtney's few seconds of puzzlement to dash out from behind the mirror, give Courtney a hard shove, and run back down the hallway.

Once again, she could hear Courtney behind her.

I have to stay out of sight, she thought, trying not to panic. The moment she sees me, she's going to pull the trigger again.

As the footsteps grew closer, she darted into the first room she came across. A big sign over the door read JUNGLE ROOM.

It was well named. The walls were lined with the heads of animals. Dead animals. Big, scary-looking animals, too—a lion, a bear, a tiger, and a panther, all of them with their mouths open and their teeth bared. A large leopard skin lay in front of the fireplace. Even the furniture stayed true to the jungle theme. The leather couch with shiny metal studs was festooned with fur-covered throw pillows. A footrest was also made from the fur of some unlucky beast.

From the footsteps growing louder in the hallway, Mallory knew Courtney was getting closer. Frantically she scanned the room, looking for a weapon, a way out, a place to hide...anything that would buy her some more time.

And then she spotted a switch on the wall, half hidden behind a curtain. It was much too big to be a light switch, so she suspected it was the control for one more special effect.

Her eyes darted around the room as she tried to figure out what effect pulling the switch might have.

When she glanced upward, she realized she'd just found exactly what she'd been looking for.

As she heard Courtney coming up behind her, she leaped over to the switch, pulled it down, and ducked behind the curtain. Then she watched as a giant net dropped from the ceiling at the same moment Courtney rushed into the room.

"Ah-h-h!" the younger woman cried, her limbs suddenly tangled up in netting that was heavy enough to catch lions and tigers and bears, including the ones whose heads now hung on the wall. As she tried to free herself, she slipped and fell to the floor.

"Get me out of here!" she screeched.

Not likely, Mallory thought, nimbly skipping over the edges of the net that spilled into her path, determined to flee.

As she ran through the doorway, however, she struck something hard.

"Ooph!" she cried, glancing up.

It wasn't a ghoul she had collided with. It was

Detective Martinez. Coming up behind him were two uniformed officers, one male and one female.

"Ms. Marlowe!" he exclaimed, surveying the bizarre scene before him. "What have you done?"

"Captured Phil Diamond's murderer, that's what I've done!"

A look of disbelief flashed across his face. But before he had a chance to speak, Courtney's muffled voice rang out from beneath the thick folds of net. "He had it coming!" she growled. "Phil Diamond ruined my life. He deserved to die! I'm *glad* I killed him!"

The detective's expression quickly changed.

"Get her out of there," he barked.

The two uniformed officers pounced, thrashing through the netting to get at Courtney. The woman cop already held a pair of handcuffs in her hand.

Mallory turned to face the detective. "How did you know what was going on?" she demanded. "What brought you here?"

"The sound of a gunshot," he replied. "Somebody called it in and I came right over. This place is closed, so I immediately knew something was very wrong."

Mallory and Detective Martinez paused to watch the police handcuff Courtney and lead her away. She was sobbing so hard that Mallory actually felt sorry for her.

Courtney was a killer, all right, Mallory thought, but she'd killed Phil because she sincerely believed he was responsible for destroying her family.

The fact that she had been wrong only added to the tragedy.

Once they were gone, Detective Martinez folded his arms across his chest. "Okay, Ms. Marlowe. Would you mind telling me exactly how you managed to identify Phil Diamond's murderer? And then would you tell me how you caught her—in a *net*?"

She was only too happy to fill him in on the details of

her investigation, leaving out the suspicions she'd had about Frieda, Annabelle, Desmond, and Wade. Then she told him about Patrice's claim that in Phil's eyes, David had been responsible for his first business failure, which accounted for Phil's years of hoarding articles about her husband. She also explained David's role in Phil's latest get-rich scheme, saying she believed Phil had even traveled to New York City last summer to confront him.

"We'll contact the police up there and look into that," Detective Martinez assured her. "What was the exact date of your husband's death?"

"June twenty-ninth."

She'd barely gotten the words out when a wave of exhaustion swept over her. The shock of being held at gunpoint and then being chased through a haunted house, as well as all the other events of the long, grueling week, suddenly caught up with her.

"And now, if you don't mind, I'm going to find my purse, drive back to the hotel, and start packing," she said. "First thing tomorrow, I've got a plane to catch."

22

"A man travels the world over in search of what
he needs, and returns home to find it."
—George Moore

Now, *this* was a trip I won't forget soon," Frieda
announced as the three female journalists gathered in the lobby with their suitcases to say
good-bye early Friday morning. "And believe me, at my
age I've got so many memories filed away in my head that
there isn't a heck of a lot of room for any new ones."

She sounded as cheerful as if what had made this particular press trip so memorable was something along the
lines of another skinny-dipping adventure—or perhaps a more personalized activity, courtesy of Alligator
Zeke.

While Frieda was her usual bubbly self, Annabelle
seemed even more subdued than usual. Still, her somber
mood didn't stop her from sashaying past the front desk,
snatching a dozen books of Polynesian Princess Hotel
matches off the counter, and dropping them into her
purse.

"I suppose I owe you a thank you, Mallory," she said

begrudgingly as she rejoined their little group. "For finding out who murdered Phil, I mean."

"You don't owe me anything," Mallory assured her. "I just hope knowing who the culprit was makes it a little easier for you to cope."

"It does." Annabelle sighed. "To be honest, I don't know how much longer Phil and I would have been an item, anyway. After all these years, I'm ready for something more. In fact, I'm thinking of signing up with one of those online dating services when I get home. Maybe my soul mate is out there waiting for me."

I wonder if there's a budget dating website, Mallory mused. Something along the lines of CheapDate.com.

"Mallory, you did an amazing job," Frieda gushed. "Imagine figuring out who killed Phil all by yourself! Who would have guessed we had a Nancy Drew in our midst?"

"Very impressive," Wade agreed, coming up behind them. "Then again, outstanding sleuthing skills are just one of the things that make this lady special."

Mallory noticed Frieda and Annabelle exchanging a knowing look. She didn't care.

Wade looped his arm around hers and drew her a few steps away from the others.

"You know, Mallory," he said in a low, earnest voice, "I feel as if you and I have some unfinished business."

She nodded. "I feel the same way."

"Is there any way I could talk you into staying on for a few days?" he asked. "To give us a chance to get to know each other better before we both take off?"

"I have to get home," Mallory said. Her heart felt strangely heavy, as if regret was weighing it down.

"Ah, yes. Home, that distant place," he said lightly. "Rivington, New York, which happens to be far, far away from Toronto."

She smiled sadly. "That's where my life is. My two children, my house, and now, it seems, my career."

"You know," Wade said lightly, "I could come down to New York sometime. Sometime soon, I mean. I bet I could even find some luxury hotels to write about. Just say the word."

Mallory squeezed his arm. "I think I still need some time, Wade. I've got a lot to digest right now. Not to mention the fact that I have a travel article to write. Don't forget, it's my very first one. I'm still not sure I can pull off that part of the deal."

"I have no doubt that you'll be magnificent at it. And that you'll continue doing this as long as you want. And who knows, maybe you and I will end up on another press trip together."

Mallory was about to reply, when out of the corner of her eye she noticed a familiar silhouette. Her stomach tightened at the sight of Detective Martinez striding toward her. She quickly reminded herself that the worst was over, that she no longer had anything to fear.

"Ms. Marlowe! I'm glad I caught you," he boomed. "If I could have a few words?"

Mallory glanced at Wade apologetically, then turned to the detective.

"Should we go someplace private?" she asked.

"Right here in the lobby is fine. I can see you're on your way out."

Still, he waited until they'd stepped away from the others before he resumed speaking. "Ms. Marlowe, I had a conversation with an individual in the New York police department. It seems that Phil Diamond was indeed in New York City at the time your husband died."

Mallory drew in her breath sharply. "Go on."

"Apparently, he had a meeting scheduled with a David Marlowe the night of your husband's death. The cops up there questioned him at the time the incident occurred but couldn't come up with any evidence that linked Diamond to the crime."

It took her a few seconds to digest the implications of what he'd just told her.

"Detective Martinez," she finally said, her voice wavering, "are you telling me that David didn't die accidentally? That Phil Diamond murdered him?" She loosened her hands, which she realized she'd balled into fists.

"We don't know that for certain," the detective replied. "And to be honest, with no evidence or witnesses—and no suspect for us to question—I'm afraid we'll probably never know the whole story."

Wade hurried over as soon as Detective Martinez left.

"Are you all right?" he demanded.

"I'm not sure," she said in a strained voice.

The trill of her cell phone, combined with the familiar sight of her home number on the screen, reminded her that she had two children who still needed her.

She'd barely gotten out the world *Hello* before Amanda demanded, "Mother, when are you coming home?"

"I'm about to leave for the airport," Mallory replied, warmed by the sound of her daughter's voice. "I'll be back this afternoon."

"Too bad," Amanda said. "I won't have a chance to see you." She hesitated before adding, "I decided you were right. About school, I mean."

"You're leaving so soon?" Even though Mallory was relieved that her daughter had finally decided to go back to school, she was disappointed that she wouldn't have a chance to see her off.

"I'm packing up my stuff right now," Amanda told her. "If I hurry, I can make my one o'clock economics class."

"Does that mean you've finally decided between law school and business school?"

"Actually," Amanda said hesitantly, "what I've decided is that I'm not ready to make a decision." She paused to take a deep breath. "I'm thinking that after I graduate, I might take a year off to figure out what to do next. Find a job, get a little real world experience . . . there's no reason to rush into anything. Not when I'm still not sure what's best for me."

"That sounds very sensible." It also sounds as if the old familiar levelheaded Amanda is back, Mallory thought.

"If it's okay with you," Amanda continued, "I thought I'd come back home to live. I could get a job in the city and take the train in every day. That way, I'd have a chance to save some money. It would also give you and me a chance to spend some time together."

The fact that her soon-to-be-adult daughter still wanted to spend time with her made Mallory's eyes sting. It also lessened the pain of Jordan going back to school in a week.

"Is that okay?" Amanda asked anxiously.

"Of course it's okay!" Mallory cried. "I'm already looking forward to it."

"Then it's settled." It was clear from the sound of Amanda's voice that she was smiling. "By the way, how was your trip? I hope it wasn't totally boring."

"It was anything but boring," Mallory assured her.

"I can't wait to hear about it. But for now, I'd better get moving if I'm going to make my econ class."

Mallory suddenly missed both her children terribly. "Can I say hello to Jordan?"

"He went out to get some things he needs for school," Amanda said. With a little laugh, she added, "I guess he finally got tired of sitting on that stupid couch."

What's that old saying about the best thing parents can do for their children is give them roots and wings? Mallory thought. I guess I managed to do that.

And I'm lucky enough to have both roots and wings, too, she realized. My home and my children are the roots that keep me grounded. And now, I'm learning how to fly.

She'd barely said good-bye to her daughter before her cell phone trilled again. Another familiar number flashed on the screen.

"Hello, Trevor," she answered calmly.

"Mallory! Is everything okay?"

"Everything is great," she said sincerely. "I'm going to write a fabulous article for you. By the way, you'll be pleased to know the old Florida is alive and well. And as much fun as always."

"I'm glad you considered your first press trip fun," Trevor said, "given everything that went on. When are you getting back?"

"I'm on my way," Mallory replied. "I'll be home in a few hours."

"Great. As soon as you get settled, give me a call. I want to talk to you about another trip."

"I'll do that," Mallory said. "I can't wait to find out where I'm going next."

In Search of the Old Florida

PIRATES AND DINOS AND CROCS, OH MY!

by Mallory Marlowe

Once upon a time, Florida was the ultimate children's fantasy, a land where rugged men wrestled alligators, caged tigers were displayed at gas stations, daredevils on water skis built human pyramids, and ice-cream stands were shaped like gigantic ice-cream cones.

But in today's high-tech world, all those delightful attractions have vanished. Or have they? Does the kitsch Florida from the 1950s, '60s, and '70s that so many of us remember fondly still exist? Has the phenomenal success of the Disney and Universal theme parks wiped out the somewhat tacky but always fun Florida of our childhood?

In short, does kitsch—best defined as bad taste in good fun—still live on in Florida, in the form of alligator farms, seashell-covered boxes, mango-flavored coconut patties, and dinosaurs glowering inside snow globes?

If you're someone who still treasures such childhood memories, rejoice. The old Florida is indeed alive and well. Below is an overview of eight roadside attractions that are throwbacks to the Sunshine State's simpler times—yet even today manage to bring in the crowds.

Gatorland

In this age of video games, DVDs, and countless other forms of digital fun, it's reassuring to know that people of all ages still get a kick out of watching good old-fashioned gator wrestling. Gatorland, billed as the "Alligator Capital of the World," not only treats visitors to down-and-dirty matches between humans and reptiles; it offers a variety of exhibits, shows, and hands-on activities that still embody the kind of fun that can be found only in Florida.

In fact, since this roadside attraction first opened over fifty years ago, the park has just gotten bigger and better. Visitors enter through a humongous pair of gator jaws, setting the tone for the adventure that awaits them. In addition to serving as a preserve for hundreds of alligators—still among the creepiest and most fascinating creatures on the planet—Gatorland is home to crocodiles, snakes, insects, parrots, and even a bear, all in a lush, swampy setting. And besides real life alligator wrestling, the park features a show called Upclose Encounters that stars tarantulas and a snake so long it takes four people—unwitting volunteers from the audience whose eyes are closed—to hold it. In another outstanding exhibition, the Gator Jumparoo Show, alligators shoot into the air to snap raw chickens from the hands of the park's braver employees.

Even the snack bar, Pearl's Patio Smokehouse, gets into the spirit, serving up smoked gator ribs and deep-fried gator nuggets. An open-air train chugs through the Jungle Crocs of the World exhibit, with crocodiles up to twenty-seven feet long lying in wait for their next meal—hopefully not a camera-wielding tourist. All in all, Gatorland truly delivers the "Swamp Stompin' Adventure" it promises.

Gatorland is located at 14501 South Orange Blossom Trail, Orlando (Phone: 800–393–JAWS or 407–855–5496; www.gatorland.com).

Ripley's Believe It or Not! Orlando Odditorium

The amazing, the amusing, and the downright atrocious are all celebrated at this unique attraction, one of several Ripley's Believe It or Not! museums throughout the country. In the Orlando branch, brazenly called an odditorium, curiosity-seekers will delight in the portrait of Lincoln made out of Lincoln pennies, the life-size Rolls-Royce constructed from over one million wooden matchsticks, and the genuine shrunken head from the Jivaro Indians of Ecuador.

The museum also pays tribute to Robert Ripley, who launched his long-lived cartoon series in the *New York Globe* in 1918. While his cartoon originally applauded outstanding sports achievements and was called "Champs and Chumps," his editor suggested changing the name to "Believe It or Not!" It was an instant success, leading to several books and, in 1929, syndication in many of William Randolph Hearst's newspapers.

In the museum, there are enough crowd-pleasing oddities, including a vampire killing kit from 1850, an awe-inspiring collection of bedpans, and a chunk of the Berlin Wall, to make it worth a visit. The Odditorium's ongoing ability to fascinate with the same type of exhibits that folks marveled at nearly a hundred years ago earns it a three flamingo rating.

Ripley's Believe It or Not! Orlando Odditorium is located at 8201 International Drive, Orlando (Phone: 407–363–4418; www.ripleysorlando.com).

Shell World
Orange World 🦩 🦩 🦩

Looking for a seashell night-light? Need a plastic lobster or a mermaid snow globe? Then Shell World is your place to shop.

Shell World boasts that over one million seashells from around the world are for sale in its 12,000-square-foot emporium. Although it's probably too time-consuming to count, shoppers will undoubtedly agree to take Shell World at its word as they cruise aisle after aisle, marveling at all the new, unusual, and at times questionable uses for seashells. Earrings, tissue boxes, jewelry boxes, wind chimes, wedding favors, Christmas tree ornaments... if it can be made out of seashells or decorated with seashells, chances are good that Shell World stocks it. An amazing variety of seashells in their natural state are also sold, from sand dollars to starfish to conch shells.

The Shell World experience includes a seashell museum, housed in a 600-foot tiki hut that looks like it was stolen from the set of *Gilligan's Island,* and a 1,000-square-foot pier, on which Florida's largest selection of seashell creations is on display. Parked outside are a Volkswagen Bug and a golf cart, both covered completely with—you guessed it—seashells.

Just down the street is Orange World, which has the distinction of being shaped like a huge orange—or at least the top half of one. Outside are bins of freshly picked citrus fruits so perfect they look as if they're made of wax. The merchandise inside covers the gamut of souvenirs, from T-shirts to postcards to baseball caps. Much more interesting are the shelves crammed with local specialties, like Anastasia's Coconut Patties in mango, piña colada, and key-lime flavor, chocolate alligators, guava jelly, and coconut toast spread.

Shell World is located at 4727 W. Irlo Bronson Highway (Hwy 192), Kissimmee (Phone: 407–396–9000; www.shell world.com). Orange World is at 5395 W. Irlo Bronson Highway, Kissimmee (Phone: 407–239–6031; www.orange world192.com).

Titanic: The Experience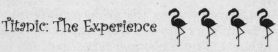

As just about anyone who lives on planet earth knows, on April 14, 1912, shortly before midnight, the supposedly unsinkable ship, the *Titanic*, collided with an iceberg on its maiden voyage from Great Britain to New York. It sank off Newfoundland, with only seven hundred passengers surviving and the other fifteen hundred drowning in the deep, icy waters of the Atlantic.

Titanic: The Experience, purportedly the world's first permanent *Titanic* attraction, recaptures both the glamour of the luxurious ship and the unimaginable horror of that historic night. Exhibits include a full-scale re-creation of the *Titanic*'s Grand Staircase, immortalized in the 1997 film *Titanic*, along with more than two hundred artifacts related to the famous ship.

Visitors actually experience some of the horror firsthand as they hear the rumble of the tremendous engines, touch an actual iceberg, and shiver on a dark, frigid deck that re-creates the conditions of the infamous night. The displays also include movie memorabilia from such films as *A Night to Remember* and one of the costumes Leonardo DiCaprio wore in the movie *Titanic*.

Upon entering, each visitor is assigned the name of an actual *Titanic* passenger and at the end can check the Memorial Wall to see whether or not that person survived.

Titanic: The Experience is located at the Mercado at 8445 International Drive in Orlando (Phone: 407–248–1166; www.titanicshipofdreams.com).*

*Since my visit, Titanic: The Experience has moved, and is now temporarily located at the Orlando Science Center at 777 East Princeton Street (Phone: 407–895–2610).

Dinosaur World

The creatures that inhabit Dinosaur World don't move. They don't make unearthly sounds. They don't even have a particularly menacing look in their eyes.

Yet even though the park doesn't provide an over-the-top Jurassic Park–style experience, visitors who make the one-hour drive from Orlando to Plant City can nevertheless have a pleasant outing. There's plenty to enjoy here—particularly for those who are looking for the old Florida. First, the grounds are spectacular. Strolling among the lush plantings along meandering pathways and across wooden bridges would be delightful even without a prehistoric creature rearing up at every turn.

Second, while these dinos may not make the ground tremble, they are all spectacularly detailed models of some of the most fascinating animals that ever stomped across the planet. And there are certainly plenty of them—more than 150. A film shown in a Fred Flintstone–esque building features paleontologists who dig for dinosaur fossils, and a small museum manages to instruct visitors about millions of years of prehistoric times in a surprisingly simple and straightforward way. All in all, Dinosaur World is an unusual yet serene spot that goes a long way in helping us understand these intriguing beasts.

Dinosaur World is located at 5145 Harvey Tew Road, Plant City, off Exit 17 on I-4 (Phone: 813–717–9865; www .dinoworld.net).

Pirate's Dinner Adventure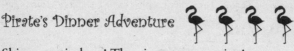

Shiver me timbers! The pirates are coming!

The real pirates who terrorized the seas in the late 1600s were basically street gangs who knew how to tie knots. Yet there's no need to fear any of the muscular marauders at the Pirate's Dinner Adventure, one of the many theme dinners that continue to thrive in and around Orlando. These pirates are too busy singing, dancing, performing stunts, and swashbuckling to do much pillaging, much less any plundering. They put on a spectacular show that demands audience participation, at times even more than audience members might prefer. There's a plot hidden in there somewhere, something about evil Captain Sebastian the Black kidnapping the fair-haired, white wedding dress–wearing Princess Anita. But with a spectacular, life-size pirate ship that floats in real water, nonstop action, and all those hunky pirates, who needs a story?

Other theme dinners in the Orlando area transport tourists to a multitude of other times and places: Chicago during the Roaring Twenties at Capone's Dinner and Show, a castle during the Middle Ages at the Medieval Times Dinner and Tournament, and Hawaii during tourist season at the Makahiki Luau Polynesian Feast and Celebration. There's also a Sleuths Mystery Dinner Show, Arabian Nights, Dolly Parton's Dixie Stampede Dinner and Show . . . in short, an evening that caters to every imaginable fantasy a kid—or, let's face it, an adult—ever had.

The Pirate's Dinner Adventure provides a wholesome

evening of adventure, fun, music, and stunts that would have been as at home in the 1950s as they are today.

Pirate's Dinner Adventure is located at 6400 Carrier Drive, Orlando (Phone: 407–248–0590; http://www. piratesdinneradventure.com).

Cypress Gardens Adventure Park

Seventy years ago, Cypress Gardens was nothing more than a swamp. But visionary Dick Pope, Sr., saw the thirty-five acres of marshland for what they could be: a lakeside park famous for both its well-tended gardens and its world-renowned waterskiing show.

During the forties and fifties, Cypress Gardens featured gorgeous flowers, photo ops with young women in antebellum gowns, and a sprawling banyan tree that Pope planted himself. But the highlight of every visit was the spectacular waterskiing show that included daredevil stunts, like human pyramids on water skis; the lovely Aquamaids, who danced on water; and the antics of water-borne clowns.

Today, Cypress Gardens Adventure Park has two separate identities: Kids will enjoy Adventure Grove, which has rides with names like the Okeechobee Rampage, Storm Surge, and Swampthing, as well as Splash Water Park; but the other half of the Park retains all the charm of its original incarnation. Plantation Gardens features manicured gardens and paved walkways with lovely views of Lake Eloise and Wings of Wonder, a butterfly house. The Topiary Trail weaves among huge animals sculpted from bushes, including a scarlet cardinal, a seal balancing a ball on his nose, and a colorful peacock. In the manicured Botanical Gardens, curving pathways wind past tall, graceful trees, fragrant rose gardens, and even a swamp that somehow manages to look as pretty as the rest of the place.

Cypress Gardens has been forced to update by adding shops in the unfortunately named Jubilee Junction, roller coasters, carousels, and train rides. Yet this one-of-a-kind attraction remains true to its original mission, offering breathtakingly beautiful botanical gardens and a waterskiing show that is as thrilling as it is original.

Cypress Gardens Adventure Park is located at 6000 Cypress Gardens Boulevard, Winter Haven (Phone: 863–324–2111; http://www.cypressgardens.com).

Acknowledgments

I would like to thank Liz Langley for her hospitality when I visited Orlando in order to see it through Mallory Marlowe's eyes. I would also like to thank Carolyn Jeffries and the members of the Whodunit Mystery Book Club at the Winter Park Public Library for both welcoming me and encouraging me. Their enthusiasm about Orlando is contagious.

And special thanks to Susan Breslow, my editor at Honeymoons.about.com, for sending me off on travel writing adventures of my own, as well as to Lyn Dobrin for suggesting it in the first place.

I would also like to acknowledge the enjoyable book *Weird Florida: Your Travel Guide to Florida's Local Legends and Best Kept Secrets* by Charlie Carlson, which clued me in to the fact that there really is a dark side to the sunshine state—albeit an entertaining one.

About the Author

CYNTHIA BAXTER is a native of Long Island, New York. She currently resides on the North Shore, where she is at work on the next mystery in the *Murder Packs a Suitcase* series, *Too Rich and Too Dead,* which Bantam will publish in April 2009. She is also the author of the *Reigning Cats & Dogs* series—look for a new mystery on sale in Summer 2009. Visit Cynthia's website at www.cynthia baxter.com.

Don't miss Mallory Marlowe's
next mystery!

The intrepid travel-writer-turned-sleuth
takes on glamour—and murder—
on the ski slopes of Aspen in

Too Rich and Too Dead

A *Murder Packs a Suitcase* Mystery
by
Cynthia Baxter

On sale in April 2009